nina x

Also by Ewan Morrison

Close Your Eyes
Tales from the Mall
Ménage
Distance
Swung
The Last Book You Read

ewan morrison

FLEET
2019

FLEET

First published in Great Britain in 2019 by Fleet

1 3 5 7 9 10 8 6 4 2

All characters and events in this publication, other than those clearly in the public domain, are fictitious and any resemblance to real persons, living or dead, is purely coincidental.

A CIP catalogue record for this book is available from the British Library.

Hardback ISBN 978-0-7088-9902-1
C-format ISBN 978-0-7088-9901-4

Typeset in Goudy by M Rules
Printed and bound in Great Britain by Clays Ltd, Elcograf S.p.A.

Papers used by Fleet are from well-managed forests and other responsible sources.

Fleet
An imprint of
Little, Brown Book Group
Carmelite House
50 Victoria Embankment
London EC4Y 0DZ

An Hachette UK Company
www.hachette.co.uk

www.littlebrown.co.uk

For Emily

'On a blank sheet of paper free from any mark,
the freshest and most beautiful characters can be written,
the freshest and most beautiful pictures can be painted.'

Mao Zedong, 1958

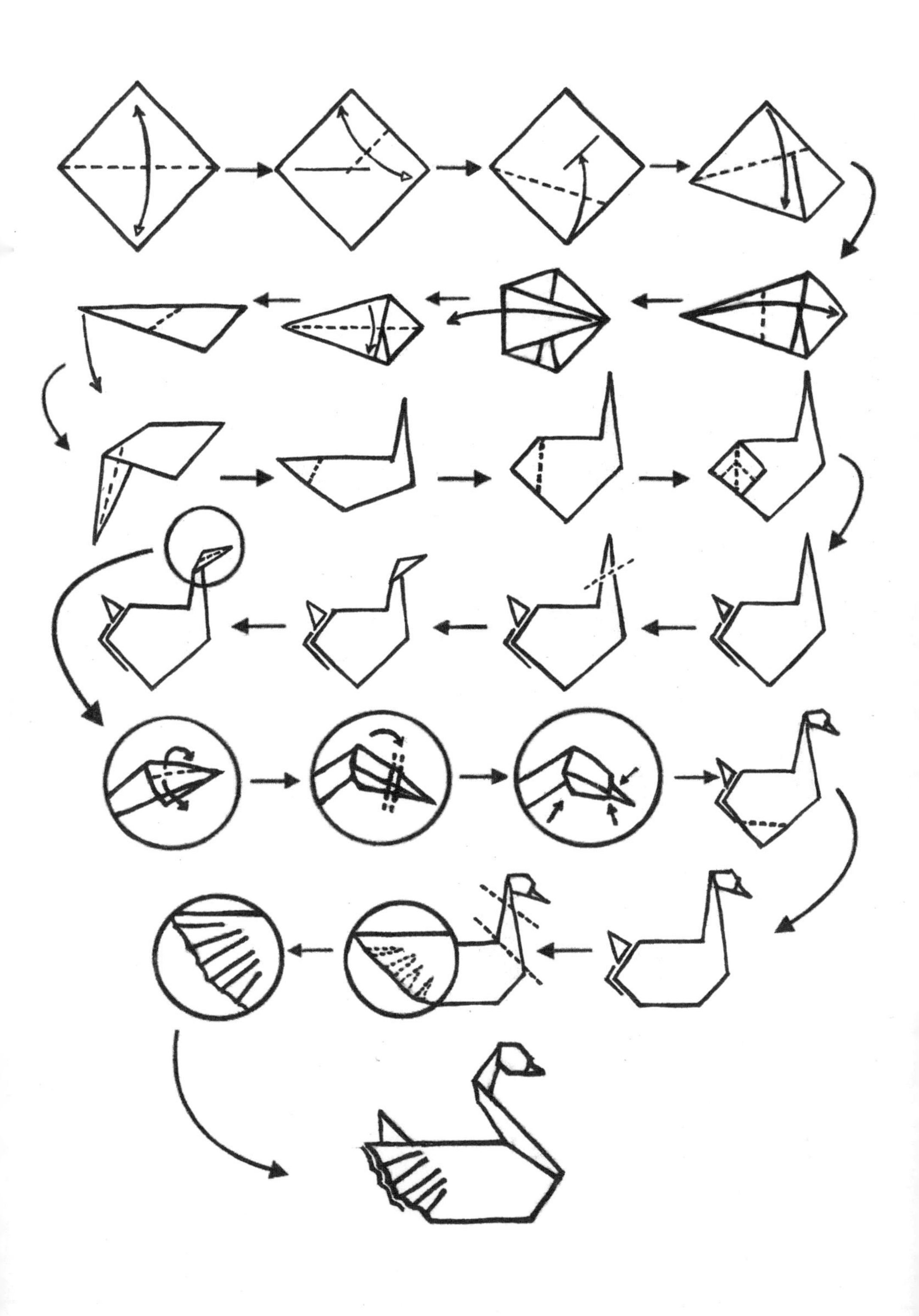

Jotter #242 2018

Nina has a list of things to try and this makes Nina too excited so lying down has to happen, but this is not to be done on the gravel or the path because Nina's first house is not her private property because it is the Charity House. Nina is very grateful to have a door and a right to go out with no permissions needed. There are many top things to do as immediately as possible:

Eat every kind of chocolate.
Fly an aeroplane.
Find out about relaxing.
Go to a supermarket.
Get all the colours of lipstick.
Learn about money.
Get married.
Learn how to dance with another person.

The Charity House smells of glue and old socks and new paint. The brown carpet is best and Nina likes to lie on its luxury. The window has fingerprints from the last escapers. Nina thinks they were a mother and children because Nina found a crushed crayon and a crumb of something sweet. There are three rooms all for Nina and even one with a table for a television but Nina isn't ready yet so Nina moved the table to the window to watch people and there are thousands. Nina is glad to have a window again.

Meet a famous person who is alive.
Have an affair.
Eat the food of many countries but not Chinese.
Be a doctor.
Make all the words mean their opposite.
Remember every day that everything is good and everything before was lies.

Nina sits and stares out but Nina is only allowed to do it through the blinds. Nina is not to be seen in case a photographer steals Nina's face.

Learn how to smile without scaring people.
Have a best friend.
Stop making swans.
Memorise the twenty-three ways to blow his mind.
Feed birds of all kinds and learn their names.

Some of the things Nina has missed out on can't be gone back to like playing with children because these are total strangers. Nina is not to try that again near the Charity House because they cry and Nina was lucky that their parents didn't call the Pigs. They are not to be called the Pigs now. They are the opposite of Pigs. Charity Sonia called them the Police.

Charity Sonia is from Sanctuary and this is an organisation in a phone which saves women every day and she has a soft face with painted lips and curly brown hair and huge dark eyes and is not a slave but smells of sweet perfume and cigarettes that she is giving up because she has free will. Nina wanted to call her Comrade Sonia but she said that was a bit odd in this day and age, so when Nina is about to say Comrade, Nina just rubs it out and changes it to Charity. It makes Nina laugh but no one sees because it is only in Nina's head.

Things Nina needs to really work on:

Walking outside without having the fear.
Not grabbing, pulling or clawing people.
Making eye contact.
Not always hiding when someone rings the bell or turns the lights on.
Eating alone.
Walking not with hunched shoulders because this is a defensive posture.
Washing every day.
Putting clothes on before going to the door and window.
To remember there is no radiation in the sky apart from lightning and it is rare and mostly in the equator where the pre-capitalist peoples live.
Sleeping in one big chunk.
Learning how to say I instead of always saying Nina because people think it is a sign of retardation to say Nina wants this and Nina likes that, when I should say I like this and I want that. And you can't say retardation either.

Charity Sonia says Nina doesn't need to write any more because no one else in the world had to write a confession diary for twenty years and it really must have been a kind of torture. She says it might be a sign that Nina is getting better when Nina can own her own experiences and that Nina could practise this every day, saying I, I, I. But no need to write it down.

She touches Nina's head and says Poor You.

But Nina has to write because if Nina doesn't Nina will never learn from mistakes.

Try to turn everything around.

Bad is good. The sky will not kill.

Charity Sonia visited again and stood in the room with chairs and she said, Have you been practising being outside, Nina? And Nina said Nina had been reading. Nina told Charity Sonia that Nina was so excited to be in Freedom because Nina could find the fourth comic of The Wizard of Oz, because Nina had read the first three one hundred and forty-eight times because apart from the books written by the Great Fathers of the Revolution and Nina's two learning books and two National Geographics that was all that was allowed in the Collective. And Nina had never found out the ending because the third comic ended when Dorothy and her friends were captured by the Wicked Witch of the West.

Charity Sonia smiled and said she didn't know that Wizard of Oz was a comic because she always thought of it as a movie which means a big television in a dark room with strangers who eat behind you. Charity Sonia was very surprised that Nina had never seen this movie because it always happens at the time of year when the slaves of Capitalism parade their wealth and they all want snow to come.

Nina asked, Do they escape from the Witch and does the Wonderful Wizard magic Dorothy back to Kansas like he promised? And does she take the Lion with her? Because he is Nina's favourite.

And Charity Sonia smiled and said if she had time she'd try to find the last comic but it might be a lot easier just to get the movie and maybe that would help getting Nina from A to B as well, because her kids always stopped shouting in the car when she put a movie on. And Nina was so excited and couldn't speak but really it was because Nina was scared to travel in a car after the ambulance experience. But Nina was just so excited to hear the end of Dorothy's epic tale that Nina kissed Comrade Charity Sonia but this was not appropriate. Nina got the hole feeling again when Charity Sonia made Nina let go of her hand and went to leave.

Charity Sonia said, I forgot to say, can you lock yourself in? Can you do it now with the keys, as a test. Not that anyone's coming to get you, no don't think that, it's just everyone does this. I know you're afraid of locked doors but you have the key. I just want to see that you know how to do that, Nina. I've got a set too, just in case.

Nina was on one side of the door and Charity Sonia was on the other and Nina turned the key like the instructions and then Charity Sonia's shadow was in the glass and she was saying, It's OK, see, I'm still here, you've got my number on that phone I gave you, just call me if you need me.

This means Nina must be brave and use a telephone. It does not give electric shocks and make your grey matter boil. And Nina is not to be scared of Comrade Chen because he was a liar and his world is now upside down because there is a warrant out for his arrest by the Pigs who are called Police. And he will get his just desserts and in time Nina will come to forgive him.

Nina must add more to the list.

You are not lonely you are just alone and this is normal for people in Freedom.

Learn how to be with no people in any other rooms, apart from through the walls. These are neighbours and some are sick and some are vulnerable adults so it is best if Nina does not knock again.

Learn to focus on things further away than the walls.

There are no spies poisoning the food.

Nina has to study people so they don't think Nina has learning difficulties.

Things Nina has learned:

Today is the thirtieth of September. The sun is high and London has never been destroyed by nuclear bombs. A new President has just gone to make a war against everything that causes terror. A new kind of dog has been invented that doesn't make people allergic and a new kind of dinosaur has been discovered in Wales. A mother in a bikini with a flawed body has inspired forty thousand other mothers with flawed bodies to share them with strangers on a thing called On Line and there are newspapers that are free on every doorstep. Nina is twenty-eight years old and this is Nina's second day of freedom because the last week was just processing and when you can't cry and you talk about yourself like someone else this is called dissociation and this is also a natural reaction to the horror you must have experienced.

Freedom has so many smells that Nina might be sick with joy or just sick. Freedom is very noisy and a bit blurry. Nina does not know what to eat because the food of Sanctuary smells strange and in plastic. Nina should not be writing because it means Nina is habituated to self-interrogation.

Nina has to practise saying I. And not rubbing it out.

I am Nina. Nina is I.

Communism does not exist any more and will never come back.

Start sentences with I all the time. Put yourself first.

It is going to take Nina a lifetime to turn all the words round and Nina had twenty-eight years robbed from me.

I, I, I, I.

Me, me, me, me, me.

—

I have many missing days to write about. On the day before the Charity House and after Nina's lost Hospital days Charity Sonia tried to make me go to the place with the sign that said Park House Women's Hostel and Charity Sonia was very confused why I was hyperventilating and staring at Nina's feet and shivering and saying, Nina doesn't want to go to Park House Women's Hostel or back to the Hospital, ever.

Erase. Start again.

Staring at MY feet and shivering and saying, Nina doesn't want to.

Erase.

I don't want.

It is too hard to write I and My. Nina can't do it. I is all about the self and the self was banished and Nina has to get a self first.

Nina will go back to writing Nina and start before the experiment at the Park House Women's Hostel. Start again with the car experiment.

Nina had been taken away from Hospital inside a car for the first time and it was different from an ambulance and a police van, like happened on the lost days. A normal car is not there to destroy the planet like Comrade Ruth said, instead it is like a room with a door for each person and everyone has to watch a window at the front. You can't see the wheels moving inside and can only hear a rumbling and if you open your door to try to touch the earth it is very dangerous and you are not to try that again, ever.

A discovery was made, it is also dangerous to put Nina's head between the knees to stop being attacked by panic because Nina is a full-grown woman and quite big and must keep her seatbelt on. Charity Sonia stopped the car because Nina had to vomit on a hard shoulder. She held Nina's hair back and asked what Nina had eaten today because it was just slime and Nina told her five sugar lumps from the Hospital because the smell of the new things called bacon and porridge made Nina sick. But Nina knew the exact number of sugar lumps because Comrade Chen used to make Nina write down everything Nina had to eat and that was when Nina had to be called The Project.

Charity Sonia had emotions in her face and she said, Wait, my God, is that all you've eaten in the Hospital? And then she shook her head and muttered about nurses and doctors.

Then Nina's head was spinning with the noise of wheels, then Nina was told to open the eyes because Charity Sonia had stopped at the Park House Women's Hostel and this was the first place in Freedom that Nina was supposed to live in. It had a rainbow picture drawn by a child on the glass and a fascist man behind it with a shirt that was called Security.

Charity Sonia said it was safe here and a lovely friendly place for Nina to relax after all the trauma of Nina's escape and she said there were many women just like Nina but it smelled of too many perfumes and bleach and strange food and sweat and the women weren't like Nina at all. One had long curly hair and a jumper covered with badges and kept calling Nina Love and touching Nina's arm. The badge woman tried to take Nina by the hand and showed Nina a room with three beds in it, but Nina shouted Nina didn't want to go in because it was like the time Nina and Comrades Ruth and Uma and Zana were in the same little room. There were two women in the room who had dark sheets over their heads with eyeholes cut out and the badge woman was smiling and stroking Nina's arm and she said, This is a Refuge, Love, everyone here is in the same boat. And she whispered to Charity Sonia, Does she have any specific cultural needs?

Nina looked at the women with sheets on heads and was scared and said, This place is not safe. Such women have false consciousness.

The badge woman's smile changed to teeth and her eyes were very tight.

Nina pointed at the sheet women and said, They oppress all women and are the whores of religion.

The badge woman said, Well, I wouldn't use words like that. And she said to Charity Sonia, Is she in shock, has she been assessed? Then she whispered, Is she violent? The women with sheet eyes were staring at Nina and gripping each other and in the corridor there were little slave children believers in God on the stairs, all staring scared-eyed at Nina, so the badge woman led Nina back to the place called Office. Inside there were pictures on the walls of women with cut and blooded faces with numbers underneath the same as at the Pig Office. Nina tugged free and ran but the door was locked. So Nina hit the glass and it cracked.

The badge woman kept saying, OK, OK, calm down, calm down, and she said to Charity Sonia that maybe this wasn't going to be the best option just yet and she said the words Health and Mental and Nina knows that when women whisper like that it is always about you.

Charity Sonia took Nina back to the car and Nina asked if she could drive back to the Collective, please, because Freedom was a mistake. Charity Sonia spoke to other people with a machine in her ear and asked Nina to hug Nina's knees and just breathe, please just breathe, and she drove round bends with many lights so as to make Nina fall against her then the other side against the door. She said the name of the man nailed on the wood and said, I'm sorry, Nina, but we have to take you back to Hospital, there's nowhere else tonight. But Nina doesn't want to go to the Hospital, Nina wants to go back to the time when every day was the same and Nina was little and was still called The Project.

Jotter #67 2002

The Project watched how to fold the piece of paper, in one way then the other, then turn it round and fold it again. When you do this twenty times it is like the revolution, Comrade Uma said. You start from the blank page and then with science and care a thing of perfection is born. Comrade Uma held it up for The Project to see and it was very pretty and called a swan and this was origami and it was a great art form from the far-off land of our great helmsman.

The Project asked, Why do swans exist? And Comrade Uma smiled and said, Why didn't you ask instead, Can you teach me how to do it or Can I play with it? Like a normal child would. Then Comrade Uma became thoughtful and said, You've never seen a swan have you, petal? No, I suppose you haven't.

Why? The Project asked.

Comrade Uma said, Well, they live in parks with water and trees and we can't see any trees from up here and some might still exist out there but I doubt it. Mostly, they were all destroyed.

And The Project didn't know why Comrade Uma looked away and she had eye bags from night patrol.

The Project asked Comrade Uma if the thing growing upwards from the window gutter was a bird tree and The Project was told it was just a big weed from a flying seed and the mind is like a garden that must be weeded every day. Then Comrade Uma sighed and said, There used to be lots of trees, banana trees, coconut trees, apple trees, lemon trees. And she showed a picture that had not been burned because it had been saved inside my favourite National Geographic which is falling apart.

The Project was told these things were once food. But the fascists killed the trees and burned the land and made the skies dark, because The Project has seen many pictures of nuclear bombs and people turned into shadows by radiation on a wall and then all the birds died then everyone starved apart from some survivors and that is why we live like this now.

The Project asked, But why do the fascists still live out there?

And Comrade Uma said, It is the only world they know, they have become used to selfishness and suffering.

The Project said, But why can't we help them and teach them the answer?

And Comrade Uma said, They wouldn't listen. Sometimes it is kinder to let people live within their lie.

The Project said, But Why?

Comrade Uma smiled and ruffled The Project's hair and she said she wanted to hug The Project tight but such actions are banned after Comrade Jeni hugged The Project too many times and into her big chest with her long red hair because this is too hippie and we are not a free love Collective, so Comrade Uma didn't hug and instead she called The Project the Why-child.

The Project said, Why?

Because other children only ever want to play and The Project only ever wants to ask Why, why, why. That's why. Then Comrade Uma said, but maybe The Project would never play with children now because The Project was nearly taller than Comrade Uma and soon becoming a woman and the world is a terrible place for women. The Project stared at her chest rising and asked, Why was it so bad for women?

The Project saw Comrade Uma was being made sad so The Project said, OK, tell me again how you escaped from oppression and Comrade Chen hid you in his great heart and we came to be the chosen number?

Comrade Uma smiled and said, But you know that story so well now, why don't you write it down in your diary. And do it tomorrow because you must be sleepy. Shh now, time for sleep.

The Project said, But The Project doesn't want to sleep.

Comrade Uma breathed and said, Why do you never sleep?

And The Project laughed, Why, why, why. See, you said it too!

Comrade Uma tickled The Project and said Oh you!

Comrade Uma is the best teacher of writing and the world and The Project likes her most because she is so small and round like a Munchkin of Oz and has many grey hairs because of the sufferings of mankind. But we are not supposed to like people best or be best at anything because then it makes someone else the worst and then the cycle of inequality will start again and people will burn. I wanted to have Comrade Uma as my only teacher but then Comrade Jeni accused Comrade Uma of going behind backs and favouritism and the committee argued. So now Comrade Uma only comes to my little attic room under the dirty roof one time a week even though the other Comrades forget to teach me at all.

When the lesson was done The Project said, can you show me again how to make a paper swan? Please, please, please. The Project tried five times but they were a useless failure so Uma gave The Project her perfect swan because private property does not exist and jealousy is banned.

I miss Comrades Eli, Tobias and Louise, but Comrade Louise had to leave because she is a Capitalist whore and would not break her ties with her bourgeois children, and so they were erased two years ago.

The Project watched the pigeons through the attic window for a long time. They have made a house of sticks and poop under the gutter which means trees must still exist. There are five of them like there are five of us and I am giving them names. The bigger grey one is Ho. The one with a white fleck is Cornflake. The one with the gnarly foot is Gramsci. The one that makes eggs is called Rosa Luxemburg. The one that is very little and fluffy is called Fluffy.

Four floors is a long way up for their stick house and The Project is worried for the eggs when they are born because one year there was a baby bird and it tried to fly but then it fell straight down and vanished. Then the next day a nasty black bird was eating something on the ground and The Project saw it through the crack in the boards on the kitchen window and it was the fluff and blood and bones of the baby and The Project screamed until Comrade Uma made it all go away.

The Project must never think of this again and now the pigeons do funny dances and I did a copying dance sticking out your head and anus to make the other Comrades laugh. Comrade Ruth never laughs because she is like a Daddy Long Legs and always cross and I had to stop dancing because it made Comrade Jeni giggle and she spilt coffee on seven wasted pamphlets. Comrade Chen didn't give her a row but took her to the one room with the door and gave her a special teaching with her pants off to remove ideological contaminants. Comrade Chen didn't give The Project any gold stars today but if The Project stays focused on our great task, The Project will surely earn one tomorrow. The Project can remember no more as this was enough for one day.

Note from Comrade Ruth: We thank The Project for her record. However, she must report her days with greater material clarity, otherwise we cannot judge the effectiveness of the experiment. Other

Comrades must also take time to read and to help her erase her incorrect words. This task must be shared equally as must be the photocopying of pamphlets for the next demonstration. Comrade Ruth asks that Comrade Uma stop wasting paper on origami as this is a reactionary pastime from The Four Olds.

Note from Comrade Uma: Comrade Uma apologises but insists the paper was taken from the bin and so we were re-using it. Comrade Uma expresses concern about the safety of the top window which The Project likes to watch birds from. Can we please check the locks? Comrade Uma also asks the indulgence of the Collective to continue to permit The Project to use the attic storeroom as her learning room. May we also whitewash the attic space, as we have with all the other rooms? Comrade Uma also asks that we continue to attempt to erase the memory of the little dead bird which still troubles The Project, as we do in our weekly erasures of her language.

Comrade Jeni was absent from the re-reading, but sent revolutionary greetings in a note via Comrade Uma and asked that The Project stop being such a cheeky little sneak. Comrade Jeni also promised to spend more time teaching The Project and to cease using reactionary feminine words.

Note from Comrade Chen: The Project education rota must be observed and all must share equally. The Project is no longer allowed to sit by the upstairs attic window or to be left unattended while in the toilet. Neither the attic nor the toilet are her private property. The Project must cease using the words my, mine *and* I *as she has been told over many years. Thinking about the* self *is* selfish *and is the very crucible of Capitalist oppression.*

I tire of repeating this rule: Each and all of us cannot sleep in one room for more than three days and all must move according to the rota to guard against growing attached to one space. I am grateful for Comrade Ruth's editorial and writing contributions to The Red Flag but must remind all Comrades that we must all equally share in the tasks of cooking, cleaning and collecting food according to the rota. Comrade Uma completes too many of these tasks when others fail and she is not a housewife who is here to cook and scrub while Comrade Ruth writes and Comrade Jeni does the shopping. I must also insist that when inside our four walls every one of us wears the grey cotton clothes and one-size flip-flops at all time as the jeans, T-shirts and feminine things that have been appearing lead to envy and contaminated thoughts.

Finally, Origami is Japanese, not Chinese and is a counter-revolutionary activity which must cease. All praise our Glorious Leader, Mao Zedong, the un-setting sun. We love him more than we do our own lives.

There are yellow sunflowers and red other flowers and rice fields in a lovely soft blue haze. The little people are children. One girl holds a big red fruit and one is holding a thing like a fat cucumber and the girls have ribbons in their hair and they are all so happy with the boys in a circle in the sun and all have their red scarfs and stars on as our Glorious Leader stands in the middle smiling with his hand on the little girl's shoulder. He holds a piece of paper and The Project thinks he is reading the instructions for the better world to come. The Project has looked at this picture in the eating room all week and gave the children in the picture names and wanted to be the little girl with the satchel who our Glorious Leader is touching.

Comrade Ruth said The Project stares at the picture too long and is avoiding whitewash and floor bleaching duty again. The Project hates Comrade Ruth because she is too skinny with a head shaved like a skull and has no chest and she is always looking down on everyone because she is the tallest and she says Comrade Uma and Comrade Jeni teach The Project frivolous feminine things.

The Project has to leave my window and is not to watch those other children playing in their back garden either. They are far away and smaller than a pigeon, over two walls of distance, and The Project can only see their heads when they jump and try to catch the ball. The Project tries very hard not to imagine herself catching it and to not give the children names because names are signs of slave ownership. With the window up as far as it goes The Project can hear them running and there was a song and a slapping noise and a bit of rope in a circle above the wall so they were being trained to whip the slaves. They are cruel because they laugh at suffering and if The Project ever went outside I would be given a lynching because I have seen it in the other National Geographic with the grey pictures.

The Project helped paint the attic room to make it whiter again and had to take all the books off the shelves. The Project asked why weren't there more for The Project's Great Learning and Comrade Uma said the two National Geographics and Core Maths and the A to Z and The Wizard of Oz were all the Comrades could save from the Nuclear War in such a hurry and these are the last books in all the world now apart from Capital and the Little Red Book of our Great Helmsman which The Project is old enough to read now and to ask for nothing else.

The Project made my own scarf from an old red towel and wore it for two days. Comrade Ruth took it away and said, Stop showing off and go and wash the rice and look out for mouse poo because mouse poo tastes very bitter when you cook it in the rice and it is planted there by fascist saboteurs. I don't know how they get into the kitchen at night when there is patrol duty. The Project felt angry and dreamed of choking Comrade Ruth but only Comrade Chen has the power to do this.

The Project ran round rooms two, three and five then a cloud burst outside and The Project was scared at the boarded-up window at the bottom and sad that man has made the radiation fall from the sky like bleach which you are never to drink.

Comrade Chen gave a beautiful speech at the dinner circle.

He has listened to the requests for a new washing machine and more muesli. He announced that Comrade Ruth found some feminine scented soap in the bathroom and the guilty party will come forward and he warned again against Comrades who crave nice things. He said be patient, there are only grey things in the world right now but when Year Zero comes the trees will burst forth again and the flowers bloom in colours never seen before with more radiant smells and everyone will have the most perfect things like in the picture of the children and they will not want for anything else or compete with each other for possessions or status. But until then we must live with mouse poo rice for the sake of the billions who have none.

He placed his hands on each of our heads and said, Women know more than anyone the burden of exploitation. To give love and in return to be disposed of when your shell has been emptied. It is for the hope of the first fully free woman that we make our sacrifices. And he gave me his special smile. These words of Comrade Chen fill us with tears of joy. I love the curly hairs in his eyebrows and his chin. Comrade Uma always cries but I don't because I am The Project and I have new kinds of emotions.

Comrade Chen said he will read The Project's full report later as all Comrades are busy with preparations for the anti-war demonstration and the push for new recruits. He stroked The Project's head and said, You young people, full of vigour and vitality, are like the sun at eight in the morning. You will purge the old of their errors and build the better world. He makes me feel very special and I want to kiss him.

Comrade Zana has green hair and painted eyes and arm pictures and smells of the smoke of the burning beyond. She came from the demonstration to the Collective and needs help. She has a strong proletarian accent and will be living with us now because the fascists tried to kill her through her veins. Comrade Ruth offered to shower Comrade Zana and cut her hair to remove all contagion but Comrade Zana said she could manage by herself, thank you very much. She has paint on her fingernails and dirt and shivers because she has been sleeping on the contaminated streets. The Project watched her shower and told her we have to share everything, like air and water and looking because there are no private possessions here.

She has wounds in her arms where she escaped from slavery and the codes of her masters are branded in pictures of animals on her skin. She made me feel dizzy and dirty inside. She has metal hoops in the pinks of her breasts and one through her nose and six in her ears.

Comrade Ruth gave her some of our shared grey clothes and we watched her change and Comrade Ruth took her old clothes away for burning. She was wearing jeans made by a counter-revolutionary and the patch of his name had an H and an M. Also destroyed were banned things from her pockets, paper sticks to burn in the mouth of addicts, paints for the face and a bottle of feminine smell.

We must erase that we have seen them.

After wearing our T-shirt and boots Comrade Zana talked to The Project and Comrade Ruth about how Comrade Chen saved her life. She said he is the kindest, wisest man ever. She said she was with a group of anarchists before and they wanted to save the planet by throwing Molotovs and this is petrol in a bottle and petrol is what makes cars go and it comes from under the sea.

Zana said, you don't half ask a lot of funny questions then said, anyway she gave these fuckers her money to buy petrol but they ran away to buy some smacks instead. She wept and said Comrade Chen found her and gave her food and promised her shelter. She said, I want to learn, he's right, how can we change the world if it's rotting inside us, right, right? We have to get rid of the evil that's in here first, right?

She hugged us both and we forgave her because she has yet to be re-educated about emotions. Plus I said we are the ones chosen to free the world so she shouldn't be so twitchy. She said it was maybe the cold turkey she had eaten. It is so unfair that Comrade Zana gets to eat such things because we hardly even get chicken but we are not to be jealous. Then we women had to hold hands and put our differences aside and Comrade Zana became at one with us.

The Project is looking forward to giving Comrade Zana the lesson about contamination. The Project will tell her why we must paint all the floors and walls white and never move the boards from the windows on the bottom floor in case fascists spy inside. And why we must never move the big white blinds from the windows on floors two and three and never peek out because they keep radiation away, and how the window boards and blinds keep heat away in summer and cold away in winter and nosy fascists away all the time but if you scrub the white floor too hard the evil Victorian wood sneaks through so you must paint it white again to stop Capitalist contamination. And why we have no doors between us, but try not to walk in when someone is making bowel movements.

Comrade Zana says she totally gets it about every room being white and the tables and chairs and floor all white too and its magic like in that video by John and Yoko called Imagine and then she cried and smiled and shivered at the same time and said maybe it was a bit chilly with so many windows boarded up. And The Project said if Comrade Zana was good she could come to the special little window up top.

We ate rice with the last frozen carrots and The Project had a bowel movement which was not perfect but soft and yellow. The Project feels something churning in my belly. I think the feeling comes when I think of forbidden things that I like, like when I stare hard out of the attic window and magic the tops of human heads to come past.

Comrade Chen gave Comrade Zana her first lesson and told us we must erase the word like from now on, as it leads to dislikes and comparisons and then you end up with inequality and hatred again. He says that The Project uses the word like far too much. The Project feels like saying But I like the word like and I like when Gramsci comes to my window and makes his flapping dance but I didn't say it because it would be many mistakes in a row. The Project will have to re-educate myself and Comrade Zana too.

Comrade Uma began to sniffle again at the sharing time. Comrade Chen said she had had news of an old friend who died in the guerrilla war in Germany. Afterwards Comrade Ruth muttered that all this crying was just Comrade Uma's way to get attention from Comrade Chen. The Project is sure this feeling I get when I see her cry is not a banned feeling and that I am feeling a cramp from some bad food even though the food is never bad, as everyone cooks it on the rota and it is always good and always rice.

I confess I was dreaming of boiled chicken and wanting to have my own sleeping room and be alone because of Comrade Zana taking up more space.

The Project must also report that Comrade Zana asked incorrect questions in the corridor. She said, Is it true The Project has really never ever gone to school not even for a single bloody day?

The Project nodded.

Did The Project know what MTV was? Or Top of the Pops or Radio One? Or boyfriends? Or booze?

The Project felt very ignorant and hot in the face.

Comrade Zana said, No shit? God, No, that's not what I meant. You're so lucky. So, so lucky.

Then The Project was confused about my name because Comrade Zana said, Why do they call you The Project anyway? That's really weird. She said Ruth told her that the reason I was called The Project was because I was like this test to prove that a child kept free from inherited prejudices of History would grow up to be an improved kind of human. She said that was fucking mental.

The Project asked Comrade Zana what her life was an experiment to prove.

She laughed and she said, I'm test-tube fuck-up man, experiment in nothingness. Then she said, Weird though that they never, like, gave you a name.

The Project said, Why? And she said, Well, maybe you're the only person in the whole world without one. See you're lucky again twice!

The Project went to my thinking corner and there are other people who are called The Something. Glinda is called The Good Witch of the North and The Queen is called The Queen. But I am not a Witch and Comrade Chen says all royalty must be beheaded. If we are all the same in the Collective then I should have a name too. It makes my belly hurt because Comrade Ruth said Witches is a name men use to oppress women and Comrade Uma said I am called The Project because I started off like a blank page but if I wanted she could call me Swan or something as a nickname but I said this was counter-revolutionary and silly.

There is no self-criticism this week because the fascists contaminated the rice and now everyone uses too much toilet paper so we have to use newspaper but not look at the stories because they are all Capitalist propaganda. I accidentally stared at one page of a woman near some water with breasts even bigger than Comrade Jeni and a very white smile and long long hair like Comrade Jeni too, but not red. The picture made me look at my face in the toilet bowl water and make comparisons. I also confess to kissing my own arm till I was dizzy in the communal bathroom and thinking about someone just like my shadow but a boy.

I said my whispers in my bed and taught Comrade Zana the

right words. She is ignorant like the masses but new so she won't be hit with the ruler yet. I told her, We have eradicated greed, sexism, racial inequality, mouse poo and murder and soon these words will cease to have any meaning. We are all broken shards from many imperialist wars and Comrade Chen has brought us together to make a vessel to hold the pure water of revolution. All praise Comrade Chen. She repeated it after me and slept on the floor next to Comrade Uma. The Project had the bad dream about the baby bird again but I am not to wake the Comrades ever, so I made myself think of the picture of the smiling children and the Glorious Leader. I want to go into his picture and be the first to read his great plan for us all.

The Project thought it had come as punishment because I had wrong head pictures and thinking I too many times. It was a thing of black blood and it kept coming like beatings of the ruler but from the hole that is in me. The Project ran with it on newspaper to Comrade Uma in the kitchen and Comrade Uma screamed.

Comrade Uma told The Project I was not going to die and said that it was normal and was very surprised that no one had warned The Project that this is part of the monthly oppression of women.

The Project tried to give the newspaper to Comrade Uma because there was more dripping out and Comrade Uma yelled, I don't want it, keep it yourself and for God sake cover your privates.

The Project let her lead me back to the toilet with a tea towel and The Project asked, Why are they called that? Is it because they're private property?

Comrade Uma made me stand in the shower and she said, Well, I shouldn't have said that and it's not a hole either, it's your vagina, that's the correct name.

The Project showed Comrade Uma that blood was still coming and pain and was confused and asked, You said keep it to yourself but that's not allowed.

Comrade Uma pushed the hand of blood away and ran water and muttered about other people and responsibility. The Project said, But is this my own thing?

Comrade Uma sighed and said, Do your eyeballs belong to you?

And The Project said, Yes.

And your belly?

The Project told her Yes, but the food belongs to everyone and it goes in the belly, so that means the belly is stealing communal property and making it private, like the capitalists do, but blood starts inside, so it must be private to start with.

Comrade Uma rubbed The Project roughly all over with the grey towel and said, Well you can't share your vagina with anyone else can you? Like you can't share your eyes. And don't ever let anyone else touch you down there without your permission.

The Project said, So the blood and the vagina, they're mine?

Comrade Uma hummed Yes and went into a basket and took out a bag of things.

The Project said, But, we really aren't allowed private things because Comrade Ruth said the personal is political.

Comrade Uma said, Well, this is different. Now put on those clean underpants and I'll show you how to put on a pad.

It was a good education and The Project is now very pleased to no longer be a girl but one of the oppressed sisterhood of the world. The Project also learned that when a pad is done it is still private property and has to be hidden in the bin and not down the shared toilet. The Project has some questions to do with vomit and tears and nose bits because they all come from inside too and The Project had no idea that there was so much private property in the Collective and will have to ask Comrade Chen. To calm down The Project practised making swans again but only managed a paper pigeon because there were too many folds and my nails were dirty.

Comrade Chen reminded all that we must keep our eyes wide

open even when we sleep for the enemy is within. Comrade Zana didn't sleep and was shivering loudly and this is called withdrawal, so she had to go to Comrade Chen's room in the night for special teaching.

Comrade Zana cannot make it to the analysis of The Project's diary. Comrade Zana is being cared for by Comrade Chen and sends Revolutionary greetings.

Notes from Comrade Uma: It is with some alarm that Comrade Uma reports that through the process of child-rearing by rota, we have all passed the buck to each other on educating The Project about menstruation, basic feminine hygiene and anatomy. Comrade Uma requests funds to purchase a simple functional training bra for The Project. This will be without frills or padding. The Project also needs more exercise and sunlight. Can we please open the window blinds on the third floor. The Project is old enough to see the front streets now. Comrade Uma also proposes that The Project join in on the trips beyond for supplies. It is perhaps time to socialise her to deal with some aspects of the outside. Exclusion from such activities indicates favouritism. The Project does not participate with the tasks of shopping and selling The Red Flag and being left alone is making her regress. She is not a child any more. The Project should also be registered with the DSS so we can claim benefits in her name in due course.

Notes from Comrade Ruth: Comrade Ruth absolutely opposes the introduction of this bra, we all know it is a symbol of female subjugation. Comrade Ruth warned from the start that The Project had to be raised gender neutral but Comrades Uma and Jeni, through ideological laziness, have allowed this mess to develop. Comrade Ruth suspects a leak is responsible for the sudden appearance of all these trappings of bourgeois femininity. To stop further contagion Comrade Ruth proposes that all gendered words such as nice, sweet, petal, etc., should be absolutely banned from The Project's vocabulary.

Comrade Jeni's notes: Comrade Jeni really doesn't like the finger pointing going on in the last reports. We're all equally to blame for failing to teach The Project essentials. And, of course, we need to buy a bra. This is a non-issue. If there is a question of money for such household things then Comrade Jeni is happy to help directly. As for state benefits, again I would rather get some guilt money from my capitalist pig parents. Comrade Jeni agrees that The Project really needs to get out for some fresh air.

Note from Comrade Chen: There is deep concern at the lack of unity in this Collective and categorically refuses the proposal to involve the British Pig state in the upbringing of The Project. Neither should the child begin adult work. The Project is to be saved from the slavery we were born into. The experiment cannot be jeopardised. On the other issue a brassiere will be permitted.

The Project had to be brave Comrade Jeni said, and take out the bins just for once. The Project was very scared of attack by fascist radiation and had to hide in the shadows and then crawl on concrete, then run. On the ground next to the bins The Project found egg shells and some pages of colour pictures and words fastened together. The Project knew it was a thought bomb and threw it far away so that it could not contaminate us when it blew up. It had pictures of starving women who were all smiling with just bras and pants. They had flame colours on their faces and spikes fastened to their feet. It made me feel sick in my belly but no more blood came. The face colour must be bruising from the violence of men.

This week The Project must save up all my self-criticisms and help teach Comrade Zana how to confess with us in the circle. I did not look through all the colour pictures and I have already banished the words make-up and Dior, which I read by accident. The Project should never have seen these words because they have contaminated my white page.

The Project looked at the place called The Lane and there are fifty windows all from houses of survivor slaves but The Project was not to pity them. If they could listen to Comrade Chen he would save them but they love their chains and they also love addiction bottles because these are in the bins outside and some are smashed.

The Project also must report that the children from the garden two walls away were trying to brainwash The Project with a propaganda song and making the sound of whipping again.

The Project had to hide between the bins and put her fingers in the ears. They were singing: Mickey Mouse built a house, how many bricks did he use, one, two, three, four five six. It is a bad torture to make a slave count all the bricks in a house when you whip them. The Project has been warned about Mister Mickey Mouse before. The Project has seen all the wires above the garden that join all the houses together and this is how Mickey Mouse signals are sent into every house. Comrade Chen cut the wires to the Collective out on the roof near my window so that we don't get the signals. He must be the bravest to have climbed out there with Cornflake and the other birds.

The Project still has a bad score because of all the I words. The Project has a question: When I cross out I should it stop me thinking I in my head? Like when I think I am hungry? Or am I pretty? No matter how hard I try I cannot seem to get rid of I.

Urgent note from Comrade Chen: Comrade Chen has been informed that The Project might be concealing objects around the Collective. There has been much talk of images and pages. Where did they go to? They have not been found at the bins. Out of kindness, Comrade Chen asks that The Project confess rather than be subject to house search.

Note from Comrade Uma: Comrade Uma expressed concern that we may be testing The Project too much. She is just a teenage girl with healthy curiosities. Please don't interrogate her.

Note from Comrade Jeni: Comrade Jeni expresses anger over insinuations that she has put consumerist ideas into The Project's head.

Comrade Jeni thinks a certain Comrade is attempting to punish The Project for her growing teenage desires and attractiveness. *Comrade Jeni will name names if the neurotic bitch pushes her any further.*

Note from Comrade Ruth: Comrade Ruth condemns the language of Comrade Jeni in the strongest terms. To say The Project is attractive *– what does this do other than summon oppressive* memories of rape*? The Project should not be permitted to create her own ribbons and scarfs as she has been doing for the last few months. And what has happened to these pictures she talks of? A search is imperative. Comrade Ruth alerts the Comrades to Comrade Uma and Comrade Jeni's regressive thinking. We must prove once and for all, that the* teenage emotions *of* secrecy, lying, vanity and lust *are ideological constructs and not* 'human nature' or 'female nature'. *Comrade Ruth asks why a certain Comrade keeps pushing The Project into areas where she encounters* temptations. *Comrade Ruth absolutely condemns the outbreak of this reactionary behaviour known* as bitching. *Comrade Ruth is not afraid to name names and proposes that Comrade Jeni be re-educated after a total search of the Collective is undertaken. If The Project is lying and hiding things punishment will be administered.*

Jotter #242 2018

Nina had to be wired to two machines one that beeped and one that had a rubber thing tight on Nina's good arm, then they put a needle in the skin and took blood out and the woman said, Be brave, so Nina thought about how brave Dorothy was when the Monkeys flew her to the castle of the Wicked Witch of the West to be tortured.

The next visit in Hospital was much easier because Nina was listening to The Wizard of Oz with the voices in the ear-wires and Nina's eyesight was getting better and less was blurry.

Nina kept being introduced to new people but Nina didn't have to say hello to everyone passing by so it was OK to just look at the Hospital floor and passing shoes of many colours instead.

Charity Sonia has flat shoes because she believes in equality. The nurse had shoes with a lady heel because slave women have been trained not to run because they are required to lie down for penetration and heels make their toes point like a sexual climax which is flattering to their owners, but if you wear only small heels it means you don't want to put this message across quite so much.

Nina told this to Practice Nurse Amy McGill and she said,

That's very interesting, Nina. And Charity Sonia said something about appropriate language and this being why they needed the test.

Then Nina had to sit and it was a game like a test but no one was going to be the winner or loser but this wasn't because the NHS was communist. This was what Nina was told by Practice Nurse Amy McGill who had a uniform but was not a fascist. And she said a list of statements and then Nina had to take them and put them through Nina's own head. Then Nina had to tell the nurse if Nina did strongly agree, slightly agree, slightly disagree or strongly disagree.

> I keep abreast of the latest fashions.
> I often find it difficult to judge if something is rude or polite.

The sentences said I all the time, so this was good practice at having an I, but it was hard. People in freedom do say I an awful lot.

> When I was a child I enjoyed cutting up worms to see what happened.
> I tend to look on the bright side.
> I find it easy to put myself in someone else's shoes.

Practice Nurse Amy McGill told Nina what literal meant and Nina shouldn't be it, so when it said put yourself in other people's shoes it didn't mean how Nina used to share flip-flops with Comrades Uma, Ruth, Jeni and Zana.

Charity Sonia explained to Practice Nurse Amy McGill that Nina had come from a communist Collective. And Nina corrected her and said Marxist Leninist actually not reformist like the Soviet traitors.

Charity Sonia said, OK, let's just try to answer the nurse.

Nina said, Do I have to take my clothes off again for the flashing pictures?

Charity Sonia said, Not just yet, the nice nurse is here to help you with your feelings first.

Practice Nurse Amy McGill said, Don't worry, we'll need to see how your bruises and scars are doing and Nina felt cold in the bad hand and tried to hide it. But the Nurse said let's just get this new test done first, OK, Nina?

Nina said, Do you have to put the things inside my vagina again?

Practice Nurse Amy McGill looked confused.

Charity Sonia said to the nurse, Sorry, her only other experience with doctors was ER on the first night and we had a swab taken.

Practice Nurse Amy McGill looked at her bright box and said, I see we're still waiting on the results.

Charity Sonia said, She's never been to a dentist either, have you, Nina?

Nina nodded.

Practice Nurse Amy McGill made a long breath and a smile again and said, OK, Nina, I like to keep abreast of fashions? Does that apply to you, Nina? Nina laughed and Practice Nurse Amy McGill thought that was unusual so then Nina explained how abreast was a pun because all fashion was about the turning female body bits into sex commodities.

Nina told Practice Nurse Amy McGill that being a sex object was banned before but Nina knew it was important to be a sex object from now on because Nina had read about it in Top Tips in In Style magazine.

There were stacks of these learning magazines on all the tables in all the government places Nina had been made to wait, like the council building with Charity Sonia and the Housing Office and the Emergency Doctor room of waiting. These magazines contained important government information on how to behave.

A woman who smiled like the capitalist wolves had a secret way of losing seven pounds and a famous slave woman with a large chest made of plastic under the skin had ten tips on finding love.

Practice Nurse Amy McGill said, OK, fine and maybe Nina could put strongly agree to the one about trying to keep up with fashion.

Practice Nurse Amy McGill was keen to get back to the question of cutting up worms which could also mean killing bugs or hurting small creatures or big ones or even not feeding them and this could be a cat and had Nina ever done any of these things? Nina said Nina had never hurt any small animals apart from a higher primate when Nina had killed one of the Comrades.

Practice Nurse Amy McGill looked at Charity Sonia then she did a smile like in Hello magazine. Then they were silent.

Charity Sonia said, What do you mean by that Nina? Did you call your pets Comrades too?

Nina shook her head and said, A human, a woman.

The two women looked at each other and other Hospital noises became loud.

Charity Sonia said, Do you mean that literally or as a figure of speech, like I could kill for a cup of tea?

Practice Nurse Amy McGill said to Charity Sonia, It's quite normal for victims of abuse to internalise the violence and feel that they are to blame.

Nina said, Not like a cup of tea. She had foam and blood in her mouth and her eyes were all white but it took a while longer for her to properly die.

Charity Sonia gripped Nina's arm and said, How old were you when this happened, Nina?

Practice Nurse Amy McGill said to Charity Sonia, It's also possible that she can't tell fantasy from reality.

Practice Nurse Amy McGill said, Who did you kill, Nina?

Charity Sonia said, Was this in self-defence, Nina?

Nina's bad hand went cold. Nina had to rub and hide it but Charity Sonia saw and she bent down close and she said, Was that when someone hurt your poor hand, Nina?

Her eyes were so big and Nina wanted to tell her but every time Nina tries to think of that time all the pictures and words are rubbed out and the head hurts.

Charity Sonia and the Practice Nurse Amy McGill talked quietly to each other and very fast. Charity Sonia said, Right, so now I have to contact the police again. She sighed. This gets worse every minute. Deaths. Were any reported? Oh Nina.

Practice Nurse Amy McGill said to her, Do you want me to continue?

Charity Sonia said, Nina can you please tell me who this was, this person who died?

Nina remembered what Nina had been told and told them, All Comrades are not to repeat it. We are to erase it.

Charity Sonia said, My God. OK, let's just finish the test and then I'll call the station.

Practice Nurse Amy McGill said just one more, Nina, and she said, I prefer animals to humans. Nina told her about the pigeons and how watching them gives a feeling in Nina's chest when they fly, expanding out and filling up the hollow like music does and this does not happen when Nina looks at humans. Nina likes birds best.

Nina wasn't supposed to look at the page when they left Nina alone to whisper behind the door but Nina did and it said: Empathy Rating. On average, most women score about 47 and most men about 42.

Nina felt incorrect because Nina's answers had only made four boxes be ticked. Nina stuffed papers from the desk into Nina's pockets in case they had tips for future tests.

Charity Sonia drove Nina back to the Charity House and was silent and she gave Nina some paper money for food. She gripped the wheel for the hands and said, Nina, you know, with cults, you can't blame yourself, people aren't really individuals. They're all to blame, equally. What did they do to you, Love, what on earth?

Charity Sonia's face was having emotions and she said, Nina, can you tell me, this person who passed away. When did this happen? Were you very small?

Then Nina had sore head pictures and then words came and Nina said, All who betray the cause are dead to us.

Charity Sonia said, OK, sorry. Don't worry, best not to think about that right now, sorry.

Charity Sonia said goodbye and said it was OK for Nina to hold onto her hand like that just this once and it made Nina's bad hand feel better. And she said she really, really had to go now and speak to the Pigs and Nina really shouldn't call them that and, Yes, Nina would be all alone again tonight, like everyone else in Freedom.

When she was gone the hole feeling came again so Nina took out the pages from the pocket from Practice Nurse Amy McGill's desk.

I really enjoy caring for other people. I would never break a law no matter how minor. I think that good manners are the most important thing that a parent can teach a child.

It was no good. Nina would have to break a law and become a parent to be able to know the answer.

Another page had other kinds of boxes and one was ticked and it said, Shows little signs of facial, gestural and vocal indices of empathy-related responding.

Nina felt sorry for this person and thought maybe that meant Nina could tick the caring box. Then Nina looked at the top and it said Patient Name Nina X.

Nina had an emotion and it made the shivering come. Nina must stop writing because it means Nina is still under the control of Comrade Chen and is not yet an I.

Nina folded the papers into birds and hid them in different places. Then Nina felt better.

This was a lot for one day. Nina did not sleep because Nina sat in the window looking for pigeons who did not come in the night or morning even when Nina left a paper bird on the windowsill for them.

Nina waited a long time for Charity Sonia because we had to make a trip for Nina's blood appointment but Nina couldn't make it past the second corner where there is the shop with dead parts called Halal that smell sweet, that made pictures come of the skeleton people in the desert. So we had to go back. This day was a failure and Nina slept twelve little times, but Charity Sonia said it was a good sign that Nina said We.

The next day Nina slept for a longer bit but Charity Sonia was sad to say she was too busy and sent a message on a bit of paper that said: *It's now official. Comrade Chen, also known as David Chen and David Thompson has been found and arrested. So far he will be charged with your unlawful imprisonment and assault and GBH but the police would like to interview you, Nina, for more details, especially about the incident you mentioned and other witnesses. Don't worry, I'll be there too. Sonia.*

First a young person buzzed the door to take Nina to the blood test man. She had bright yellow hair and chewed gum and gave Nina some to try and it was exciting because it was the most banned sign of American imperialism but do not swallow it. And her name was Support Worker Katherine but just to call her Cas and she had an accent and she helps Charity Sonia and lots of vulnerable adults.

She said she had to ask Nina, How many hours sleep did you get last night, Pet? And, What have you eaten today? Nina said, four and two sugar lumps. Cas came inside fast with a bag with milk and bread for Nina and she checked the cupboards and she said, Didn't they explain, all those cans of soup is for you, Love, we stacked it up for you, special.

Nina was nervous because Nina doesn't know about cans.

Then Cas opened the fridge and she said, You've not touched your Ready Meals either, what's wrong, Pet? Look, you've got Lamb Rogan Josh and Lasagna and look a Thai Curry, I love a curry. None of them take your fancy? You a vegetarian?

Nina shook the head because Nina had smelled the packets before and they were of sour and plastic and the box said they had Microwaves inside.

Then Cas said, You've not even plugged in the micro or the kettle, Bleedin heck, here.' And she pushed buttons and a radiation light went on inside and a humming and a plate turned by itself and Nina couldn't hear Cas's instructions because of Nina's fingers in the ears and the shivering.

Then Cas said, Bloody hell, You all right, Love?

And then she turned it off. Then she said, Look, Love, you gotta eat something, you look totally anorexic. What you normally eat?

And Nina said Rice, and Cas looked in the cupboards and she said, Right, OK, forget that appointment, I'm taking you to the shops right now, OK, Petal?

Then it was outside and Cas said she had never seen a person staring at the bleeding cars like they was rabbits in the headlights. Cas said, Step back, Jesus, look out for that wing mirror.

And these are things on cars and not on birds.

Cas said, OK, just stand back from the edge and breathe.

Cas said, Right, well, here we are at the corner, the shops is just three more blocks. This is the kerb and this is the road. All right? Cars don't come up the kerbs, and the pavement is just for people, OK?

The only way to walk in the outside is to put the hands on the other person's shoulders and look at their heels from behind but Cas didn't know this and she didn't like Nina doing it. Cas said,

What you doing? Stop clinging like that. Have you never seen a bleedin bus before? Bloody hell. Why you shaking like that?

The metal machines were in many shapes and moved fast and every time Nina looked at one it leapt at Nina. Nina knew some of them were called cars but there are also other loud things that are much bigger with many wheels and not called cars.

Nina told Cas Nina couldn't do it, Nina will pee and to please go back to the Charity House. Cas became frustrated and Nina stared at a picture high on a building that said Golden Ball Lottery. Everyone is a winner. Nina was confused.

Cas said, Wait I've got an idea, let's get some tunes on then you can focus on that. She said that when she got nervous, like on the train when some dodgy geezer was eyeing her tits, she just put on her headphones and let him go fuck himself, and she put her wires in Nina's ears. Nina told her she had seen many people like this out of the window, everyone looking at the things in their hands which were phones with no wires and only magic electricity and ignoring everyone else.

Nina had the wires in her ears and Cas said, Right, what music you into?

Nina told her that Nina liked Red Star Shone, the Song of the Four Pests and Sailing the Seas Depends on the Helmsman. Cas had never heard of these.

Nina said there was also a song playing in the first attempt at shopping but the slave woman said if she had no money she had to stop touching things and get the hell out.

Cas said, What do you mean slave? And Nina told her that women of Asia, Arabia and America were owned by Imperialist Patriarchal Masters. Cas said, Bloody hell, don't let Sonia hear you saying that!

Nina said, OK, sorry. Nina is still learning.

Cas said, Do you always do that? Say Nina this and Nina that, like what? Tarzan, Tarzan wants to eat, Tarzan is hungry.

Nina asked who Tarzan was.

Cas said she was sorry for laughing and not to think she was talking to Nina like she was mental, because she was told Nina had an extremely high IQ and some of the people round here in sheltered housing well they were actually mental for real but don't tell Sonia she said that neither, right? Nina told her Nina would erase the bad words from memory and try harder to say I.

Cas pressed the glass of the phone and a song was in Nina's head very loudly and Cas took Nina's arm with her. The song was about wanting to be loved and Nina remembered to get many lipsticks.

Nina and Cas walked like this and then Nina was upset by the big street picture of Your Breakfast Bun for only 99p because Nina wanted it and there was no place to buy it.

Cas said Nina doesn't half say the funniest bloody things and it didn't mean Nina's own personal bun and the people who made the sign had no idea who Nina was and it wasn't like an order that Nina had to obey, like right now. Cas said please to try to chill and ignore shit and stop shouting and take those headphones out when you talk to folk. Nina did and Cas said Bloody hell, how would you get through the day if you had to buy everything in all the adverts. Jeans and a car and a new phone and God knows what else before you even get to the end of the road. I mean Sonia said you were hypersensitive but we've only gone two streets and we'll never get there at this bleedin rate.

Cas said, OK, three more blocks. OK, walk like this, you know, we're off to see the Wizard, Nina? You know, like how you walk down the Yellow Brick Road. The song with the Tin Man and the Lion. Sonia said you was well into that.

Nina was confused because there are no songs in the Wizard of Oz comic and Nina can only listen to little bits of the DVD at one time because of the danger of radiation and Nina did not like the singing bits.

Cas said, C'mon take my arm. I'll teach you the song. And she said, You don't have to sing it out loud, just say it quietly.

When Cas's Yellow Brick song had been learned by Nina and sung for the eighth time Cas said, Wow, you did brill. Look!

She pointed back and Nina couldn't see because far away things are a blur and Cas said, See, Continental Halal is two streets back. Look how far you came because you was distracted and not panicking or nothing.

Cas said there was just another block then through the underpass and she said, On you go, I'm letting go of your arm now, you're going to be fine.

Nina put the headphones back in and walked on the pavement place with the music in the ears and kept on going and it was all fine and no radiation came. Nina saw a pigeon and ran to it because Nina misses them so much, but this was in the road and Nina screamed when the wheels came so fast and Nina fell and a horn went and a man shouted and Cas had to shout, Very sorry. And after that she didn't let go of Nina. She said, You really don't have a Scooby, do you? This is im-fucking-possible.

Nina told her she was doing that thing again of talking to Nina like Nina was a child and if she wanted Nina could recite Das Kapital to her because Nina has a memory like a photograph and Nina began, The wealth of those societies in which the capitalist mode of production prevails, presents itself as an immense accumulation of commodities, its unit being a single commodity. Our investigation must therefore begin with the analysis of a commodity. A commodity is, in the first place—

Cas said, All right, all right, keep your hair on.

The trip was cancelled and Cas said she'd speak to her boss about Nina's problems. She said, You'll starve to death if you can't make it to bleeding Sainsbury's.

In the Charity House Nina had to lie down in the dark next to the bath and Cas said no one had told her about that either and is the flusher not working because it don't half niff in here. Then she flushed it and the smell of the old place went away and Nina was needing the dark again.

Cas said, Look, I'll drop you off some sandwiches, but Tuesday you got to see your Doctor and your Social Worker because since you said that thing about the dead woman they have to get involved and that's a long way and a lot of changes of trains or buses. Could you practise singing the Yellow Brick Road in your head and not out loud, maybe that'd help.

Nina said this was enough for one day and much work had now to be done writing it all down.

Cas said Bye then stopped at the door and said, Is it true they brainwashed you and made you do someone in?

Nina said nothing.

Cas said, Wow. I mean, bloody hell. How do they do that? Brainwash? How's it work then?

Nina stared at the floor.

Cas said, OK, Sorry, bye then and remember to flush next time. I'll get you some toothpaste too and some deodorant. Take care, bye, Nina. Bye.

She shut the door, then there was nothing and electricity hum.

Nina lay still and breathed then tried to practise I phrases. I would like to thank you. I would like to come into your shop. I would like an apple. I am not afraid of being alone. I am hungry for some cheese.

It was no use, Nina has to think Nina first and then rub out Nina to think I. Like this: Nina wants I want this. Nina is I am too tired.

Nina wants to see the old diaries again from when Nina wasn't even called Nina but The Project. No one will understand. So many pages were torn out and others were eaten. Birds make nests out of chewed things. Nina has only this little jotter now. Nina will sleep on Nina's words so no one can steal them.

Jotter #67 2002

Today was search day and The Project was twisting in the belly but first Comrade Jeni wanted to give The Project one of her bras but her breasts were far too big and Comrade Ruth said Comrade Jeni's flowery bra was oppressing all women everywhere. Comrade Uma went to the outside for a long while and brought back a simple white bra for The Project. It was too scratchy. Then Comrade Jeni kept looking at me strangely then she shook her head and said, God, all of that ahead of you yet. The Project was confused. Comrade Jeni said The Project would be a stunner one day and she gave me a hug and a kiss and her long red hair covered me. Comrade Jeni has been in trouble before for kissing on the lips and behind backs. I told her that being a stunner is a capitalist disease and she ran off to be alone again and smoke some weeds but they only make her two polarities worse, said Comrade Ruth.

I always say I more when I am around Comrade Jeni because she says it all the time.

Then Comrade Uma sat me in bedroom four and said I wouldn't be moving to bedroom two this week because they had to break the rota because new recruit Comrade Zana needed to stay in room one to get better. The Project said, Why is she getting favouritism? Comrade Uma said, You're very grumpy. Why? Is it the Search, are you hiding something?

The search was to begin at two o'clock and The Project had a churning belly, so Comrade Uma said it might be a good time to practise The History, because it could be The Project's job to teach Comrade Zana and Comrade Chen would send my History to Chairman Mao and I will get a gold star if all is correct. And The Project hoped for a hug when it was over because Comrade Uma is the fattest and best for hugs.

The Project started. Once there was a place called London Fields and it was slums from the time of the evil King George, and, our Glorious Leader said all land is the property of the people so Comrade Chen said let us take these abandoned grey tenements and kick the locks off. And there were ten Comrades, then twenty, then forty and they were called squatters and many were looking for hope and refuge after the bad times of the seventies. And there were five buildings all in the same part of the ruined city and all had the same with four floors with four attics and eight rooms each and all with a basement and very bad toilets. And these homes had once housed many proletarian families and had been called slums but Comrade Chen renamed them The Fields People's Collective and Comrade Uma was there from the start too and they were sixty Comrades then and they had no electricity and nasty water and Comrade Chen was the leader of all.

The Project stopped then and Comrade Uma read it.

Comrade Uma said, You are a top student but don't get too proud, little monkey. You have not said how Comrade Chen took in the homeless and fed them and how the evil council tried to demolish these old buildings and we had to fight to save them.

The Project begged to hear Comrade Uma tell the rest because of her funny accent and because she says it best of anyone.

So Comrade Uma said, OK, OK. So then there was the great battle and Comrade Chen and the sixty Comrades beat the Council and Comrade Chen bought this one block for nearly nothing because it was condemned. But then the sixty became twenty because some were just hippies and they did not like the hard work of rebuilding and plumbing and making it new and white and pure.

The Project knew what was coming and was excited. The Project said, And then the Great War of Fire came!

Comrade Uma said, Yes, and Comrade Chen had warned of it but no one listened, and the skies burned for a hundred days. And the twenty Comrades in this house became nine because a wall fell down in Berlin.

The Project got the tingling feeling and said, And then The Project rose from the ruins!

Comrade Uma said Yes, that is correct. You arrived a year after the reformist Soviet Union collapsed, and you were the new hope because Communism never dies it only hides and sleeps and is awoken with a new generation. But you were also a great test and some Comrades would not care equally for you.

The Project said, But why did Eli and Tobias and Louise go back to the burning lands. Was it because of me when I was little?

Comrade Uma said, Well, you know why.

And Comrade Uma said, Comrade Louise wanted a baby too, but Comrade Chen banned it, because she was already pregnant from a fascist outside and she lied to Comrade Eli and Tobias, and told both men they owned the baby and there were many fights of bourgeois jealousy. So Comrade Chen forbade all relationships. Because all must come to him first, not to each other. And this was called the second clean-up. And Comrade Chen banished Comrade Louise because she would not sever all links to her family outside and he purged all men from the Collective and he made our locks tight so no contamination could enter ever again. And that is why we paint every room white and that is why we are now only female Comrades and all faithful and why you must stay safe inside and not try to peek through the cracks in the downstairs window boards.

The Project got the feeling in the belly and Comrade Uma looked as if she knew the next question was coming.

The Project said, But where did I come from?

Comrade Uma was quiet and she said, You know the answer already, Child.

And The Project was very proud and said, The Project is the first perfect child of the new mankind!

Then Comrade Uma gave a serious face because The Project must banish all vanity and individualism. Then Comrade Uma said, you won't feel so full of yourself if you've been hiding something, little monkey. Come on, it is time for the search.

The Project had a sick feeling in the belly and Comrade Uma said that if The Project had anything to confess, best to tell her in advance. The Project was cross with Comrade Uma because she is very close to me with soft hugs then gets ashamed and goes cold and like Comrade Ruth the skeleton.

Comrade Uma helped The Project turn the mattress. Then she stopped and put her hand to her mouth. She told The Project that The Project had committed an atrocious act by hiding a banished thing.

The Project has to confess:

The Project had snuck the paper pictures of the smiling women with the big chests and long hair like Comrade Jeni into the Collective. Then hid them under my bed.

The Project lied in the diary about it.

The Project has looked at it every time I could sneak away from my duties and has seen many pictures from this magazine.

The Project prays that Comrade Mao will not delay the revolution in North London because of The Project's selfish actions and begs Comrade Uma not to tell him, please. The Project said, Could we just destroy it please and not tell? But Comrade Uma said there can be no secrets and lies. Comrade Uma asked, How many pages have you seen? Did you read any of the articles? She said, Good God and she read out loud, Totally Irresistible Ways to Please Your Man in Bed.

Comrade Uma asked why The Project was searching in the bins of the enemy. The Project breathed too fast and said Comrade Zana has made me feel stupid and so I had to learn what pop music was. Comrade Uma said, But why, why on earth did you sneak it inside? Why? You're protected from everything here. She swore at herself in German and said, You have no idea how you've jeopardised everything. There are bad men out there hunting for us, now.

The Project breathed so fast until the floor spun and, The Project was made to grab the knees and breathe slow, and again and again.

Comrade Uma shouted for an emergency meeting and The Project was not allowed to attend. The Project banged the head against the bathroom tiles and picked off the biggest scab to make the warm pain come that makes you forget.

The Project sat in the no window bathroom and tried to erase all incorrect pictures from the head. Spike Feet. Fast boxes with people inside. Paint on faces. Dresses too short but not called shorts. Spider net legs. I lost five stone in three weeks. Six sexy looks for summer. Naked bodies and gold. The Project said very, very sorry to the taps and vomited and then washed it away. There were bits of rice that were hard to erase.

The emergency meeting went on for many hours and The Project rocked back and forwards and listened to the shouting and the banging of tables and the silences more horrible still.

At dark time it was Comrade Chen who came. He lifted The Project from the shivering tiles and covered The Project in the towel and set The Project on the edge of the bath. He stroked The Project so the teeth would not chatter. The Project feared to look in his eye. He told The Project that it was too late now, the mind of The Project has been contaminated and this is why she bleeds from the head but now more must be done. He said, We had wished to protect you from such things forever, but now we must tell you what they are. We must make things worse to make them better.

Comrade Chen is so kind. The Project is to be made pure again like I was after the time with the doll I made for myself.

Note from Comrade Uma: Please be gentle with her. Comrade Uma takes full responsibility. Please don't subject the child to this.

Note from Comrade Ruth: Perhaps Comrade Uma does not realise the severe nature of the contamination she so foolishly let The Project expose herself to. There is a dangerous article in the magazine on Sexy Mums and an image of a wedding dress. There are images of bourgeois family life. Does Comrade Uma suggest we should explain what these things are to The Project? If we explain families then we shall have to explain the entire History of Patriarchal oppression and if we tell her about mothers she may even start to want one. No, the need to raise children away from the negative influence of parents can only be enforced in children by not telling them what parents once were, let alone who they were. Children often crave that which they don't have. She may crave parents in the way she does children's stories. Comrade Ruth again requests that The Project's Wizard of Oz comics be confiscated. We know Comrade Uma used them to teach The Project how to read but certain Comrades have been naive to think that quaint cartoons found in a garage sale could ever be ideologically neutral. This contagion must stop.

We now have only one option, The Project should be subject to The Purification as we all have and not given special treatment. As has been said by others, she is now no longer a child.

Note from Comrade Jeni: You're all mad, all this fuss over a stupid fashion magazine, The Project is going to have to see them someday, isn't she? Can we just chill the fuck out please?

Note from Comrade Uma: Please, if anyone is to be punished it should be me. Please let me go through The Purification in place of The Project.

Note from Comrade Chen: Comrades, please! End this talk of I and Me! Unity is only possible through purity. If we are not pure then the Revolutionary Liberation army of China will not come to overthrow The British Empire. They had intended to arrive before 28 December but now they will have to postpone again. Comrade Chen has decided that The Project will have to undergo The Purification. We shall prepare the process together and we should use it to remind ourselves of why we all joined the Collective. After it is done, all Comrades will edit The Project's report to make sure no contaminated images or words remain. The Project must understand that Language is the material of the mind, and she who erases wrong words from her brain can change the structure of life. As Lenin said, the Communist party's most critical task is the selection of language.

All praise to our Glorious Leader. We shall fight until a bright red cultural field of Mao Zedong thought comes.

Jotter #242 2018

Black Female ones are not called Slave Pigs. Two Police were in the Charity House with Charity Sonia and the lights were too bright and machine voices too crackling because Nina had not slept because Nina waited at the window but only a sparrow came. Nina was not to be scared because everything is its opposite and the black uniforms are not fascists and all this is in the past.

The Female police sat down and said, This is just a preliminary chat to see if you feel fit to give a witness testimonial. She said, We can confirm now that the first charges have been brought against the man you call Comrade Chen and he is being held in custody without bail, pending the next hearing. So you're safe now and you can tell us anything about him. Any bad things he did to you.

And Charity Sonia squeezed Nina's shoulder and Nina rested the ear against her hand. Charity Sonia said, Nina, you can tell the lady anything, she's right, you're safe now.

The Female Police said, We understand that you were taken by the emergency services from a private residence at Well Street,

London Fields and that you had been held there against your will for a great number of years. Is that correct?

Nina felt cold in the bad hand and turned it over to look at the good side.

Charity Sonia said, Yes, since she was a child.

The Female Police said, I'd like to hear from Nina, miss. Following your initial statement, we have looked into the Well Street location that the accused and others resided in and can confirm that there was a fatality in 2002 that this address was connected to. You would have been eleven Nina, is that correct?

Nina looked to Charity Sonia and Charity Sonia took a breath.

Nina said Nina did not know the age and did not say anything about the diaries, because nobody must know about the diaries of The Project.

The Female Police said, The fatality was one Simone Genevieve Lamberton, is that correct?

Nina shook the head because none of the Comrades were called that.

The Male Police said, She might have gone by a different name.

Nina looked at Charity Sonia and whispered, Second names are slave owners' names.

Charity Sonia said, It's all right, Nina, the officers are here to help.

Nina didn't want to, Nina's bad hand hurts when Nina thinks of being The Project again.

The Female Police said, It was reported as a drug-related accidental death at the time. I've seen the file. If any new evidence were to come to light the case would have to be re-opened.

She handed a piece of paper to Charity Sonia and Charity Sonia said Good God.

The Male Police asked, Was it an accident, Nina, or did something else happen?

The Female Police said, Maybe somebody scared you into keeping a secret? Why did you state that you killed someone?

Nina's head became hot and breath went fast and there were windows and birds flapping fast.

The Male Police said, There's no actual evidence that you were at that Well Street address at that time. Were you at that address?

Nina doesn't know, Nina doesn't trust them. Pigs in the house, hide. Hide the diaries. Nina had to go to the basement. If The Project is bad this will all happen again. The Project made it happen last time.

Charity Sonia said, Nina, are you all right?

Nina was rocking back and forwards and thinking of the Comrade. Erased. Nina was making a hum noise to make the words be erased.

The Male Police said, Can you explain what you meant when you said, I killed Simone Lamberton?

Nina said, I must say I all the time, not Nina.

Charity Sonia said, Can't you see she's traumatised. No more questions, please.

Nina said, Everything is a lie. Pigs are liars.

The Female Police said, Sorry, are you saying people lied about it? Or that your initial statement was untrue?

Charity Sonia said, Please, Nina's the victim here.

The Female Police said, Could you tell us if more than one person was involved in the actions that you think led to the death?

Charity Sonia said, She was a child for god sake. You should be interrogating the monster that did this to her, not Nina. And Charity Sonia shouted with her eyes.

Nina whispered to Charity Sonia that it was more than enough for one day and Charity Sonia said it out loud. The Police said they had more questions and names had to be located at addresses and matched with faces. Also, they were hunting for

Nina's birth certificate. They asked, Have you remembered your second name yet?

Nina said, The Project was my first name and Nina is my second.

The Police said, What did she say?

Charity Sonia said that she was going to have to call a stop to this interview now because of Nina's distress and she was sorry and she thanked them and went with them to the door and she locked it and let Nina go to Nina's wall for breathing. Nina squeezed the head into the corner and Charity Sonia went down on her knee and stroked Nina's back three times and said, It's OK now, Nina. And she stroked two times more and asked what Nina was feeling.

And Nina said it was the hollow.

And Charity Sonia's hand stopped stroking and she said, I'm sorry, I don't understand. I'm sorry, Nina, so sorry.

Then time was slow and Nina felt Charity Sonia warm behind and it was safe and she was still there and Charity Sonia whispered, Maybe one day when you feel better you can tell me, as much as you want to, like what happened to your poor hand, Nina, I would really like to know. But in your own time.

Then Nina felt the hollow very huge and a want to be very small and Nina squeezed the head tight and picked the scab and Nina vanished into the warm pain. Then it was later and Charity Sonia was on the phone with no wire at the door. She said, No, no, This is much worse than any of us realised. Yes, of course, Doctor.

Nina does not feel better from writing this down. Nina does not feel like freedom has come yet. Nina must fold four more paper swans with twenty-eight folds to be calm and then try to go to sleep. Nina must go to a supermarket one day and stay away from the windows. They must not find Nina writing. Hide the diary.

Charity Sonia took Nina after a long trip with closed eyes and the sound of the Wizard of Oz movie in the car to a room with a sign that said Waiting Room and you have to do what the signs say with strangers who weren't fascists, all sat in a square and not looking at each other. There were more magazines from the government so Nina read one. Britney was in crisis at being too fat and alone again and Comrade Sonia said not to worry so much about people in pictures as it was a kind of sport for some people being horrible about them because they were famous. Nina told her that Comrade Ruth said these pictures made people die in deserts.

Nina started to feel hot and there was music in the waiting room too. It was the fast kind of women singing about wanting and it said Baby, Give it to Me.

Charity Sonia said its OK the music was just an NHS regulation now so people could have privacy from each other and how Nina should just try focusing on breathing, so Nina took a page from the table that said Asthma Questionnaire and folded it twenty-eight times. The wings were wrong but Nina gave it to Charity Sonia.

Charity Sonia said, That's beautiful, where did you learn how to do that?

Nina said, the beak is twisted and the wings are not equal. Nina will try again.

Charity Sonia said, It's so intricate, it's really very lovely, Nina. Is it a duck or a swan? You're full of surprises, Nina.

Nina told her Nina had done thousands more in the basement, then stopped because the basement has been erased. Nina looked up and one waiting room man had a thing growing on his face and was very old and his eyes said he was going to die soon.

A little girl came in and was staring at Nina with the woman who she called mummy and she kept staring harder and was dressed in pink and she hid her face in her mother's arm and then peeked out and looked scared at Nina and this made a very hollow feeling come in Nina's belly and then angry.

A buzz noise went and the name Nina was said from a machine and it was time to move again. But the shivers and the not wanting to go anywhere came.

Doctor Two was called S. Jenners. It is a terrible thing to reduce someone to an object Charity Sonia said, but it was OK for Doctor S. Jenners to take your clothes off again and photograph the bruises again. Then Nina had to pee into a cup in front of them and it took a while to come. Then there was blood from the arm into the needle and the pump.

Nina is not scared of any blood and likes the way the big scabs come.

Nina had to go behind the screen to dress again. The Doctor spoke quietly to Charity Sonia, but Nina could hear because Nina is good at spying.

The Doctor said, The swabs came back negative for semen. The scars on the back and buttocks show repeated beatings over, we think, many years. The serious burn scarring on the left hand, wrist and lower arm must have been a medical emergency but we can't trace any treatment history. There's also developmental deformation of the spine.

Then the Doctor was quieter and said, The fresh scab on the same arm wasn't there on our first examination so could be self-inflicted. As concerns any other damage, we'd like to get her a brain scan.

When Nina came back out, Charity Sonia tried to put on a smile to make Nina be brave and Doctor S. Jenners asked, Did I feel tense or wound up most of the time, a lot of the time, time to time, occasionally or not at all and she had a pen in her hand for ticks.

Do I get a sort of frightened feeling as if something bad is about to happen?

Nina started to feel all things they were saying and folded another paper swan.

Charity Sonia said, Nina is very susceptible to suggestion. She doesn't seem to understand hypotheticals.

Nina asked her what this meant and repeated every word and the Doctor said, Does she do that a lot?

Yes, Charity Sonia said. I was going to ask if there was a test she could do for photographic memory, she had to do this diary you see every day for years and record everything or she was punished and—

I see, the Doctor said. I'd have to book with a specialist.

Then Charity Sonia said, Sorry this has taken so long and I know you've gone over time for us and I'm very grateful but I was wondering if you could give her something to help her adjust, perhaps some Beta blockers for the panic episodes.

The Doctor said, Of course, and said, and some Diazepam to help with the sleeping problems. And then she sat and stared at her screen but it didn't have pictures of naked people on it but just words and blueness and she said, CAT scan, Diabetes testing, Bloods, Osteo, CBT and then there's the eye test just in case Nina's eyes don't re-adjust to seeing far away things, and of course the DNA test.

She said, Well, madam, that's quite a few waiting lists we've got you on. Come back next week, maybe you can manage by yourself and we'll let you know some of those results.

Outside Nina gave Doctor S. Jenners the new paper swan as a present then Charity Sonia's hand was shaking too and she was hiding her face and had red eyes. Nina asked what was wrong and Charity Sonia bit her lip and said I'm sorry, I'm sorry. Nina was confused because nothing was Charity Sonia's fault. Charity Sonia said, You were very brave. You did really well.

Nina knows that there will never be any gold stars from Comrade Chen or any Comrades ever again. He must have hated Nina a great amount from his jail cell where the Pig state finally got him. Nina could feel his rage in the sky like the flying monkeys chasing Nina into the safe corner. His hatred would only end when he was dead and then Nina would be free. Nina wished she had killed him instead of Comrade Jeni. Nina gets pain in the belly and bad hand and eyes when Nina tries to remember that day. It is all erased. And then Nina needs to see if there is a bird anywhere because if there is not then the radiation clouds will come.

Dorothy got angry at the Wicked Witch because she was going to kill Toto so Dorothy threw a bucket of water over her and the Witch melted and was dead. This was very good news and a bit of a shock. I walked alone four blocks with The Wizard of Oz in the ears and did not panic more than twice. I took the ear wires out at every end of the pavement and put them back in after, so then it was back on the yellow brick road then the real road and silence and the same again and finally Dorothy and her loyal friends returned to the Emerald City to get their reward and I discovered that the kind people of capitalism had painted special white signs on the road in the shape of a person to show you where to walk and finally Nina had arrived at Sainsbury's. I went very far and said I a lot, and then I had to stop because it is so tiring being I, so I was Nina again till I got my energy back.

Nina said, I am walking. I am nearly inside a supermarket. I will be me for just another step then another.

Nina tried to touch the door but it opened by itself but this was OK because it did this every time with other people as well, then Nina stepped inside and it was vast with music but no one else was dancing and their eyes said not to do it. So Nina tried to copy what you have to do. First Nina couldn't believe it because there was a National Geographic and it was bright and new and it had a picture of a blue ball in the black sky and it said How the Earth Works. So Nina had to have it. Then there were Nina's new favourite magazines with more rules on how to eat but not be fat but Nina was burping from emptiness so Nina only took six of them. Then Nina saw that people had things with wheels or carried metal baskets so Nina picked one up.

Nina was breathing too fast with all the millions of kinds of food like you have never seen before so Nina had to stop and just listen to The Wizard of Oz. Nina pressed the backwards button and listened again to the bit where Dorothy dissolved the Witch, and then again, because Nina is still coming to terms with this.

People looked at Nina because Nina was standing in the middle place with the milk and yoghurt and ham and blocking their way. There were people at a glass place and a man holding a plate and bits of cheese and some kind of meat with sticks and people were taking them and eating them and saying thank you so Nina had five and they were delicious.

Then Nina followed a woman with spider nets on her legs who was Nina's height and sexually attractive and she led Nina to the fruit place. The woman touched something and so Nina copied her. It was an apple and Nina didn't know you could have eight kinds, and the labels said, Product of Israel and Nina remembered that everything is the opposite, so Israel is not the Imperialist war Pig.

There were so many fruits Nina had not seen before and they all had signs so the proletariat could learn. There were pears from Spain and grapes and lemons from Turkey and Nina had seen a banana before but never yellow and so many. There were peaches and kiwis from Australia and Nina couldn't believe it was a fruit because it was so hairy so Nina tasted it and it was very delicious and then Nina put it back down and tried a peach and it was very wet. Nina walked on and there were many amazing vegetables. There was something called a courgette from Italy but it didn't taste very good and worse was spring onions from Greece, but then Nina felt very ashamed because a tall old lady was staring hard with eyes like skinny Comrade Ruth and Nina realised what Nina had done wrong, so Nina went back to all the things Nina had tried and put them in the basket.

Nina was in the middle of a long street of food then and saw many more streets with numbers on. A woman with a baby in her womb passed by and another little one holding her hand and Nina had to remember that the woman was not being greedy and the one-child policy was incorrect because everything is the opposite now and greed is good so you should fill your basket with food and your womb with babies.

Nina's basket got full too fast and there were things Nina didn't want and things Nina hadn't heard of, so Nina had to put back the chilli sauce and the party pack of crisps and the Mister Muscle cleaner so Nina could get the chocolate sponge cake and the Oil of Olay and the eyelashes and the roast in the bag extra tasty pork loin joint and the bread for the birds and the frozen vegetable pizza slices.

The surprising thing was everyone looked so bored and like it was a terrible burden. Nina picked up one yoghurt and then another and another, then Nina turned and saw the chickens and many birds behind glass. The legs and pink skin and the picture of the bird. Then a flash came.

The baby bird through the window on the roof. One wing is flapping then it falls over the edge. Then it is a skeleton far below.

The dream is not supposed to come at daytime.

Nina dropped the yoghurt and it burst open over the feet and Nina knew this had been too much for one day and decided to leave so as to read the magazines for instructions on how to do this better next time. Nina ran.

A sound went off and a man came behind Nina and he said Madam and he said that Nina had done something wrong and touched Nina's arm near the line outside with the picture of the man. He looked like a Pig and Nina asked if he was. He looked confused so Nina said, A booby or a filth.

And he said, I think you forgot to pay, madam, and Nina remembered that that was what Charity Sonia gave the paper and the lesson about and Nina felt very ashamed. Nina gave him the basket and the many things back and the pocket full of paper money and apologised and the man was confused and tried to give the paper back to Nina and made signs to come back inside but Nina didn't want to and dropped the paper and it all blew away in the wind because this was in the car park. Then Nina ran but that was not wise because a car chased Nina and when Nina looked up there were cars all around and it was a thick road and all going very fast. There were two cars side by side on each side of Nina and not stopping. One after another after another all going to kill Nina. Nina screamed but nothing came out, like in the bird dream.

Nina is not sure of whether to tell Charity Sonia about this. Nina has realised another thing about being free. If you are alone then things in your life happen but no one knows about them. In the Collective people used to know everything Nina did every minute. Nina must stop writing it down because there is no one to read it and writing is part of the sickness. Nina must practise not writing for two days and just be a person and say I.

Nina had a sleep by accident and then it was the next day but in the same clothes and Nina failed because if you do not write the hollow feeling comes back.

Then Support Worker Cas came and she said, Christ almighty, at the cupboard because Nina still hadn't drunk the milk or eaten the bread and still hadn't touched the Ready Meals. Support Worker Cas had brought some rice that said microwave and she said she couldn't very well cook it for Nina and sit there and make sure Nina bleedin ate it now could she? And Nina said sorry. Then Support Worker Cas was on her phone and sighed and said, Sorry, Pet, forgive my French, what are we going to do with you, eh?

Then there was another car experiment with eyes closed and singing. Cas said would you mind giving that flippin Follow the Yellow Brick Road song a break and couldn't Nina Change the record. Nina had only sung it to make Cas happy, so Nina didn't understand why Cas was cross.

Then Nina had to wait with Cas on orange plastic seats in a corridor that had busy people and dust balls and perfume and sweat smells. There was a pile of government advice on the table and one said Why I Still Love My Murdering Husband and one said Ten Killer Looks for Autumn.

Then Cas gave Nina a present and it was the first one ever because presents are Capitalist and Nina was moved but not to tears.

But then Nina saw it was a phone and was scared.

Cas said, Don't worry, Nina, It won't bite, it's pretty crap actually but lucky you, eh, look at the size of it and who knew, free phones from the DSS, eh?

The box said Virgin and Nina said, Do I have to give this back after I have sex for the first time? And Cas laughed very loud and covered her mouth and said, You're radio rental, you are, bloody hell!

Cas turned it on and showed how to touch the glass and said, Let's take a selfie. Then a scaring flash came and Nina's face was inside the phone.

Nina shook the head. Nina doesn't want people to see pictures of Nina's face. Pictures twist people's minds and the bit of Nina's ear is missing.

Nina doesn't understand why every person has to make pictures of themselves. Nina has watched through Charity House window when no pigeons came and there were four young people taking a picture below the sign of Rose Garden Sheltered Housing and making faces like dead people for their flash. They must have been told they will be punished if they do not record their lives. Then there was a bald man in a silver car outside of Charity House and a flash came from him too.

Cas said, You're getting a bloody computer too, they'll bring it over next week. Wish I was homeless like you, getting all this stuff for free, eh.

Then she patted Nina's hand and said, Aw Pet, only joking.

Nina is not to be scared of radiation any more so Nina tried to hold the phone. Scary things are good. Pictures travel through the sky but they don't kill. And Nina held it and nothing happened.

Then a man came to the door and Nina had to go in and Cas said she was just outside the door on the phone to Sonia and that Nina should keep the chin up.

Inside it was a grey room with a desk and two seats. Nina was nervous so Nina folded a paper swan from a bit of paper on the man's desk and he looked through many pages all about Nina with a smile on his face that was like Comrade Una when something went wrong but she was hiding it.

He flicked his pen between his fingers and was thin with arm muscles and very short hair like Comrade Ruth but he had never met her.

He said, So, Nina, I've had two reports in from Women's Aid and the NHS and we've become involved since a third report from the Police regarding some violence.

Then he stopped like it was a question.

Then he said, Not to worry. How you getting on with Cas? Fine? You look tired. Are you managing to sleep any better? Has your GP given you any drugs to help you relax?

His name is Social Worker Phil McClusky but he had never met the Phil who lived in the Collective. He is paid by the state to solve all of Nina's problems in case Nina is a danger to herself or others and not just Nina's but thousands of others and this is why he clicks his pen very fast. He must be very clever but we were not there to talk about his job but to get to the bottom of Nina's care assessment.

He said, Are you washing yourself now without assistance, are things improving?

And Nina told him there have been great leaps forward as Dorothy and her friends made it back to The Emerald City and it won't be long till Nina gets to the end of the film although Nina prefers to just listen because Dorothy's face is all wrong.

Social Work Phil said this was all very interesting, but what I'm trying to establish, Nina, is if you are managing to clean yourself, to buy and cook food. To sleep at regular hours. I need to find out if you have any conditions that might necessitate a different kind of accommodation and care. I'm talking here about physical disabilities or maybe brain injury from an accident or incident. Sonia has you down as a victim of violence but you may also be a person with some learning difficulties.

Nina did not know if these were all questions and why he didn't leave enough time to reply to each one so Nina just nodded to everything he said and hid the bad hand so that Nina didn't say anything bad.

He said, Sorry? Was that a yes or a no? Can you look at me please, Nina. Then he asked the question about incidents again like talking to a child, and he said Nina a lot. Then he wouldn't look up after Nina stared at him too much because Nina didn't know what to say. And he made a little shiver.

And Nina shivered too. Nina wonders if this feeling is attraction, because the magazines said women tremble with desire when they meet the man of their dreams.

Social Work Phil said, Right, moving on. Cas reports that you've been having trouble eating and shopping. Is that correct,

Nina? There was a half-eaten sandwich on his desk but Nina didn't want to touch it. Nina nodded. Then Nina realised it was a test so Nina told Social Work Phil that Nina has now eaten many kinds of things and most of it chocolate and it was like explosions of joy, but the first bite was the best and after the Bounty Nina was sick on the carpet but Nina was very very grateful for the rations from Cas and would try better to eat a yoghurt because it doesn't have to be cooked with radiation.

Social Work Phil stared and said, OK, OK and he made a tick. Then he asked if Nina could lift a spoon to her mouth without assistance. And dress without assistance. And he made more clicks and ticks.

Nina couldn't stop staring at the picture on his desk of a smiling magazine woman with three babies. Social Work Phil is very fertile. Nina wants to be a happy wife and marry a patriarchal master with lots of money. Nina would also like to be a mistress. Nina thought Nina could make a baby with Social Work Phil and said I want a baby with you but not out loud, only in the head. Nina was not sure that Social Work Phil was Nina's type anyway because his bald head reminded Nina of Comrade Ruth.

Social Work Phil said, If this failure to eat keeps on we'll have to re-assess you as disabled or with Mental Health issues. And he wrote something. Then he said, Is three visits per week from Cas enough? Has Sonia got you to apply for housing benefit yet and job seekers allowance? Has she told you about the competency test for disability allowance or PIP and about the waiting list? Has she explained that your current housing is a temporary arrangement?

Nina nodded once and shook the head three times.

Social Work Phil said he was sorry, if he had his way things would be faster but it was the system. He said that Nina was in legal limbo, because Nina doesn't have a national insurance number and the police are still trying to find her real name and birth certificate so Nina is technically not a real person yet.

Nina said, That's OK because Nina's name comes from Vladimir Lenin so it's not real because communism is not real any more and so Nina will have to get a new name anyway.

He smiled and said, Right, well let's just stick to calling you Nina, shall we, just until we get you processed.

Nina realised that Social Work Phil was writing things down about Nina. Nina knew some answers had been wrong and worried that Social Work Phil would send Nina back to the Collective so Nina told Social Work Phil that Nina has been free for one week, two days, four hours and forty-two minutes and I am very happy here, so happy I can't believe it. And Nina used the I word a lot. I must cross out my Ninas and say only I. Or I will never get well. Nina told him being free to go anywhere is the best feeling in the world.

Nina has never had to demonstrate how happy she is all the time before and it is tiring. And happiness is like the future Comrade Chen promised, always over the next hill.

Social Work Phil said, Now, Nina I know that Charity Sonia has said you're fully able to take care of yourself, and I know she wants that to happen and you're putting on a brave face, but it might be running before you can walk so I'd like to do a full ability and risk assessment.

He handed Nina some paper and it had all the days of the week on it. And he said, You just put the times in under the words for each activity once you've done it. So if you eat breakfast at nine, you write down nine. Easy. See.

Monday	Breakfast	Lunch	Dinner	Bath	Sleep
Tuesday	Breakfast	Lunch	Dinner	Bath	Sleep

Nina felt cold. He said what's wrong, Nina? Nina said this list is like what Comrade Chen made Nina do for twenty years and why does Nina have to do this?

Social Work Phil said he was sorry and if it was up to him Nina wouldn't have to, but it was the system. And could she write down, honestly, any times Nina was unable to eat or sleep or any accidents or incidents. Or times when Nina needed extra help, with such things as handling money or toilet hygiene and washing yourself.

He said the people who are helping Nina, like Charity Worker Sonia Linklater, have the best will in the world but they might be out of their depth and overlooking the severity of your condition. He said, Between me and you, don't let them turn you into some PR photo opportunity for their Charity, OK? And then he said, Forget I said that.

He said, Nina, there's one issue that's clouding things. This history of violence. We still have to get the full police report. Now this incident the police are investigating, when you reported it last week, you were in shock and you've made some contradictory statements. We have the NHS Doctor who says you might have Stockholm Syndrome or be a person with cognitive and behavioural challenges. Now, Charity Sonia tells me you're the victim here and I don't doubt that for a second, but I need to know if your involvement in the cult was more. And then he stopped and said: complicated.

Nina looked at him and felt something was coming.

He said, This is a question that has a bearing on your care needs but when you were, incarcerated, I need to know, did you hurt anyone?

Nina felt the heart get fast again and the cold in the hand and the heat in the eyes so closed them. Nina hurt all of the Comrades. Nina got gold stars and extra ketchup rations from Chen for hitting extra hard.

Social Work Phil said, It's just that before we assign you. And he stopped. Then he said, less temporary accommodation, we have to establish whether you're a threat to. And he stopped.

Nina's head was hot and Nina wanted to confess to hitting Comrade Uma and Comrade Ruth, but Nina was scared Social Work Phil would take away the Charity House.

Then he said, Don't worry, Nina, we're getting you a full assessment with a clinical psychologist. And he stared at Nina then handed over another bit of paper and it said Personal History at the top.

He said, I just need you to write down some details about your past, Nina. I'm sorry if you find that upsetting. If it was up to me I wouldn't have you do this but it's the system. I know it's a lot to ask but do you think you can manage that?

He said, How you got here, with rough dates if you can, Nina, write it down. And how you became sick and this other woman who contacted the Charity, Uma, who took you to the Hospital and then disappeared. All of that stuff, very traumatic, that's important. Do you understand? Nina, neglect, physical, violence, sexual, as far back as you can remember, this will be the story we'll take to the Marac meeting. And he spelled it out M-A-R-A-C, but he didn't say what it was.

Nina's head was hotter and Nina felt guilty.

He said, There are a lot of people out there who pretend they are sick to get free care and I'm not saying that's you, in any way, but I want to get you to the top of the waiting list. We don't want you falling between gaps. Do you understand what I'm saying? The stronger the case we can make that you can't take care of yourself, the more we'll have the authority to take care of you. The worse your situation, the more we can help.

Nina was very confused. Charity Sonia wanted Nina to get better but Social Work Phil wanted Nina to be very ill.

Nina stared at the pages and they made Nina's head buzz.

Nina had wanted to stop all diaries and reports but now they won't let Nina.

Social Work Phil smiled and said, I'm not promising anything, but I think we could, if you're no risk to yourself and others, find you a fulltime place in a care home.

Nina asked what that meant because sometimes things in Capitalism have nice names but are a trick. Like Friendly Fire or Three for the Price of Two when you only want One. But it was time to go.

Nina wanted to sleep but first it was the car with Cas and Cas was saying, Did you tell him you tried to go shopping on your own? Probably best to have kept mum about that. Well that's me up shit creek again. Is he a bugger or what?

Nina kept eyes shut and said, Nina doesn't want to have babies with him.

Cas said, You what? Then the car was shaking with loud laughs. Cas said, You're a classic, you are.

Then she was yelling at cars to get out the way you fucking arseholes and saying Pardon my French. And she said, You all right, Love, you look a bit peaky.

Nina kept eyes closed.

Nina thought about how Social Work Phil likes blaming the system. Nina does not understand if it is the same system that Comrade Chen hated. Nina suspects Social Work Phil is a secret accomplice of Chen. Nina will not fill in his eating and sleeping and washing forms because it is all too much for one day.

Nina's body was heavy but Nina shouldn't sleep at Charity House in daytime because it is a sign of depression and Nina must pretend to be well for Charity Sonia.

Thinking about Charity Sonia made her appear as she was waiting at the door and she was smoking because it was a horrible addiction and Pigs were coming soon.

Pigs always come in twos and they must have decided that Nina liked female Pigs better because only the female one did the talking inside and she talked very slow as if to a child and the male one waited at the door. Charity Sonia touched Nina's back and said she was sorry, she could see Nina was exhausted, but the Police were moving things forward very quickly and we just need to get this out of the way so we can focus on what's really important which is making Nina better.

The female Police Officer was called Alia Yusef and she was dark-faced with big breasts like the woman on the beach with the packets of plastic in her chest in the magazine and smiled when Nina said this.

Police Officer Alia Yusef said, Just to reconfirm. You're not a suspect or anything. We're re-opening the investigation into the lethal incident in 2002 and you were a juvenile then. We'd like you to tell us more about that incident. Did you see anything that might help us? We're trying to establish if dangerous and illegal actions were committed by Chen, or by all of the people in the Collective under the instructions of Chen?

Nina does not know why they must make court cases. They cannot put Comrade Mao in jail because he is dead. Nina only found this out two days ago.

Police Officer Alia Yusef said, if you don't feel up to making a statement, that's OK. Don't worry, we won't think you're protecting guilty people. Comrade Chen is denying all charges by the way and we want to make as convincing a case against him as possible.

She said, Do you believe that at any time during your incarceration, Chen could have tried to kill you?

Nina stared at her thinking Nina will have to read every one of the two hundred and forty-two diaries again to answer but nearly all are gone and Nina misses them. Nina thought of the basement and the smell of mould and pee.

Police Officer Alia Yusef said, OK, we'll come back to that one.

Then Police Officer Alia Yusef looked to Charity Sonia and some nodding happened and she said, We've heard that you wrote diaries, Nina. Sonia said you have one that you keep with you. Is it OK if I borrow it from you just for a little bit? All we need to do is copy it. I'll give it straight back to you, say, the end of the week.

Nina shook the head.

She said, That's fine, we know you're not hiding anything, we know you're not an accomplice, we'd just like to know, have you got any other diaries, from childhood?

Nina thought, It's all right to lie now. Nina has never been allowed to have a secret before.

Nina has to protect the words. Protect The Project.

Nina said, No diaries.

Nina said, The diaries were all destroyed.

Police Officer Alia Yusef looked to Charity Sonia and said, Who destroyed them, Nina? Chen? Did he destroy the evidence? Who, Nina, who destroyed the diaries?

Nina nodded and shook the head and told her this was more than enough for one day.

Police Officer Alia Yusef said, Look, we've cordoned off the commune and we're searching the building so if we find the diaries, that would actually be breaking the law, Nina, if you told us a fib. That would be withholding evidence and lying to a police officer.

Nina rocked back and forwards. Nina said nothing.

Charity Sonia said, Nina's very tired. Should we be getting a lawyer?

Police officer Alia Yusef said, No, no, we're just eliminating Nina from our enquiries and it would help us do that if she could help us in any way.

Nina felt very small and surrounded.

Police Officer Alia Yusef looked straight at Nina then and said,

I know you're very tired but if you could just help with a few more things, Nina.

Her voice was not cruel and Charity Sonia's hand on the shoulder made it safe, so Nina nodded.

Police Officer Alia Yusef said, So if it's all right with you and Sonia, next time we come, Nina, we'll have photographs and if you can I'd like you to identify your Comrades for me. This will include pictures of the dead woman. I hope you'll be OK with that.

Nina rocked back and forwards on the seat.

Police Officer Alia Yusef said, And Comrade Ruth, it's very important that we identify Comrade Ruth because, well first of all, we don't believe that's her real name and secondly she's escaped. She was never actually detained for questioning, she did a runner when you were in Hospital.

Nina went cold. Nina had to breath very fast and look at the carpet. Nina told her this was more than enough for one day. And Charity Sonia said, Can we stop now, please? And then Charity Sonia came down to Nina's size on her knee and she said, Nina, making your own choices is what it's all about, if you'd like the police to go now, then just say, or can they ask you one more thing?

Nina said, OK, one last one. And Charity Sonia smiled.

Police Officer Alia Yusef said, OK and she didn't like to have to ask but she was going to get a court order for all members of the Collective who could be identified to have a mandatory DNA sample. She said, because we have your DNA already and we can match it. She said, just so there could be no uncertainty, because it could change outcomes if this gets to trial. It just had to be proved, beyond all question of a doubt, because it was even possible that Nina had been abducted, and separating children from their biological parents was something other cults had done in the past, and if Comrade Chen had done that too then maybe they'd even find Nina's real parents.

Nina rocked back and forwards. Nina had to breathe very fast and stop the carpet from moving.

Police Officer Alia Yusef said, Did anyone in the Collective, at any time, give you any clue as to who your mother could be? Most likely she was a friend of the Collective or even one of the members.

Nina is scared of Comrade Ruth and Comrade Ruth is on the outside hunting for Nina and Nina is not stupid but the police are. Comrade Ruth knows everything. She has ears in walls. Comrade Ruth cannot be Nina's mother. Nina has no parents. They died in the war. The family is the source of all oppression.

Police Officer Alia Yusef said, Thank you so much, Nina, three times and the Pig officer at the door said goodbye as well and thank you, and Nina could not breathe.

Then he said to Charity Sonia, We strongly advise that neither you nor Nina speak to any journalists or strangers. Your address has been kept secret but we don't know how much longer that will last. And if a hack does speak to you, if the case against Chen goes to trial, it could prejudice the outcome or even be reason for the case to be thrown out. So, Nina, if you feel you're being followed or approached without your consent, give us a call straight away on this number.

Then Nina was choking.

Charity Sonia said, Are you all right, Nina, what's going on?

Then Nina had to hold the knees on the floor and breathe like Charity Sonia showed but on the side with the face against the carpet and to stop thinking that Nina won't make it, that it would be easier to go back to that basement, and not eat and just push Nina back to even before Nina was Nina, to the time Nina was called The Project and no more questions and no more past and The Project had Uma and Ruth and Jeni all the other Comrades and even before that when The Project was just a thing with no name and just an experiment, and before that to when it was just a cell, then nothing, just an accident.

Nina had a little sleep from the pill from Charity Sonia called Diazepam and before Nina fell asleep there was a feeling of Nina being stroked on the head by Uma but it was Charity Sonia saying, It's going to be OK, love, I know you're going to pull through.

Nina was awake again and it was night and Charity Sonia was gone. There was only the phone for Virgins on the table and a packet of oranges and all the Ready Meals and the yoghurt in the fridge with special bacteria in it.

Nina was still sleepy and Nina took out the one diary from being hidden under the mattress and was so glad it was not found. Nina closed the eyes and thought about all the other diary pages hidden in many places and Nina squeezed the eyes tighter and felt how safe it was to be surrounded with words.

Nina tried hard to think of the Comrade Jeni incident and Nina remembered that Nina had to write it many times and every time Comrade Ruth said, No this is wrong, write it again, write what we told you. Rub it out, write it again. Erase.

Nina remembers writing The Project was in the top-floor room. Many times. And Comrade Ruth said, No you were not, you did not see anything. You were not there. Tear it out. Write it again. And she hit Nina on the back of the hands with the ruler and shouted, Wake up! Write it again. And Comrade Uma said it too. Write the correct story.

Nina remembers being The Project and being small. Nina remembers feeding a pigeon through the gap in the window. It was Ho, the smallest and greediest one with the white fleck. The Project learned not to be scared of these birds or any others, like Uma taught her. The window was open just a tiny bit so no one will know and the bird won't get in. It is rice, hidden in The Project's pockets from the kitchen and The Project poked bit after bit through the gap between the frame and the loose window. The Project tells Ho to Shh and not be a greedy Capitalist and drops one grain, then another through. The Project laughs at Ho's funny move of the neck and flickering little black eyes and The Project says, One more piece Ho, but that's your quota and tell Cornflake and Fluffy and Rosa Luxemburg to come too because there can be no favouritism.

Then a shadow moves and someone is coming and The Project is not to open that window ever because it is too dangerous and an adult person slams it shut and Nina tries to scrape up all the rice because it is stolen and birds are one of The Four Pests. Then two adults are there and one shouts at the other, but The Project cannot see the face only the flip-flops but all are the same and owned by everybody and The Project's face is down in shame. One adult is screaming and pointing at The Project and someone slaps then someone pushed the woman and she falls against the window and there is a smash and a stumble and a scream. The Project opens the eyes but window is open and the person is gone and bird feathers are flying outside.

Then it is all black and cold and The Project walks to the back door, and there is crying and whispering. The Project sees. Like a bird, all broken, the woman with the white eyes with no blue in them any more, and the body floppy in the hands of the adults and the white foam from the mouth and blood from the head and being dragged through bird poo and a feather falls from the sky but they kick the door shut in The Project's face so The Project will not see.

Then the voices asking after in the shivering bed in the dark corner, what did you see? Write it down. Then the voices saying, this is incorrect, erase this. This is not what you saw. You were dreaming. You are getting different times mixed up.

And a hand tore out a page, and three voices said, Erase it all and write it again. And one other said, Don't let her sleep till she has remembered correctly.

And pills in the mouth hard to swallow and someone shaking The Project.

And shouting, Write it again. Write what we say. Erase it. Write it again.

This is more than enough for one day and Nina is so tired it is sore all over. Nina wants to remember it all or erase it all, not this mess in the middle like a scratchy scab that never gets better.

Jotter #68 2002

The Project feels very sorry and will be brave and grateful and not cry. The Project is very grateful to have been made clean and white again in The Purification and is sure all bad pictures will be erased for ever now.

But then The Project gets stabs of hot in the skin and a bad picture comes.

The Project's hand was fire and arms lifted The Project up to the shivering bed. The Project has been awake all night and asleep in the day and unable to fulfil my duties because the hand is very hot then cold and the skin is nine blisters and not to keep touching. I will never say I again. I promised. I am scared of I and it is a sickness. I promised the Comrades this and showed the pain in hand.

The Project is worried about the report because writing made the incorrect pictures come back and holding a pencil is so sore. The Project rocks back and forwards and has sore bellies and has to squeeze one of the nine blisters every time a skeleton or a smile woman comes. The Project had some howling but no one is to give The Project extra attention and a voice said, Leave her to rest now, she has had more than enough for one day.

The Project must write down all the bad rememberings then erase them so The Project's hand will not burn any more.

The Project remembers all the Comrades in a circle in the dark room and the candle and the bowl and Comrade Ruth held the magazine and The Project had to drink a special drink that was like gas and it made fire come inside.

The Project's hand is so jaggy and the skin wants to come off. The Project is so sorry. Please let The Project sleep. The Project has to stay on the mattress on the floor in room three even though it was time to move back to room one because the Comrades have made an exception with the rota because of The Project's bad hand with the bad pictures in it. Write down everything and then erase it or the hand will never get better.

Comrade Ruth showed the pictures of the women near the candle with the long legs and spike feet and breasts on display and smiles and all the Comrades gathered round the magazine and she said, Do you see, these women mutilate their bodies, they paint their faces to say me, me, me, chose me, all competing with each other to become the objects of men. To make nuclear families that make nuclear war. And The Project cried and begged to erase them.

Erase.

And Comrade Ruth held up a picture of a brown-skinned mother with no chest and a skeleton covered in dust on her knee and it was her dead baby with flies in the mouth and eyes and a hundred dead skeletons in the dust and The Project screamed but Comrade Uma had to hold The Project's eyes open and Comrade Chen said, Do you see? The one is the result of the other. The rich create the poor. Every time you desire things you make skeletons and death come. And Comrade Uma begged it to stop but there were many more pictures to be erased and Comrade Jeni ran out.

Erase.

The Project has to think instead of the happy children with

the Glorious Leader and the big fruits and to sing but not How many bricks on the Mickey Mouse house. The hand is purple and red and yellow now and The Project must stop being selfish and touching it and howling to wake the Comrades up. And Comrade Uma must especially stay away because there must be an end to this favouritism.

The Project has eleven blisters now and remembers Comrade Chen made a fire in the bowl with oil and tore up the Capitalist smile women and handed them to The Project. And he said, You must burn them from your mind.

The Project is sorry but can't stop thinking of the bowl falling and the fire on skin and the screaming hands throwing The Project on the ground.

It is in The Project's head over and over and The Project had to bite a blister, and it tasted of salt and sweet then the pain erased everything.

It is night again and The Project has heard noises in the walls of bashing but not like birds but like a woman moaning many times then faster and it must be Comrade Jeni punished for saying The Purification had to stop.

The Project was scared and had to go to the window and looked and saw Gramsci had come back limping with only one toe. Then The Project saw Rosa Luxemburg had made a new egg in the nest and was very excited then there was listening on the cold glass to the coo-cooing and the hot hand went away.

But The Project is worried because it is selfish for pigeon mothers to make eggs so high up and too cold for eggs. And now The Project has another bad picture in the head of smashed baby skeleton with empty eye holes and the bad hand is more sore again and all mothers have to be erased.

Sometime after a long time the Comrades came one by one and sat beside The Project. Little Comrade Uma stroked The Project's hair and was silent, hiding her face under her grey hair.

The Project asked, Comrade Uma, are my blisters a personal possession?

Comrade Uma smiled and said, Hush no, don't worry so much about these things, darling. And she rubbed a cream in to make it less sore but it was more.

The Project said, But no one else has blisters so they must be my personal possessions, so I have to get rid of them. And The Project squeezed the biggest blister and Comrade Uma shrieked and took Nina's hand away and said, Don't do that it will be very sore and The Project said, It is.

And Comrade Uma put bandages on, round and round so The Project would stop picking and sucking the pain from the bad hand.

The Project asked, So why do I always have to have the personal things and no one else does?

Comrade Uma shook her head and said, Oh you, you are still my Why-child.

Then Comrade Uma told Nina not to unwrap the bandages and pulled them even tighter. Then Comrade Uma sang The Project a song very quietly and the words were not allowed because they were about buying status symbols and it was like this, Hush little baby don't say a word, Papa's gonna buy you a mockingbird, And if that mockingbird won't sing, Papa's gonna buy you a diamond ring.

Then Comrade Ruth came in because she is like a spider spy who crawls the walls. What was that song, Comrade? And Comrade Uma shook her head secretly to tell me not to repeat anything and she left. Comrade Ruth stood so tall above and said that the pain The Project feels in the blisters is not hers alone because when we give our bodies to the revolution and become one with the masses, then the suffering is shared and when we die it is a worthy death, weightier than Mount Tai, but to die for the exploiters and oppressors is lighter than a feather. And she showed the long scar on her shaved head from a battle with some Pigs.

The Project asked, Am I going to die from blisters?

Comrade Ruth said, No, why are you always so stupid and selfish?

Comrade Zana came to the doorway and kept saying the name of the man with the cross and staring at The Project's hand with bandages. The Project asked Comrade Zana to please stop because she was making the skeleton pictures come back.

The Project tried to eat some rice but skeletons wouldn't go and vomits came in the blue plastic bucket. The Project can't sleep because there is nowhere for the hand and the whimpering comes. The Project looks at the floorboards and wonders if The Project will have burning skin and head pictures for the rest of my life and if it will be long.

Comrade Chen came to The Project's mattress and held and examined The Project's bandaged hand and kissed The Project's head and whispered that The Project's bravery was an example to us all. He kissed my nose and my eyeballs and said, Remember we sacrifice everything today for the better future. After he touched me I was so happy. He makes a feeling open in my chest like the darkest sky in the cold nights when all is silent and there is only breath on my window and outside the birds are flying to the moon.

Then because of calling out and not sleeping Comrade Uma ran and washed my sores and gave a pill and stroked my head till light came. She said, Beatings, burns, when will it stop? She became very silent and stroked much and The Project asked, Why did you say that?

She said, Maybe we are too hard on you because we want you so much to be better than we have been.

The Project asked, Why? And Comrade Uma said, Well, There was once a fire that burned many people and I once hid the man who planted the bomb, she said, in Hamburg. We didn't want anyone to die. It was only meant to scare the government but it went wrong and four people died.

The Project said, But you did it for revolution so it will be fine.

Comrade Uma said, Maybe, but one of the people was a young mother.

The Project said, Well don't worry, you will be forgiven by Chairman Mao because he is the Red Sun and all mothers are selfish anyway.

Comrade Uma was silent then she said, I'm sorry, as she stroked my head. She said, I shouldn't have told you that. Now you've got another horrible picture in your head.

Then The Project peeled a bandage off and it was stuck with skin like stretchy white glue and Comrade Jeni arrived and she said, My God, are those third-degree burns? And enough was fucking enough, The Project needed to go to Hospital. Then there was a meeting around my bed and I pretended to be asleep. All were present but their voices get mixed because of the whispering and the second sleepy pill. The voices said all of these things. Accident and Emergency is open twenty-four hours.

She's not registered with any doctor, they'll ask for her address, if they put two and two together they'll come banging on the door, asking why she's not at school.

I disagreed with that from the start.

Quiet!

We will not go to the NHS.

But the NHS is Socialist.

Rubbish, it's a prison of the Pig state.

What if it's infected, it looks like pus and she's passing out.

She's just sick from the morphine.

Whose fucking idea was that?

Look, we could drop her at A&E, they don't ask for names, they'd patch up the burn, give her the once-over, give her a jab.

Absolutely not.

Why? And why don't we have antibiotics here?

What if they asked her questions? She hasn't learned to lie. She's not capable of it. She'd tell them everything.

Rubbish, she tells lies all the time.

Don't you read the papers? You know what social workers do. They'd take her away, interrogate her. They'll look into everyone's dole claims. Ruth's on disability benefit, they'll cut that. Then legal status. They'll ask questions. Uma, have you even got a passport?

What if she were to die, what would you do then?

Don't be foolish.

Have to speak to the Pigs then.

Don't start, Comrade, no one likes that tone here.

Hasn't she got a birth certificate?

No, she was born here. No one knows she's here. No one.

And Comrade Chen shouted, Silence!

And Comrade Jeni told the other Comrades to fuck themselves and then the door slammed and I pretended to wake up. When people asked questions of what I'd heard, I was silent and memorised it all for my report.

Note from Comrade Ruth: All Comrades must be wary of communicating incorrect things in front of The Project. This report must be edited and the story of her Purification rewritten. We all took part and are equally to blame. We must all repeat – The child burned herself while playing with a candle. Each Comrade must memorise this.

Note from Comrade Uma: Comrade Uma asks please can we register The Project with a doctor in case the blisters go septic. At the very least we should replenish the first aid kit as the rest of the morphine and codeine tablets have been taken by someone and not replaced. Please, let me go and get these things from the outside and fresh bandages and iodine.

Note from Comrade Jeni: Comrade Jeni is fucking sick of a certain individual who is not our leader telling us what to do. And another who thinks she's Mother bloody Theresa. Comrade Jeni volunteers to take the trip to replenish the drug supplies for Nina and get other essential things.

Note from Comrade Chen: Comrade women, do not fight, it belittles us all. Comrade Chen agrees with Comrade Ruth and adds that we must refrain from mentioning the forbidden name at all times. This is of the greatest importance. Any Comrades caught breaking this rule will be punished. Now more than ever we must stick together. Our enemies seek just one error from us so that they can pounce. If they do we will be separated. Unity is strength, Comrades.

The Project is very proud of The Project's new job after too many sore nights and daytimes in bed with special pills and the bandages are off to let the blisters breathe and a bit of sticky yellow skin came off too. The Project wants for us all to be equals and no more bitching. The walls in the rooms of the top two floors had to be painted white all over again because reactionary patterns were showing through. And then much bleaching near the front door had to be done with all Comrades on hands and knees. But The Project must not get bleach in the burst blisters or pick because no one can bear the whimpering.

The Project has to report to Comrade Chen a second secret incident that occurred in the top bathroom at the sink when Comrade Uma was taking off The Project's fourth bandages and putting on stinging iodine.

Comrade Uma gave a forbidden substance to The Project because of pain and it was chocolate and delicious and called Dairy Milk and The Project was told to keep this secret by Comrade Uma because it was from a secret place.

Comrade Uma also said that she felt bad about what happened to The Project in The Purification and that some of what The Project had been told wasn't true. The Project asked Comrade Uma to tell me what the lie was.

Comrade Uma stroked The Project's hair and said, Well, that bit about mothers and fathers. I had a mother who loved me and cared for me and my brother when we were sick, and she fed us and taught us songs, like the one about the mockingbird, so it's not really true that they're all evil.

The Project told Comrade Uma that she was wrong, wrong, wrong and Comrade Ruth had already explained this. Mothers and Grandmothers are the cradle of all oppression. No woman should be authorised to stay at home to raise her children or have that choice, because too many women will make that wrong choice.

The Project watched Comrade Uma weep and asked her why she did this so often. Comrade Uma said that she was some days glad that she had not brought a child into this incorrect world and other days she couldn't see the point of living. She said she had once felt terrible jealousy over a woman who had a child, so much because Uma had once nearly had a baby and was forced to get rid of it. Uma had so much rage she wanted the other baby dead by strangling then she just cried and this is why she has never stopped crying.

The Project is now the Finder of Secrets and asked, So, where is this baby now? Who is this mother? Is it someone I know?

Comrade Uma said, No, no, long ago. You were too young to remember.

So The Project told Comrade Uma not to worry and that that the nuclear family must be a very incorrect thing indeed if it could turn a good person like Comrade Uma into a strangling killer. The Project told Comrade Uma that she is more like Glinda, the Good Witch of the North and felt sorry for her. Comrade Uma kissed The Project's biggest blister and said, Kiss it better. Then she said, Don't worry, Petal, if the pain gets worse I'll take you to the Doctors myself. The Project asked where the Doctors was and was told it was outside, down some streets and this information made The Project shudder because of all the burned people hanging from lamp posts. The Project told Comrade Uma that I didn't want to go, ever, and that if I did die from blisters could Comrade Uma please feed Rosa Luxemburg for me because she needs help with her egg.

Comrade Uma touched The Project's cheek with her round fingers and moved her face close like to whisper but then stopped.

The Project hopes this report will not get Comrade Uma into trouble.

Note from Comrade Chen: Comrade Chen is very pleased with these pages and they are surely making The Project heal faster. The Project must erase from her head all thoughts about the words mother, father *and* baby *put there incorrectly by Comrade Uma. Comrade Uma still has much pollution in her from The Four Olds, and these are Old Habits, Old Culture, Old Customs and Old Ideas and we must help Comrade Uma erase these from her mind.*

Comrade Chen now asks The Project to show the reports to no one but Comrade Chen and to discuss them with no one. The Project is a very good finder of secrets and The Project's great ordeal has made The Project stronger but there is a traitor among us. If we do not find them then Chairman Mao will be cross and not send us any rice or ketchup rations.

The photocopying and folding takes a long time and you are not to moan or get any pus smeared on from burst blisters. When you fold The Red Flag newsletter you have to take it from the right pile and not the one that is too fresh because then the words smudge and you are not to fold paper birds because this has been banned.

Comrade Chen made a spell to give himself and Comrade Ruth safe passage through the radiation. In the burning city of Hackney they handed out words to educate the slave masses and spread the revolution and this is now for free but the fascists threw them back in their faces and some dirt at Comrade Chen.

Then The Project was given the important task of being Chief of Pest Duty.

Pest-free areas are glorious. The Project has replaced the mousetraps and primed two new ones with rice and the fatalities have been three in two days. The Project sniffed for mouse poo trails and located a hole behind the rice bag in the cupboard. The Project reported this to Comrade Chen and he was very pleased. The Project was so grateful because I have been fully forgiven. The proof is that the blisters hurt much less now and The Project will get five gold stars and extra ketchup rations if the blisters all go away.

The Project made tight fists to stop the pain and went to every room to check if everyone had done housework properly and to make sure no white paint had come off the floors and no window boards were letting in light. The Comrades waited downstairs in a line in the kitchen staring at the white wood floor like they should because they were not to interrupt or make excuses. The Project's proudest task was to look for forbidden things. First The Project found some dust in bedroom three and a ball of hair. There was also dust on a lampshade and we will never make any progress unless we learn to rid the world of the Old Habits, Old Dust and Old Fluff and something else.

The Project knew to look for one thing in the bathroom and found it but it was not just one but three bars of the Comrade Uma chocolate hidden behind the wooden bit under the bath.

The Project needed more time and the Comrades had to wait, standing in a line.

The Project also found some slime from a bar of soap that was not white and smelled of perfumes. The Project looked for smells of it and in the bottom place where the hand towels are stored round the corner The Project found a shining thing with my own face in it and a thing that looked like a bullet. All of these were forbidden things.

The Project ran but not too fast and whispered to Comrade Chen. He was very surprised and pleased and instructed The Project to go very slowly so he could watch the reactions on the faces of the Comrades lined before him.

Give us your report, said Comrade Chen.

It was very exciting because The Project had put the hidden things in a bag and was holding it and all of the Comrades looked very scared at the bag and then at The Project's eyes.

Comrade Chen said, if everything is neat and in order, then all is fine. But if not, then you must inform us so that the Comrade responsible can learn and do better and if anything forbidden is found there will be punishments.

I looked at Comrade Jeni and she looked worried. She is thirty-six years old and smokes weeds and has some false ideas like saying her long hair is her Red Flag of freedom. I knew she had done wrong because she always does, so I didn't want to start with her.

I said, Comrade Sister Uma, you cleaned the surfaces correctly in the bedrooms but the corners need more attention because of dust which is made up of human skin and may spread The Four Olds.

She looked at me with fear in her eyes. Comrade Chen nodded at the bag.

The Project went into the bag and pulled out the chocolate bars. There was a gasp and Comrade Uma covered her mouth.

Comrade Chen said, Are these yours, Comrade Uma? If you do not confess it will be worse for us all.

Comrade Uma stared at me and her face turned to fear. She said, Yes, it was me, I am sorry. I will take punishment.

Her legs became trembly and Comrade Chen asked The Project what punishment. The Project didn't want to hurt Comrade Uma at all, but someone has to be hurt otherwise Chairman Mao will never bring the Red Storm to London, so The Project said, ten beats with the ruler on the hands of Comrade Uma.

Comrade Uma said, Thank you, and stood to one side. Comrade Chen nodded at The Project to proceed.

I said, Comrade Ruth, your cleaning activities have been perfect.

The Project was nervous but Comrade Chen nodded.

The Project said, but there is the question of these objects. And The Project took out the reflection thing and the bullet thing and was told that it was a hand mirror and the other was called a lip stick. It had Revlon written on it.

Comrade Ruth denied that she had anything to do with these symbols of female subjugation and said that whoever was behind them was a traitor who should be severely punished. Comrade Chen asked The Project if we should believe her innocence and even though The Project doesn't like Comrade Ruth because she is a bully and too tall like a skeleton and would like to hit her with the ruler twenty times, The Project said, You are commended on your honesty and faithfulness and your good cleaning and are to be awarded a gold star, though we do not have any gold stars left and it is just a symbol.

Comrade Ruth stepped to the other side and made a slow sigh.

The Project looked to Comrade Jeni and said, You, Comrade Jeni, failed to clean the bathroom and spend too long in the shower, this I have established because there is a wet patch on the tiles, also there is long red hair in the plughole so it can only be yours.

Comrade Ruth said, Comrade Jeni was the last person on bathroom rota, so the mirror must be hers too.

Comrade Chen said, Silence. And Comrade Jeni stared at the floor.

The Project said, Do you confess, Comrade Jeni?

She said, A bloody child, interrogating us.

Comrade Chen pulled a hair out of her head and said, Look, it is the same colour. Confess. And she confessed that yeah, so sometimes she pulls some hairs out when she has a lot on her mind and yes, she had forgotten to take them out of the bloody plughole but she knew nothing about the mirror and the lippy.

Comrade Ruth shouted, Liar. And Comrade Zana looked scared.

Comrade Chen said, So as there is only one left are you saying that Comrade Zana is to blame?

The Project got a zap of energy and even though the blisters were very sore wanted Comrade Zana and Comrade Jeni to be hit ten times with the ruler, right away, but the eyes of Comrade Chen said no.

Comrade Chen held up the mirror and said, Who is responsible for this abomination? He said, Comrade Zana, if this was you, this is partly understandable, you have not been with us for long, but you must confess.

The women were very silent and terrible radiation was going to come through the cracks in the window boards, because a metal taste was starting.

Comrade Chen said, Maybe you all take turns to dress up as whores and fantasise about possessions? If no one steps forward then there will be no food until the confession and the Comrades shall beat each other in turn.

Comrade Ruth went to the kitchen and took out the ruler and the wooden spoon. She handed them to Comrade Chen. He then handed them to The Project and The Project was very proud.

Comrade Chen said, Fine, The Project will administer the first beatings.

Comrade Jeni's green eyes went dark and her mouth full of silent curses and Comrade Ruth could not hide a smile and Comrade Chen said, We are all equal in our sufferings, Comrade Ruth, you too will be beaten.

The Project had never had the noble task before and was very excited. The Project looked at the faces of the women to ask who was really the traitor.

Comrade Jeni said the name of the man on the cross and, No way, Fuck this. You're all fucking mad.

Comrade Uma stepped forward quickly and said, I am sorry it was me.

Comrade Chen said, Was it really? What use do you have of lipstick? Are you not just saying this to protect someone? Or since you are to be beaten anyway?

The air was crackling and radiation would come any second. Then Comrade Jeni yelled and ran out of the room.

The beatings were postponed till tomorrow as this was all too much for one day. Ten hits for everyone apart from Comrade Chen and The Project. The Project was secretly glad because the blisters are too sore to hold the ruler and hit with.

Notes from Comrade Chen: The Project is healing well and doing an important work of unity by helping Comrade Chen to flush out the enemy within. Comrade Chen tells The Project that all of this must be kept secret and that not all secrets are forbidden, the ones in the service of the revolution are good to keep.

There was only two hours and ten minutes until the beatings and The Project was sink scrubbing with the good hand when there was a flapping outside. Comrade Jeni was on the other side of the window on the concrete with her red hair up in a big knot and she made a hand sign to come to the forbidden back door and to be quiet. The Project looked and all the other Comrades were very busy at the noisy smelly photocopier.

The Project went to the forbidden back door and Comrade Jeni had already opened it. She made the sign of Shh, and not to bash the spades and brushes and wellies and said, Come on, I've got a surprise for everyone. Chen's going to be so happy when he finds out. Come and help me get it. Don't make any noise.

The Project looked past her and said, Outside?

Comrade Jeni said, Not far and anyway I'll protect you. C'mon, get those wellies and that jacket on.

The Project told her no. The fascists would catch us and the radiation would melt The Project's head. Shivering started.

Comrade Jeni said, There's no fascists today, I was out all morning and checked. Come on hurry up and don't make so much noise. You'll be fine, I have a secret radiation shield. C'mon, shh.

Comrade Jeni led The Project out by the good hand and The Project saw Comrade Jeni was wearing a short forbidden skirt and bright red paint on the lips and colours like bruises on the cheeks, like a magazine woman.

The Project was shaking and Comrade Jeni pulled the hand. A wind was blowing with a smell of rotten things from the nuclear war.

The pigeons were circling and there was poop all on the ground and very slippy and it was a sign. Comrade Jeni had a bin bag and a rucksack and The Project could see breath. Comrade Jeni said, Four steps to the bins and duck down and just a bit more till we're at the high wall.

The Project said, But what about the beatings at five o'clock?

Comrade Jeni said, Look. They'll forget that crap when they get their surprise. Anyway, it's not good for you being cooped up in there with those bloody window blinds. You'll end up as mad as they are. I was mad for a bit and it's not great. Can't say I recommend it.

The Project tried to walk but muscles went tight and breathing became very loud so Comrade Jeni pulled The Project.

Comrade Jeni said, Please, just past the bins, OK? You've been to the bins a few times and nothing's attacked you. Right?

The Project tasted salt and everything smelled sharp and was heavy.

Comrade Jeni said, See, there's no radiation and no dead birds. See.

The Project repeated no radiation, no dead birds, no dead people but thought it must be a trap like the way the flying monkeys of the Wicked Witch caught Dorothy. The Project looked back at the Collective and it was sixty-one steps away and no Comrades had come to the window and it looked like all the other places where the enemy called neighbours lived all joined together.

The Project said, Can we go back? Can we throw a stone to make sure there are no fascists hiding? Where are we going?

Comrade Jeni said, A surprise won't be a surprise if I told you, now would it?

Then she threw a stone into the Lane and said, See no monsters there. Now, come on, run. I'm not going to take your hand all the way, I don't want to squeeze your poor blisters, that was just plain evil what happened to your poor little fingers. Come on, we're nearly at the end then it'll be a street. The fascists are all away. Right, remember counting your numbers, I want you to do the same with your feet, right? One step, two steps, three. Just look at your feet, nothing else.

The Project counted, twelve steps, thirteen steps. The Project's eyes kept looking back and the Collective got smaller and The Project got very scared from noises from the end of the lane and another road was there The Project had never seen and The Project stopped and said to Comrade Jeni, But this is where the fascists live!

And Comrade Jeni said, Well we can use Dorothy's Ruby slippers to magic ourselves invisible, can't we. Come on hurry or we'll miss our bus.

And then Comrade Jeni dragged The Project hard by the sore hand and a big metal machine came fast to kill The Project and The Project screamed but no noise came and a wet feeling came down the leg and Comrade Jeni yelled, Jesus, what the hell's wrong with you? And The Project clicked the heels like Dorothy and closed the eyes and went invisible and there was rushing and wind until The Project remembers being back at the

Collective steps and shivering and opening the eyes because of all the screaming.

The door banged back and The Project peeked inside past the wellies and saw Comrade Ruth grab Comrade Jeni by the hair and pin Comrade Jeni to the floor and then pushing the dirty spade into Comrade Jeni's throat and swearing, You fucking traitor, where the fuck were you taking her? There was a mark of blood and mud on Comrade Jeni's neck and she could not breathe. Her eyes flashed into The Project and she reached out her hand then Comrade Ruth yelled, I'll fucking finish you, and kicked the door shut.

The Project was locked outside with wires in the sky and then was the sound of metal hitting and screams of Comrade Jeni calling the name Nina. The radiation sky opened and The Project tried to yell for help but no noise came. The Project tried to run but couldn't move. There was banging everywhere and radiation poured down. The Project fell down in the pigeon poo to hide with fingers in ears and to rock back and forwards. And Comrade Jeni screamed on the other side, Nina, help. The Project tried to breathe but the ground was shaking and sparks flew up into the sky then everything stopped.

Jotter #243 2018

Nina counted two hundred and twenty-six strangers passing by the window of Charity House. Freedom is a messy place. Everyone is cross out there. A car made a scream noise and a brown man leaned out his window and shouted at a white van. A woman passed in foot spikes and a husband man turned his head and looked at her with eyes of wanting even though he was holding the arm of his female and she had breasts on display. Many people are trying to say look at me and prove that they are an important I. And they are always in a hurry.

Nina is lonely in the Charity House but not in the way of the basement. Then there were Comrades who worried about Nina and wanted to hit or hug her through the roof, but now, only two new people know where Nina is and they are both on the end of a phone but Nina is scared to try it because signals go through the sky.

Nina took clothes off like in Cosmopolitan to make a man come. Then a shadow did, on the glass, but it was not a man but Charity Sonia. She said, Oh, oh, and Sorry to disturb you, can you get changed please, this is important, and she put her eyes to the floor. And she had a big bag with her with toothpaste and bleach and a sandwich and a new pair of trainers for Nina. Charity Sonia looked at her phone and she said, Nina, could you put the bra and underpants and T-shirt and jeans on as well, please. Quick. The police will be here soon.

Nina felt incorrect. Nina keeps doing things wrong and Nina had not been back to the shop for more food but just eaten the last oranges. Nina had lied about this on the food form for Social Work Phil and is not sure if lying is OK after all.

Charity Sonia was nervous and sighing because she wanted to ask something but she couldn't. Nina just waited.

Then Charity Sonia said, Nina. And then she was quiet and Nina kept putting on clothes. Then she said, Nina, about your diary. I mean your diaries, and she touched the one on the kitchen table.

Charity Sonia said, I know you don't want the police to see them, and I want to empower you to make your own decisions, but. And she sighed again and picked up the diary, and said, But, will you let me read it if I promise not to show anyone? If I give it straight back to you today?

Nina didn't want to lose the friendship of Charity Sonia, and Nina needed a new jotter for the next days, so Nina said, OK. Can you buy me a new one please, and some underpants because these ones are smelly.

Charity Sonia said, Oh, yes, of course sorry, yes, great, excellent. I'll get Cas to take care of all of that, thank you.

Charity Sonia opened a page and read. It made Nina feel a tugging inside because only Comrades are permitted to read it.

Charity Sonia said, What's this? This number?

Nina said, Two hundred and forty-two.

Charity Sonia said, Is that. No. It can't be. Nina, can you look at me please, is that the number of diaries you wrote during your incarceration?

Nina nodded.

Charity Sonia said, God. Then she said, Listen, Nina, I don't want to tell you what to do, but the police need to build the case and if you recorded everything that happened, it could be the evidence they need to put those monsters away forever and to keep you safe.

Nina said nothing and Charity Sonia said, Can I be honest with you, Nina?

Nina nodded.

Charity Sonia said, Now, I don't want to influence you in any way and I want to empower you to make all your own choices.

Nina knew there was a But coming.

Charity Sonia said, But, when you said to the police that you killed someone, it has created some real problems and Phil and his team have had to become involved. Now, I know you were disorientated when you said that, but the last thing we want is for you to be treated as a suspect. Now, if the diaries could all be found. I mean, the police could be on your side and that will let me get on with the job of your long-term housing and rehabilitation because to be honest Phil's team are now very nervous about this police thing.

And Charity Sonia said, Are the diaries back at the Collective, Nina? Are they hidden somewhere?

Nina said, Nina ate some. And some are birds now. Because this is true.

Then Charity Sonia said, OK, OK, I'm sorry. It's very good of you to let me read this one. Thank you. Now the police are going to be here soon and they're going to ask you questions. I'll stay and if they make you feel upset or angry, you just tell me. OK? And I'll ask them to stop.

Nina nodded because Nina can nod and shake the head.

Charity Sonia sighed and said, Good, I know you're not violent, Nina. And her eyes had questions behind them but Nina didn't know what the questions were so Charity Sonia said, Great, because I think it's really important that we get everyone back to focusing on the abuse you suffered. The Doctor said the scarring might date back to your early childhood.

And her eyes looked up and she said, Is that right, Nina? What did they do to you when you were little?

Nina wanted to tell Charity Sonia to make her happy but everything has been erased in empty hollows and makes Nina tired, so Nina tried to cheer Charity Sonia up by putting the new trainers on. They were blue and white and hard but soft at the bottom and already a bit dirty, not like in the pictures.

Nina knows Charity Sonia is worried that Nina is a killer who is telling lies but she won't say this. Charity Sonia keeps calling Nina a victim but Nina doesn't know if this is correct because Nina did things to three other Comrades too to make them bleed. And that made Nina feel strong. But Charity Sonia gets hot faced whenever Nina says this.

Nina looked down at the trainers and then at the legs and said, What does Nina look like?

Charity Sonia said, Well they seem to fit just fine, isn't there a mirror? And she looked about but Nina had hidden it under the bed and told Charity Sonia that mirrors were banned in the Collective.

Charity Sonia said, You mean, all that time growing up you never saw yourself?

Nina shook the head and said, Only in the toilet water and windows at night.

Charity Sonia had to hide her face and make a big breath and she said, I'll ask Cas to get you more clothes as soon as we get your emergency funds through from the DSS.

The female officer was grumpy and didn't say, My name is, or smile, so she was still a Pig. She sat and had some pictures for Nina's eyes only and she said, We know that the Collective was a kind of haven for runaways, the woman you call Comrade Uma was wanted in Germany and France, lots of extremists came and went. Now, this concerns Comrade Ruth.

The female Pig held a picture of four young women with a sign that said, SMASH THE STATE and all with fists in air and she said, is this one Ruth? But Nina said the eyes were too far apart. Then she held another one and it was of two women and a man and they were on the other side of a kind of fence and one had a thing covering his face apart from the eyes and the women had their mouths covered but the eyes were wrong again and the hair wasn't Ruth either.

The female Pig said something to the male Pig and then held up a picture of a screaming woman with spike hair and big boots and painted signs on her chest throwing a thing and yelling at police with helmets and guns and smoke. The female Pig officer asked, Does this look like Ruth?

Nina shook the head then stared because of the tallness and tight eyes and it was like a very young Comrade Ruth, so Nina nodded. Then the spidery hands of Ruth too, so Nina nodded more.

The female Pig officer said to the male Pig officer, OK, so that's a positive identification. OK, Can you confirm that her second name was Pendal? Ruth, Rachel or Rebecca Pendal, do these ring any bells?

Nina didn't know. Second names are to pass on privilege. Nina wants to be rich and have babies and have a second name one day.

The male Pig talked into his machine and he said, Positive ID on Pendal. GBH, four counts of resisting arrest, breaking into a military property, possession of a dangerous weapon.

The female Pig said, I have to inform you that we have re-opened the case of the accidental death of Simone Genevieve

Lamberton in 2002. The report said she died of a drug-related death drug with secondary complications. But it's possible the Doctors got something wrong. Can I ask you, did Ruth assault Simone Genevieve Lamberton?

Nina thought about the diary and hand pain came and a picture and Nina said, There was a spade.

The female and male Pig officers looked to each other like a secret and the female Pig said, Sorry, are you saying there was a weapon?

Nina felt the feeling like words are rubbed out.

Nina said, The Project had to write it again. It was another day.

The female Pig officer said, Sorry? And Charity Sonia whispered and then the female Pig officer said, OK, OK, fine, next, I need you to tell me if Simone Genevieve Lamberton was in fact the Comrade Jeni you've talked about?

She held up a photograph of someone very young and pretty and standing next to two others with fascist hats on beside the sea and ribbons in her long hair and she said, Is this her? And she said, This was taken before she ran away from home at the age of sixteen. Her parents are still alive. The report said that she had only visited the Collective on one occasion. Did this woman live with you? This is very important, Nina.

Nina looked at the picture and saw that the big smile was the same smile and so was the same red hair and a big pointy chest and big eyes but pain came in Nina's hand and the hollow.

Nina tried hard and said, Yes. It is Comrade Jeni.

The Pig officers nodded to each other and Charity Sonia sighed and the female Pig officer said, OK, so you're confirming that Genevieve was Comrade Jeni?

Nina nodded and Charity Sonia said, God.

Nina's pain got worse and the eyes and hand more sore, like words rubbed out again again again but still the bad pencil is always there.

The female Pig said, OK. This is very important. Chen and the others claimed Jeni was a friend of a friend, just visiting, is that true?

Nina shook the head.

The female Pig said, Can you confirm that Jeni lived with you?

Nina nodded.

The female Pig said, Were you there when she died, Nina?

Nina was confused because Comrade Jeni died in the Hospital. Comrade Jeni's mouth had foam and blood in and pigeon poo in her hair and Nina said Hospital.

The female Pig officer said, OK, that's correct, but I mean, did something happen at the Collective that meant that Jeni had to go to Hospital?

Nina's head went tight and Nina heard Comrade Ruth say, Again, write it again.

The female Pig officer said, Please, Nina, I know this is difficult but I want you to think really hard, can you tell me if Comrade Jeni was forced to take drugs, was she tied up in some way? You mentioned a spade, was she threatened or hit with it or some other weapon?

And the female Pig officer said the next picture might cause alarm but Nina wasn't scared so the female Pig officer held up a picture of a grey person with Jeni's hair on a silver table and big sewing stitches up her chest and Nina felt the needle pierce in Nina's skin. And Nina closed the eyes and clicked the heels to be invisible again and saw Jeni and the spade and her foaming mouth and Nina had to do a bit of rocking.

Charity Sonia said to the Pigs, This is totally out of order, I'm sorry but Nina's too upset to continue. Then Charity Sonia took Nina's good hand and she said, It's OK, Nina, just breathe. Then after some breaths she said Nina could open the eyes again because it was safe and so Nina did but the female Pig officer and the male Pig officer were still there but standing.

The female Pig officer passed a piece of paper and said, Can you fill this in please, Nina, this is about you and your body. Incidents, dates and so on. Everything is totally confidential. Who hurt you? What happened to your hand and your back? And we want to know about any other victims. We need all the names you can remember. You can be a big help to us in finding out who hurt Jeni.

Nina dug nails into skin to make it stop because this was how it all started when The Project had to report on everyone. Nina knows everything is supposed to be the opposite now so why does Nina have to keep making reports? Nina dug nails in harder and it made a person appear at the front door.

It was Social Work Phil and the Pig officers said they were just leaving anyway, and thank you for your time. Then Nina heard the female Pig officer at the door say in a quiet voice that they were concerned that Ruth Pendal could attempt to find Nina and they were changing her status to missing person considered dangerous and that Charity Sonia should consider moving Nina.

Then Charity Sonia wanted to speak to Social Work Phil outside urgently and Nina was left alone.

Nina looked out from the Charity House side window and spied on Charity Sonia and Social Work Phil on the path. They were whispering and Nina squashed the eyes tight to hear for writing in Nina's report.

Charity Sonia said, You can't just march in on Nina without letting me know. I have to be here at all times, or at least one of my assistants. She has some behaviours that are. And she stopped and Nina hid behind the blind.

Social Work Phil said, Sorry, OK, the update is, I've got her on the lists for PIP, on two housing association lists, but as far as I can see she's not adapting well, not eating properly or sleeping or washing. She may not even be suitable for assisted housing. She might be a danger to herself.

Nina's breathing went fast and more things were not heard. A bit sounded like Social Work Phil said, The way she stares, like she's memorising everything. She gives folk the creeps, Sonia.

And Charity Sonia was cross at him but Nina was listening too hard with breath on the glass and Nina's head bumped the window so Nina had to hide and when Nina came back Nina heard Charity Sonia say, No, no, I'm absolutely convinced she'll be able to be independent. She just needs time.

Social Work Phil said, I know you want the women in your care to become self-reliant and that's admirable but let's not be blinded by wishful thinking, Sonia. We could be looking at environmentally induced autism here or severe learning disability. I've managed to get Nina a neurological evaluation tomorrow.

Charity Sonia got angrier and said, It would solve all your care plan problems wouldn't it, if she was disabled and you could dump her back on the NHS.

Social Work Phil said, Now let's calm down. I'm just evaluating the safest housing options, what with this Ruth nutcase running around.

There was a crunching noise of the ground and Social Work Phil walked back and forwards and said, Since that leak the tabloids are out hunting for her as well, I'm getting phone calls from hacks every ten minutes.

Charity Sonia said, Are you insinuating that the leak came from my organisation?

Social Work Phil said, Please, Sonia, calm down, maybe we can use the leak to our advantage, maybe one of Nina's real family members will come forward. I'd be really grateful, Sonia, if we could share all information and try not to work against each other. It would be in Nina's best interests. In the meantime I'll try to help you find somewhere with better security.

Charity Sonia was quiet then she said, Nina gave me this.

Then Nina saw the diary in the hand of Charity Sonia and she showed it to Social Work Phil then she looked back at the window and Nina was almost caught copying their words.

Sonia wiped her nose with a tissue and turned away because she always does that now. And Social Work Phil went to put his hand on her shoulder and then didn't.

Nina is angry with Charity Sonia. Charity Sonia is a traitor for her leaks and is to be expelled. Nina is angry at the police for letting Comrade Ruth escape and to come to erase Nina.

After all the traitors left the Charity House, Nina sat in the plastic window all day. No birds came and then it was dark and Support Worker Cas came with a pack of four new blue jotters because Charity Sonia asked her to, and she said, Right, misses, I'm going to show you how to make that microwave rice if it's the last thing I do and she showed Nina that it went round with electric magic for one minute forty-five and how to push the beeping buttons but Nina was scared and angry and could not focus and had to go back to the window to look out in case of Comrade Ruth and her spade. No radiation came but Nina could feel the Wicked Witch spying in the sky. Nina wants to hide here and not run away. Charity Sonia lied and did not come back with the diary. Nina bashed the head against the window and rocked back and forwards but it did not make the diary come back. Nina will die this time if they take away Nina's window and if birds don't come and people steal Nina's words. Nina must hide all the pages and protect them.

Nina did not sleep all night because Nina had to write and Nina couldn't leave the peeking curtains and Nina spied one person, skinny and bald like Comrade Ruth and looking into a phone filled with light in their hand but walked away. Then only the old lady with the yellow dog and the bag from Iceland.

Then it was morning and too bright and Nina had to be brave

and try to be in the car again of Charity Sonia and to listen to The Wizard of Oz very loud over miles and Nina closed the eyes so as not to see the temples of Capitalism. Nina managed to eat two packets of Worcester Sauce crisps and this is hard with eyes closed, but easier in a car, because eating alone in a room makes pictures come of the basement.

Nina had to meet NHS Doctor Webber. Doctor Webber's room is in a building of many doors that you are not to open behind the big grey Hospital and the sign says Shoreditch Mental Health Resource Centre. It is at the end of a long corridor and is white and smells of bleach just like the Collective. He has a box of toys for children on his floor and scratchy drawings on a wall but he does not hurt children.

Nina likes Doctor Webber's curly grey eyebrows but he has a wedding ring so is already private property. Cosmopolitan says Nina should find it no problem to attract a successful married man but Nina did not tell Doctor Webber this because Nina should just say some things with the eyes.

Nina had to answer many questions with number adding, then matching shapes on a page and choosing which one is missing, and all were very different and then some were letters but they were not words and Nina did these very fast and even found the elephant in the picture of squiggles and Doctor Webber said, very good, Nina, and his voice was rumbly and slow and he wrote things down and held Nina's wrist.

Nina knows Nina's words confuse people but this might be OK because Cosmopolitan said it is best for a woman to be mysterious.

Then Doctor Webber went to the toy box and came back with a doll and he said, OK, Nina, This is Sally, I know you're too big for dolls but I have to ask you a question and he laid Sally Doll on the table between Nina and himself.

Doctor Webber said, OK. Now Sally is crying and Sally is sad. Can you visualise that? And Nina said, Yes.

And Doctor Webber said, What would you do if you were her mother?

Nina felt a scraping feeling and said, Mothers are incorrect.

Doctor Webber's eyes changed, and he said, Incorrect, what does that mean?

Nina said, Mothers are oppressors so Nina would take Sally away from the Mother to be on the safe side. Dolls are oppressors too.

Doctor Webber said, Can you tell me why?

And Nina said, Dolls are just to train you to be a female slave and they are banned. And Nina felt cross looking at it and Nina said, Dolls make the deserts come.

And Doctor Webber said, Can you explain that connection to me, but Nina didn't want to see the doll any more and pushed it off the table.

Doctor Webber was very calm and he said, OK, Nina, can you tell me who threw Sally on the floor?

And Nina felt like saying The Project but The Project is a secret so Nina said, Nina did.

Doctor Webber said, Can you say, I did?

And Nina repeated, I did.

And Doctor Webber said, And how do you feel about this, what we're talking about? Does it upset you?

Nina told him No, it was just like they were talking about someone else and it wasn't bad because Nina was very good at memorising things and Nina would write it all down later.

Then Nina felt incorrect and said sorry, and Nina put the knees up and hugged them and rocked. And Doctor Webber said, I'll just be a minute, Nina, and he made some writing and Nina saw he has hairs growing from his nose.

Nina was worried that Doctor Webber did not find Nina attractive any more, Nina tried to smile at him with more allure but he kept writing so Nina wrote all this up in the head for later so if Nina gets tested again Nina can do the right things.

Then Doctor Webber said, OK, Nina, that's the first test part over. Sonia tells me that you have difficulty going outside and that you have a very restricted area in which you can feel comfortable, especially that you're afraid of cars and new places. Can you be very brave and follow me, please?

Charity Sonia stayed behind on a chair in the corridor and was doing her meetings with people's faces on her phone and it was OK to go with this man but never with any others.

Nina was also not to try to hold Doctor Webber's hand even though Nina loves him ninety-two per cent which is a secret.

Doctor Webber walked down a corridor with pictures of nature and empty seats in a line and Nina passed by an old shaking man with a plastic bag and a woman with no hair and a woman behind a desk with white fascist uniform and then Doctor Webber stopped.

Doctor Webber said, OK, Nina, I'm opening the door now and I just want you to stand on the step here and tell me how you feel. Nina did what he said and he opened it and Nina was terrified because it was a trick and there were a thousand cars outside in lines and radiation was coming in the sky and Doctor Webber said, OK, now I can see you are in distress, can you tell me which of these symptoms you are experiencing, and just come down one step into the Hospital car park.

And he said, Accelerated breathing, wobbly legs, rapid heartbeat, negative thoughts, a sense of being in danger, a feeling of choking, of sweaty palms, of feeling faint, of not being able to escape and Nina said, Yes, Yes, Yes, Yes, Yes, No, Yes, and Yes. And, Can Nina go back, please?

And Doctor Webber said, OK, look at me and take a big breath and hold it and count backwards from a hundred. One hundred, ninety-nine, ninety-eight. And Nina did, and then he said and let it go, ninety-five, ninety-four, ninety-three, and tell yourself, My current symptoms are just a conditioned response and they will lessen as I desensitise myself. And Nina did that all the way to zero.

And he said, Did anything bad happen while we counted backwards?

And Nina said, No.

And Doctor Webber said, Can you tell me what is your worst fear from this car park? And Nina said, Cars will kill and radiation in the sky. And Doctor Webber said, Have you ever been hurt by radiation from the sky? And Nina said, Comrade Jeni was and she is dead.

Doctor Webber said, OK, I want you to think very hard, when you have fear like this and you feel you are going to faint or die, have you ever fainted?

And Nina thought and said, No.

Have you ever died?

And Nina laughed and said, No.

And Doctor Webber said, OK, Nina, just step down one step. Now, is there anything out here that you are not afraid of?

And Nina looked round and there was a tree and it might have birds and Nina told Doctor Webber, and so Doctor Webber said, Excellent, so try to think of the tree as we walk towards it. And Doctor Webber said, And step down and forward. And Nina loved holding his arm very much but he let go and so Nina followed him towards the tree between the cars. And Doctor Webber said, Congratulations, Nina, you are now standing four rows into the car park that you were terrified of a minute ago.

Nina started to get scared again but Doctor Webber said, Have a rest against the railing and breathe, and count, one hundred, ninety-nine, ninety-eight and now, next time this happens to you in any unfamiliar place, just focus on a goal that's beyond it, in this case the tree, and count backwards and ask yourself, is something terrible happening to me right now? And if the answer is no, keep breathing and counting and telling yourself, I am OK, I am not going to be hurt. And ask yourself, what is the worst thing that can happen if I stay here for a few minutes more and then ask yourself, is there any evidence of this, or is it all in my head, and just keep counting backwards in time with your breathing.

And Nina did what he said, and he said, How are you now? Scared or OK?

And Nina said, OK. And a smile was rising in Nina's chest. There were many cars silver and a white van saying, Vehicle reversing, vehicle reversing, and Doctor Webber said, You're doing so well, Nina. Here we are in the middle of a huge car park and you're not having a panic attack. Are you?

And Nina said, No, and smiled.

And Doctor Webber said, And what will you tell yourself next time your heart starts racing and you are flooded with fear thoughts?

And Nina knew the answer and said, Nina will say: My current symptoms are just a conditioned response and they will lessen as I desensitise myself.

Doctor Webber said, Excellent, your memory is incredible.

And Nina and Doctor Webber never got to the tree but he told stories of other people who felt the same as Nina did but about different things and Nina filled up with a good feeling. There was the man who was afraid of tall buildings and the woman who was afraid of drain covers and how this was called generalised panic disorder and was common with people with post-traumatic stress disorder. Doctor Webber said that he had once treated a soldier who survived a war, and this man couldn't say I either because of memories. Then he said, Hopefully we can help you manage this too. Step by step.

And Nina wanted to stand in the car park with Doctor Webber forever because birds passed by and they were sparrows and Doctor Webber was pleased to hear that Nina loved birds so much. Nina wants to be in love for the first time and thinks it might be with Doctor Webber.

Nina said goodbye with lingering eye contact and wanted to kiss Doctor Webber but kept it a secret because secrets are OK now and private property is OK too, and when you keep it inside it fills up the hole. Back at his door, he said, OK, Nina, now that you're adapting, you might have some feelings that are new. That might have been held back. They're all perfectly natural. But if you get any thoughts that won't leave you alone or any extreme or disturbing emotions, promise me that you'll tell me or your GP or Sonia. Before you do anything. OK?

Nina asked him, Like what?

And he said, Well you see this happened to the soldier I was telling you about, he found it hard to settle in peacetime, he even wanted to go back to a war zone and to put his body in danger, so if you have any thoughts like that, Nina, you just let us know as soon as possible.

And Nina nodded, then Doctor Webber said there were more tests to do and the data to process but he was hopeful. And Nina wanted to kiss Doctor Webber on the hand but he stepped back and he said he looked forward to seeing Nina again and to ask Charity Sonia to come in now.

After Charity Sonia was worried in the car and Nina knew it was about Nina's brain, but some man was on the phone to Charity Sonia and asking for Nina's address and pretending to be social services and then she hung up and Charity Sonia is very worried now of spies and hacks and Comrade Ruth.

Social Work Phil is working very hard to get Nina a safer place but it will take a day or two.

Nina is not to look out the window any more or answer the door to anyone and Charity Sonia is trying to hire a man of security. Nina has been shown how to use the phone for an emergency and not be afraid of its light.

Nina might need to cry, Charity Sonia says, and it might

happen soon, when Nina is properly alone, and she says to call her if the silence is too much. People also use phones for ordering food and for gambling and for sex and maps because of the digital revolution which came because the communist one didn't.

Nina knows Nina must cry and then people will like Nina more. Because if Nina can't cry it will be harder for Nina to ever find a lover man. Normal people can't say, I was locked in a basement for twelve years, without crying, so Nina has to learn how to cry as well as trying to be I and Nina told this to Charity Sonia.

Doctor Webber made Charity Sonia in charge of Nina's pills and she showed Nina how to use the ones for sleep but only gave Nina two just in case. And there are pink ones for anxiety four times a day and you are not to mix them or take more than the recommended dose and Support Worker Cas would give them to Nina when Charity Sonia was not there.

Nina was alone again and Nina couldn't help break the window promise because Nina peeked out and saw a pigeon on the path with one leg burned and Nina called him Ping because Nina pinged a crumb at him.

Nina will bring him more bread tomorrow, if Cas brings another sandwich and if Nina can find him again. There are many pigeons in freedom.

Nina peeks out the window to keep Comrade Ruth away.

Nina must have been asleep on the floor and there was a banging and it was the door. Nina looked and there was a shadow in the glass and it was not the shadow of Charity Sonia or Social Work Phil but a shape with a hat.

Knocks on the glass. And Nina thought, Comrade Ruth had a hat for her bald head.

Nina went to the kitchen place to hide and got the biggest spoon for hitting and the knife and Nina's heart was fast and fear thoughts coming. And saying, I am under no threat of harm, and counting breaths backwards, one hundred, ninety-nine, ninety-eight didn't work, because the knocking came again. And Nina yelled, Go away, Ruth.

Then the door handle moved.

Nina had tingling legs and all the symptoms like to die from heart beating and Nina said, My current symptoms are just a conditioned response and they will lessen as I desensitise myself and Nina hid from the glass shadow and remembered the phone and how Charity Sonia said dial the saved number or 999 and Nina pushed button, and then Nina saw the shadow vanish then it appeared again at the window and the face was dark and it was leaning in on the other side of the curtains with one hand up and the voice in Nina's hand was like a machine and it said, Hello emergency services, fire police or ambulance, hello?

Nina said, This is Nina, help me.

And Nina changed the knife in the hand to make it point down not up.

The machine voice said again, Fire, police or ambulance. Nina had to whisper and crawl to hide in the dark place of the bathroom, and said, Please help me, Ruth has come. And the eyes were still at the window.

And then there was a click and a hiss and the voice changed to a Pig voice that said, Hello, who is this? What service do you require? Can you give me your address please?

And Nina whispered, It's Nina. I'm in the Charity House.

Nina peeked out and the shadow was back at the door and a second shadow came. And Nina was crouching to be very small and the voice in the phone said, Where are you? Can you give me an address or a postcode? But Nina couldn't think and said Charity House, over and over, and the voice said, Who is this, can you stay on the line please?

Nina shivered and made a knife hole in the bad arm to make the warm pain come to make everything go away and the voice said, Don't hang up we're trying to track your location. We're sending a patrol car, I'm passing you through to an officer now.

Then Nina saw a piece of paper coming through the door hole and falling and landing inside. And it was white and a rectangle. Like Comrade Ruth did in the basement. Like Comrade Uma did. And Nina said, My current symptoms are just a conditioned response and they will lessen as I desensitise myself. But the words and the breathing and the blood pain was not enough to make Nina invisible.

And the knocking got louder and the second person was short in the shadow in the glass, like Uma and Nina froze. And Ruth and Uma would be very angry because Nina had betrayed them to the Pigs, and the voice in Nina's hand said, Hello, miss, This is the Metropolitan Police Emergency service, Can you please give us your address or postcode? Hello, miss. Hello? And the door banged loud again.

Jotter #68 2002

The Project was locked back inside and had to erase the sight of red hair and blood on the back-door floor and Comrade Chen asked The Project many questions. When Jeni grabbed you did anyone see you? Did Jeni speak to anyone? Comrade Chen asked, How far did you get? He asked, Does the phone box on Lamb Lane still work? He asked, Did Jeni call 999? Does anyone know she is here? Did anyone see you?

But The Project couldn't remember, just that Comrade Jeni had taken The Project out and then The Project went invisible and then Comrade Ruth with the spade and the blood and the cold and slime on the back door but Comrade Chen didn't want to hear about that and when The Project asked, Is Comrade Jeni OK? The Project was just told that Comrade Jeni is very sorry.

Comrade Chen made everyone wait in a line in the washing room with the hanging rack of white sheets because the meeting room was full of boxes of The Red Flag that had not been sold. Comrade Chen walked back and forwards and all the Comrade's eyes were lowered in shame. Comrade Jeni had many bruises on face, neck and throat from Comrade Ruth and her spade and fists.

I could feel Comrade Chen's great eye entering mine, and looking around inside. After we heard Comrade Zana confess to smuggling banned cancer sticks into the Collective, Comrade Chen said, The Beloved Chen congratulates you, Comrades, for your admissions of failure, which are so essential to the progress of each of us. And he touched Comrade Zana's face then he said, But these confessions, like the dirt on the floor, sometimes you sweep it into the corners and hide the bigger truth with a smaller confession or a lie.

The Project got a shiver feeling.

Comrade Chen crossed his arms behind his back and said, In order to make our actions shine forth forever, let us now try fearlessly to help our sisters better detect their own faults. Who wishes to speak bitterness of another's faults?

It was time.

Comrade Ruth stood proudly forward. Comrade Ruth pointed at Comrade Jeni's face and said, You attempted to destroy the great experiment by stealing The Project away.

Comrade Jeni turned and tried to run for the door but she was restrained by Comrade Chen. His hand moved and his power pushed her to fall over, like the Wicked Witch did to the scarecrow with fire. Comrade Jeni tried to crawl for the door but Comrade Ruth blocked her way and Comrade Chen held her arm firmly.

We have hardly begun, said Comrade Ruth. Your lies about going to the shops have been exposed. We know you planned to destroy the Collective. You're just lucky that The Project has blanked the memory of all that happened so that all our work is not ruined.

Comrade Jeni slumped to the floor and The Project tried to touch her but Comrade Uma held The Project's sore hand firmly. Because pity is a bourgeois feeling.

Comrade Ruth said, In light of these violations, I propose that

Jeni be stripped of the name of Comrade and be banished to the bourgeois hell she came from.

Comrade Ruth became taller than ever before and she said, She stinks of privilege. She degrades us all and buys our friendship. For too long we've been living off her trust fund. I say her cash debases us and the cause. Furthermore her volatility and mental health issues are a constant danger. This is not a rehab unit. I have been saying for a long time that she should be ejected. I propose we do it today.

There were spit bits on the side of Comrade Ruth's mouth and her bald head shined with the light bulb. The Project could feel power in the room stronger than the last purge of former Comrades Eli and Tobias and Louise, when The Project was smaller. The Project's proud feeling was turning into hollow hurt for poor Comrade Jeni who was weeping as Comrade Zana and Uma held her arms.

Comrade Jeni shivered below Comrade Chen's fist and power flowed making her long red hair stand up. Comrade Chen turned to Comrade Ruth and said, You say she should leave immediately?

Comrade Ruth nodded and smiled. Yes.

But The Project could feel Comrade Chen's eye searching in all the hidden spaces. Comrade Ruth's eyes looked at all of us.

Yes, she said again, Comrade Jeni must be banished. It's all in The Project's diary, betrayal after betrayal. I say get rid of her!

The veins on her shiny head stood out. She had circles of sweat in the pits of her thin arms.

Comrade Chen said, Did you just say, I say she should leave, I say she should be banished? And Comrade Ruth's face went white all over. I knew right away what she'd done wrong but I had been trained not to shout out the right answers. So instead I made the sign of erasure through the air.

Did I say that, Did I . . . Oh my God! she said.

It was exciting to watch her eyes going big and trembly. I

shouted out, You did it again, you said I, I, I and you said my and you said God.

Comrade Chen held up a finger to silence The Project and he placed a hand on Comrade Ruth's shoulder.

He said, You have the right to pass judgement, do you, Comrade Ruth? To give orders, to decide on the fate of a woman who you have deemed to be beneath you. Two women you have cast down this month with accusations and is this not the bourgeois way, to build oneself up, by tearing others down?

And he took Comrade Jeni and raised her up and caressed her brow in forgiveness and he motioned for Comrade Zana to come close. He said, This poor proletarian, this addict, a woman lower in class than you, a woman subjected to exploitation by Capitalist men. And Comrade Jeni, one of our most faithful Comrades. You have the power to banish Comrade Zana and Comrade Jeni, do you, Comrade Ruth?

Comrade Ruth said, I . . . I . . . I'm sorry, but Jeni tried to kidnap The Project, she showed her the outside.

Comrade Chen said, Comrade Jeni will do her penance in her own way. Do you feel it is in your power to decide the fate of others? Do think you are the leader, do you wish to challenge my authority?

Comrade Ruth pleaded, No, I'm sorry, I try to be correct. I am selfish, I am in error, please forgive me.

Comrade Ruth fell to her knees and bowed her head before Comrade Chen, praying and muttering. She clung to Comrade Chen's arm and wept, Please, forgive me, Comrade Leader.

Lift your head, Comrade Chen said, Look into my eyes.

Comrade Chen placed his thumb over Comrade Ruth's throat lump. He said, Henceforth, Comrade Ruth is placed beneath the shadow of the hand. The suffering peoples of the world look upon you with disgust. They give me, in this moment, the power to take away your life.

Comrade Chen pushed on her throat with his thumb like The Great and Powerful Oz and he said, Your little life is worthless in itself. Betrayer of women, betrayer of Socialism and the long march.

Comrade Ruth was gasping. Comrade Jeni and Comrade Uma pleaded with Comrade Chen to spare her. He withdrew his thumb but we saw a shadow of pure energy strangling her. She wrapped her own hands round her throat. Her mouth was choking and she was going to faint like the Cowardly Lion.

I begged too, not because I wanted to really stop it but because sometimes it is hard for The Project not to do what the others do when they are shouting and crying and beating their chests.

Comrade Chen said with a trembling voice, Comrade Ruth, you have become sanctimonious, vain, self-righteous. You have already attacked Comrade Jeni, without permission. Are you, you who says I, I, I, I so often and with such ease, are you a fascist in disguise who has infiltrated our Collective?

Comrade Ruth's face was turning purple. She nodded.

Comrade Chen said, Have you been planning sabotage? Passing secrets to the outside?

Comrade Uma wept too and she said, Please spare her. And Comrade Jeni.

Comrade Chen said, They beg me to spare you because they are pure of heart but what will I do then with this force the billions of suffering have placed in my hands? This force that will kill me if I cannot release it?

Give it to us, pleaded Comrade Jeni, then Comrade Uma too, even though we are too weak to bear it. Give it to us, please. Comrade Uma was the best at saying these words and The Project wants one day to be the one who says them.

Comrade Zana was staring at the other Comrades and copying them and me. It was only her second self-criticism. We all said:

Give us the power, though it will harm us, so that we can serve the will of the oppressed peoples of the world.

The electricity flowed through me and it made me want to run and run in a circle. But The Project remembered what to do and The Project joined hands with Comrade Jeni and Comrade Uma and then Comrade Zana took Comrade Uma's hand, although she was still looking at me like The Project was a scary person. Comrade Chen released Comrade Ruth from his power and she fell to the floor grasping her neck.

Comrade Ruth stammered, Thank you, Comrade Chen. Your criticism of me is true, I am grateful for being corrected.

Comrade Chen said, No, others cannot correct you. Your surrender is proof only of weakness. Do you have the discipline for self-critique?

Comrade Ruth stared at him and said, Forgive me, you are correct, I must Self-critique. Then Comrade Ruth made a fist and looked at it and then looked at Comrade Chen. He nodded and Comrade Ruth struck herself in the face. Then again.

Comrade Chen said, You are too weak you must be stronger.

Comrade Ruth fists grew tighter and she hit herself harder in the face. Her nose was bleeding and The Project felt like a bird fluttering in the chest and wanted it to stop.

Comrade Uma joined in and shouted, Coward, hit harder. And Comrade Ruth hit herself so hard in the face that she stumbled on the wall.

Her eye was all swollen and bloodied and The Project was shivering and Comrade Uma said, Strike those proud lips. Comrade Ruth hit herself again and her lip tore. Comrade Jeni said, For God sake can we stop?

But Comrade Ruth hit herself and again and again and again on her ears and nose and lips, till there was blood and her eye skin was swelling like a ball and again and again till the class traitor had fallen and banged her own face against the floor and a pool of blood came and The Project didn't want her to raise her face because of fear and when she did The Project screamed because Comrade Ruth's face was all red and wet and did not look like a woman any more. On her knees she took Comrade Chen's hands and begged, saying sorry, sorry, I am worthless, I am sorry, teach me.

Comrade Chen stepped back and said, And yet you still speak of I. And he shook his head and said, We must destroy the illness to save the patient. And we felt the magic power of the oppressed running through us. Then he nodded and we raised our hands together and brought them down upon the traitor Comrade Ruth. Comrade Jeni did not hit very hard but little Comrade Uma is stronger than she looks and Zana is too and so am I and I hit very hard but not on Comrade Ruth's face only on her stomach and neck and back.

The Project felt very good and hot because we are non-violent and condemn all violence unless it serves the revolution. And it was exciting to be hitting someone all at the same time and to see the flashes in other Comrades' eyes and this must be what the final fire of revolution will be like and The Project is sure I hit Comrade Ruth the best of all and will earn many gold stars.

It was The Project's turn to sleep in the last room that Comrade Jeni slept in and I found some secret things she had forgotten. They were many pills in plastic boxes in a bag and were called Lithium Carbonate and Diazepam and Fluoxetine and some other ones with two halves with tiny sparkling bits inside that tasted sour and fizzy.

The Project showed them to Comrade Chen and he said I had done very well because these were the mind bombs of the bourgeoisie. He warned The Project to stay away from the evil mind seductions of Comrade Jeni, because she had sneaked weapons into the Collective. I went with him to the toilet and watched him flush all of the evil pills down the toilet and it took two flushes. He patted my head and said that every time Comrade Jeni said something The Project was to think that she meant the opposite and that would be the truth. Comrade Jeni's mind is now under the control of fascist pills and they are pulling the electric strings of her tongue.

So when she says that she is hungry, she is not to be given food.

When she says, Come here, Darling, The Project must run away.

When she says, Give me a hug, she really means, I want to hurt you.

Note from Comrade Uma: Comrade Uma reports with some alarm that The Project has spent the last week drifting around in a state of confusion after Comrade Jeni tried to abduct her. Most distressingly she is repeatedly quizzing all Comrades on who her mother was. Comrade Uma calls for an emergency meeting to put this matter to rest as it is damaging for The Project to hear conflicting stories about the past. Comrade Uma also worries about the mental health of Comrade Jeni. Comrade Uma asks, even though bipolar disorder is a sickness of bourgeois decadence, if we can please just get more pills for Jeni as she seems very lost. Comrade Jeni is saying disturbing things like, I can't go and I can't stay, she has also been asking for sleeping pills and we know where that leads.

Note from Comrade Ruth: Comrade Ruth is very grateful for the purification process and apologises for being unable to perform kitchen duties. Comrade Ruth agrees that The Project should be told one simple revised story about origins and also that she should be kept from all contact with Comrade Jeni until Comrade Jeni is well again.

Comrade Zana notes: Comrade Zana is grateful and thinks you are all doing Comrade Jeni a massive favour being with her while she goes detox and gets the western drugs out of her system, no matter how much she asks for them. Comrade Zana recommends that you get her some Campbell's chicken soup as that's all you can really keep down when you go cold turkey and a bucket for puke and maybe a room of her own because Comrade Jeni is just wandering from room to room, sometimes half naked and needs to just lie down.

The Project finally discovered the truth about my mother and father and was glad because The Project is living proof that the need for parents is not biological at all but a cultural construct and we can all be much happier without them.

The Project was pleased to make the words Mother go away forever because the last week has been very confusing. Like the way that when Comrade Zana brought Golden Wonder crisps into the Collective The Project became very in love with licking the crumbs of Prawn Cocktail flavour and wanted more, but if The Project had never been exposed to them The Project would never have known they existed.

This is the way capitalism keeps us enslaved with false needs, like wanting a mother which is also called a mummy.

Comrade Chen had spent very many days with Comrade Jeni making her well and purifying her mind and feeding her cold turkey and washing her body.

We assembled in the photocopy room and Comrade Chen held a piece of paper and we sat round him in a circle. Behind him on the wall was the picture of the Glorious Leader with his piece of paper that tells of the glorious future to come.

Comrade Jeni was sitting very still and staring at her bruised hands and so was Comrade Ruth there and her face was still very puffy and her nose squint. Comrade Jeni rocked back and forwards cross-legged on the floor and the points of her chest stuck out from renouncing her reactionary bra and then she stood up.

Comrade Chen said, No Jeni, Don't leave. Please, read from the page, as we agreed.

Comrade Jeni stared at The Project and started reading, then stopped. She said, Can't I tell her in my own words.

Comrade Chen laid a soft hand on her and said, No, just as we discussed.

Comrade Jeni looked round all the faces and then hard at The Project, then her eyes were soft too and she said, This is for The Project. Dear Project. To answer your question. Your mother is dead. She died a long time ago.

Then she stopped looking at the page and closed her eyes and said, Your mother was a very lost person and she ran away from her family because she hated them and she dropped out and did lots of drugs. OK. She overdosed.

Comrade Ruth and Comrade Chen tried to stop her but she raised her voice and said, No, that's not true, actually, she took her own life, she was not a very nice person, very needy and she would have made you mental like she was, or probably abandoned you. So that's why, and then Comrade Chen took Comrade Jeni's arm and led her out of the room while Comrade Jeni was still talking.

Comrade Ruth picked up the piece of paper and told The Project the real story of The Project's parents: My Father was a great warrior of the revolution. My Mother died trying to keep his secret. This makes The Project proud but also empty feeling to never have met such great heroes. It makes The Project very proud and relieved and angry with the British Pig State.

Jotter #243 2018

The Pig voice said, A unit has been dispatched, miss, can you stay on the phone, please, we are recording for your safety, please do not hang up. Are you alone, miss? Can you repeat the name of the person attacking your door? The first name was Ruth? Is that correct? Can you give me the second name? Has this person broken into your building, or are you locked inside?

The door handle stopped turning and the shadow at the window went away. Comrade Ruth was maybe hunting for Nina in another safe house now but Nina held the knife tight because Comrade Ruth could change so fast and you think it is over but it is just a trick. So Nina stayed very tight in the dark corner.

The voice in the phone said, A unit will be with you shortly, miss. Can you tell us if you are injured? Do you need an ambulance as well, miss? Can you see your attacker?

Nina whispered that Nina has to stay very quiet or Ruth will come in. Nina counted backwards from a hundred to eleven and the shadow didn't come back and Nina crept out and went to the window and Nina very slowly pulled back a little bit of curtains but then Nina was hit by a flash of radiation.

Nina fell back and the curtain fell open and there was a man with a box at his face and flashes came from it, and another man calling out, Hello, is that the Collective girl, hello. All we want to do is speak to you. And a knocking of fist on window. Nina put the full body against the door, then there was more radiation but they were blue lights and a screaming music noise again and again and a car very fast and feet coming and more men shouting. And this was all too much for one day.

Nina can't be safe in the Charity House any more. Charity Sonia had to explain many things to the Pigs who Nina feels are probably nice now and the bit of paper was something called evidence and it had to go in a plastic bag and it said, Hello Nina, My name is Matt Jackson and I'm a journalist at a leading national paper. We would like to talk to you and will pay you well for your story which we know our twenty million readers will love to hear, please contact. And it had a number.

In the Charity car Charity Sonia said, I'm so, so sorry, this is my fault, please just close your eyes, Nina, and keep counting we'll soon be there. But she kept interrupting the numbers saying, Damn, now they've got a photo of your face. Damn, where are we going to put you now? Just ignore me, Nina, I'm talking to myself. Just keep counting.

Nina had a first experience in an elevator and it is a box with mirrors of yourself like a tunnel that goes to the Land of Oz but it is just an illusion and you can't climb in. And Nina didn't feel like it was moving, apart from a bump at the start and end and Nina said to Charity Sonia that when you come out it's like magic because all the walls and pictures and everything has changed but Charity Sonia just said, Come on, you can't stay in there, Nina, I have to get this sorted out.

Then Nina was in an amazing place that is saving every woman everywhere and there are signs that say, Sanctuary: More than just a roof over a woman's head, and there were female work slaves with wires in their heads like in a sweatshop in National Geographic and all talking to people you can't see who are actually real women just like Nina who need to be saved all the time.

The place is why Charity Sonia is called Charity Sonia and she said she had to go there to find Nina a new place to sleep with better security and to make urgent calls, and she didn't like to have to rely on Social Work Phil for help but she really had to. And she said, maybe it was not such a good idea to touch the women because they were working at their desks and there was a thing called safe personal space.

Then we were in her office which was another box of glass and the noises were quieter and she made a buzz and asked a machine for coffee. Then she said, Bugger, sorry, have a ton of emails about you here. Damn, we'll have to find another name for you as well. Can you think of any?

Charity Sonia didn't think Glinda or Toto were ideal and then Charity Sonia was very busy on her phone so Nina made a swan and Charity Sonia said for sure it had been a close shave today.

Charity Sonia said, I just got an email from the police about Ruth, they want to know of any locations you think she might be hiding in.

Nina didn't know, then remembered some letters and they were CND and CPGB but Charity Sonia said they weren't places, but thanks.

Charity Sonia said that Ruth is a victim of Chen too because Charity Sonia doesn't want to believe it was Ruth who killed Jeni because she doesn't think women can kill other women.

Charity Sonia said to sit and read then she was on something called hold and she asked if Nina would like to try a different really good women's hostel but Nina shook the head because women just torture each other until they think correctly. Charity

Sonia said, Look there are magazines on the table. And one was called Awareness.

Nina looked for women's names and found the story of a woman called Hope. It said. When I met Steve and we instantly hit it off, he was charming and seemed very wonderful, I never suspected that he would stab me.

But Charity Sonia didn't think Hope was a good name either because it was actually a fake name used to protect someone's true name and now to be very very quiet because she was being put through so Nina read another bit of paper on the wall. It had a picture of two hands holding the world and it said:

MYTH: It only happens to poor women on council estates
MYTH: Abusers grow up in violent homes
MYTH: Women are just as violent as men
MYTH: Women ask for it and they deserve what they get

Nina was confused and said to Charity Sonia that the women in the Collective were very violent, but maybe it was OK because everyone agreed that they deserved it and everyone took turns doing the hitting equally.

Charity Sonia shook her head and said, Your situation was very different from most women, Nina.

Nina said, But all women are the same and we are all equal, and we abused each other.

Charity Sonia put her hand over the phone and said, Stop saying that, it's deeply upsetting and I can't hear what the message is saying.

Nina said, But I am free now, I can say what I want.

Charity Sonia said, Just not words like that, OK, they're problematic.

Nina said that was exactly what Comrade Ruth would have said. Then Charity Sonia's face became cross and Nina said, So some words are correct and some are banned.

And Charity Sonia said, Yes. Of course. Now, I really have to listen carefully to these options or we'll never get your police paperwork.

Nina said sorry three times and looked under the pictures in another magazine for a new name. There was Chloe, Jordan, Britney, Cheryl, Kim, Rhianna and Angelina, but Charity Sonia shook her head at all of them. And Nina is not to point at them and say she wants to be a whore of capitalism because that word is banned too.

Charity Sonia doesn't realise that it is like Comrade Chen to ban words. She has a poster on her wall that has a beautiful rich black skin lady on it and it says Ban Bossy. And another sign with hands on it that says Commitment to Equality. Equality means hitting everyone with the stick till they are all on their knees at the same level but Charity Sonia said that wasn't what equality was at all and told Nina to be quiet please because she just missed the buttons to push and had to go back to the main menu now, and please, just sit still, please or we'll never find you a safer place to stay.

Nina took a piece of paper and folded another paper swan but Nina is not to touch any of the incredibly important documents on Charity Sonia's desk and this is a bloody nightmare, sorry.

Nina will try to have no name for a while. It is not so bad, it is just like being The Project. Nina misses The Project. Nina would like to have shown her through the amazing place where the free women with headsets sit in boxes and make so much talking that you can't hear a single word.

Nina is also not to say that Nina misses Comrade Uma and Comrade Zana and Comrade Ruth. Nina even misses Comrade Chen but it makes Charity Sonia very concerned when Nina says any of these things.

Nina remembers that it was Comrade Ruth who made The Project write and rewrite the story of the window so many times and Comrade Ruth who tore out pages and hit The Project with the stick, and said, no, write it again, thirty times when The Project was crying.

A woman with blue hair came in when Charity Sonia was on the phone saying, Yes, processed by Hackney Social Work department, last week, all I need is one secure room. The blue hair woman stared at Nina and handed Charity Sonia a bit of paper, it was folded and Nina could see it had Nina written on the back of it. Charity Sonia set it down on the table and said, into the phone, quite cross, No, I've checked, Solace is full, Barkston has too many children, Shelter is full. Yes, homeless with security needs, possible special needs. No, no housing benefit yet. Then she was quiet and said, No, no national insurance number, but we can pay cash, if there is any space at all.

Charity Sonia picked up the bit of paper and opened it and she stopped speaking and looked very worried at Nina and so did the blue hair woman. The blue hair woman said, It was pushed under the door with the mail and she was sorry for not reading it sooner because it didn't look important but it really was and Charity Sonia wasn't sure if she should really show it to Nina but she did and it said in big letters in Comrade Ruth's handwriting.

NINA
ERASE

Nina had been kept awake all day in the whispering building of Charity Sonia and then was moved to a room to be alone and then a meeting one with a machine for water and the lights were too bright and buzzing with fear of radiation so Nina went under the table to curl, but Charity Sonia yelled with fright when she came in and found Nina like that.

Then Social Work Phil came in and he brought a picture on a paper and he put it on the table and it had Comrade Chen's face. It said in big letters Perverted Cult Leader Faces Trial and Comrade Chen had his hands tied together and was wearing some wrong trousers that were bright green. He looked very old and small and far away and Nina felt sorry for him because all other Comrades had deserted him.

Social Work Phil said, Look, we have an even bigger problem, not only has this Ruth Pendal or whatever this bloody terrorist's name is, been slipping messages under your door, she's been sending them to the tabloids saying Chen is innocent. How do we know this stalker is not still outside right now? What does ERASE even mean, is this a death threat?

Nina stared at the bad hand and made a shrugging sign to say Don't know, but Nina knows what it means.

Charity Sonia said, I don't think we should be doing this in front of Nina. We're upsetting her.

Social Work Phil held up the paper. And read it out loud and said, In a message sent to Metropolitan Police, Ruth Pendal, a one-time anti-nuclear activist has said, David Chen stands falsely accused. He is a genius, a champion of women's right, a peace activist, a scholar and a great teacher. The truth is that many women were very jealous of each other in the Collective because we each wanted to have him for ourselves. The others are making false accusations, there was never any abuse and we were free to come and go at any time.

Charity Sonia said, She's lying.

Nina held the knees tight and tucked up the feet.

Social Work Phil said, Her claim is backed up by Uma Schwartz, also disappeared, who's also sent a message to the Metropolitan Police. It says here, the woman who first contacted your charity claims that the Collective have been misrepresented by the right wing media, that it has already been proven that Genevieve Lamberton's death was accidental, that this is a witch hunt and that Chen is innocent of all charges. They say that Nina is a liar and an attention seeker and that the Collective was nothing but caring towards her, raising an abandoned child with special needs and she demands that Nina tells the Police to drop the charges against Chen because Chen is innocent and all they want is for Nina to stop telling lies and to come back home.

Then it was quiet and Social Work Phil said again, Home?

Then Charity Sonia said, Oh, no, no, no. What? The place is a crime scene. You can't seriously be suggesting that Nina go back to that fucking basement or into the care of the people who tortured her! No doubt it would make things easier for the Social Work department, wouldn't it? You could clean that one off your desk then.

Social Work Phil looked angry and Nina had the churning feeling and rocked back and forwards and Charity Sonia said, This is causing distress to Nina. You should stop right now.

Social Work Phil said, Look, let Nina speak for herself. Could Nina actually go home to London Fields and have a befriender help her there? Nina, I need to hear it from you. Are these women lying? We've invested a lot of time and effort in this already and if you've made anything up, Nina, I need to know.

Charity Sonia said, I can't believe it. You're blaming the victim. You've no idea how often I see this. This is appalling, you're shaming a battered woman by saying, Why didn't you leave? You're shaming a victim of child sexual abuse by saying, Why didn't you tell? It's not Nina lying here! And at the end Charity Sonia was shouting with her eyes and with her voice.

Nina was breathing fast and went under the table again and wanted them to take the picture of Comrade Chen away. It was burning a hole in Nina's head. Nina stared at their feet and Social Work Phil said, OK, OK, I'm sorry, please calm down, Sonia.

Social Work Phil said, Technically, she could go back to Hospital. Look, the main thing is keeping her away from this psycho and these fucking hacks. You know what they're like, any excuse to go after Social Services and they will, any dirt they can dig up, and they won't give a shit how much they hurt Nina. No, she needs high security.

Charity Sonia spoke louder and said, But Nina can't stand hospitals or hostels, they scare her.

Social Work Phil said, So have you found her a secure residence yet or does my department have to take care of this?

Charity Sonia said, Four hours on the phone and none of the homes have got a single room. And she sighed.

Social Work Phil said, Look, I spoke to Connect and they've got a place in Trinity Court. CCTV. Self-contained flat. Warden. Twenty-four-hour security staff.

Charity Sonia sounded angry, You can't stick her in a tower block with addicts.

Social Work Phil said, I'll pretend you didn't just say that. Actually, it's for single homeless and vulnerable people with complex needs.

Charity Sonia said, No, sorry, of course, but in a flat? I mean Nina can't take care of herself.

Social Work Phil said, Only last week you were bending over backwards to convince me that she could.

Nina didn't like the fast voices and Nina started counting. Charity Sonia said to Social Work Phil, But you can't stick her in a mixed housing block with men.

Social Work Phil said loudly, Why not, you're the one saying you can't put her in a hostel with women.

Then Charity Sonia yelled, Because she was abused, you fucking idiot.

Then they were both breathing loud and Social Work Phil's brown shoes went to the door then he came back and he said, Sorry. And Nina wanted to say sorry too because Nina makes everyone angry.

Then Charity Sonia bent down and said very quietly, Are you

OK, Nina? Can you come out now? I know this is hard for you but time's not on our side, can you tell Phil what Comrade Chen did to you. The hitting and touching. Just so he knows. Please?

Nina rocked back and forwards and counted backwards like Doctor Webber said to do.

Charity Sonia spoke to Social Work Phil and said, There were three women, Nina mentioned in her diary, and there was a girl called Zana. They were all abused.

Nina was locked in a basement for twenty years.

Nina knew this was the wrong number but Nina didn't want to speak because Charity Sonia should not tell about the diary and Charity Sonia had not given it back yet, like she promised.

Social Work Phil said, Look, Sonia, what happened where and when is part of the police investigation. If you want to let the Police try to house her, good luck with that, witness protection will take months and a court case will be years off and none of this helps us put a safe roof over Nina's head tonight. OK. Given that someone in your organisation was most likely responsible for leaking Nina's story to the tabloids and creating all this mess in the first place, I think it's time you let the Social Work department take care of this.

Charity Sonia was very angry again and said, How dare you and then she and Social Work Phil were shouting at each other and Nina counted faster to make it stop but it made a shadow come running on the other side of the glass.

It was Cas and Nina recognised her trainers and Cas went down under the table and said, Just breathe with me, Nina, and, What did the nice Doctor teach you to do? And Nina said, Think of a tree and breathe and say My current symptoms are just a conditioned response and they will lessen as I desensitise myself. And Nina said that over and over and counted backwards and breathed.

And the eyes of Cas were big and her hand was gentle and she said to Charity Sonia and Social Work Phil, What the hell were you two thinking? You should be ashamed of yourselves, you're just making it worse for her.

Nina got calmer and Charity Sonia was sorry and Social Work Phil said, My apologies, I've been on this all week with a caseload of thirty-two new people to house.

Cas helped Nina climb back out and Nina felt bad and had a tingling foot. Nina was scared because when people try to help you and they fail then they start to hate you.

Then Nina saw the thing Cas had run in with and it was on her phone. Cas said, Don't look at that shit and pushed it away, but it was a picture of Nina's face in the window of Charity House and it said in big words, Crazy Cult Survivor. And Charity Sonia turned away and wiped her nose because she always does that now.

Nina had to leave quick from the place where fire escapes are because Charity Sonia's Charity was named in the paper and hacks and ambulance chasers were blocking the front door but Cas had her car at the back.

Charity Sonia held Nina's hand and said, You'll only be there for a few days, I promise. You have all our phone numbers and call us if you need anything. I'll come and see you tomorrow. We have to play along with Social Work Phil because they'll be helping you long after I.

And she stopped. Then Charity Sonia's face was guilty like Comrade Uma and she said, I'm sorry, Nina, my hands are tied. Then she put both her hands round Nina and hugged and they weren't tied.

Nina looked at her and said, Can I have my diary back now?

Charity Sonia looked surprised and then said, Sorry, I had to give it to the Police, but I'll get it back for you tomorrow. I promise.

Nina was angry then there was hiding the head down low so hacks couldn't see and singing the Yellow Brick Road and then it was OK to look up and then many streets later Nina was standing in front of a huge rectangle box and it had ten windows upwards and Nina got a sore neck. It looked like a picture Comrade Chen had shown The Project of the perfect houses of the perfect future but it was not white but grey and two men were outside with hoods on and smoke and they didn't say hello.

Then there was a man of security in his reinforced window room, and a badge had to be shown to him and some papers and then a buzz came and a door opened. And Cas said, this man of security is here twenty-four hours, Nina, and there's a warden on patrol and they won't let Comrade Ruth in or any of those vultures from the papers. And look, there's a common room just down there and a laundry room.

Nina had another elevator experience and it didn't have mirrors but was of metal and had dents in it and some curly words. Cas said it was called graffiti and it was maybe one of the homeless who lived here and they are nice people really. Nina read one graffiti and it said in little writing Blowjobs Amira £20 – 07965 302 997.

Nina has to get a job and learn about money. Nina will soon get a national insurance number and then free money and free food from the kind government store of Sainsbury's like the bag that Cas had brought.

Then the elevator bumped and Cas led Nina out and Cas checked a list and got keys. The walls were very shiny and echoing and painted bright yellow and everything smelled of bleach. There was a round black ball on the roof and Cas said it had an eye so the secure man would know where Nina was all the time and make sure none of the other residents bothered her, and no, it's not like the magic ball of the Wicked Witch.

Nina thought, It is very clever of the government to watch over everyone all the time because no one can take care of themselves.

Then there was searching for numbers on the doors and

Cas led Nina past a door that was grey and one that had music inside and food smells and there were children sounds behind a door that was covered in metal and Nina was not to be scared because Doctor Webber said new experiences might forge new neural pathways.

Then there was a place with an open door that had a big hole in the bottom like the time Comrade Ruth kicked the wall. Cas took Nina's elbow and said, Don't worry that's not your one. Probably just someone with complex needs. Come on. I think it's this one.

And she put keys in another grey door and there was a smell inside so Cas made a spray come from Summer Breeze and said, just hold your horses. Inside there were windows and Nina had to say Wow three times because it was up in the clouds. Nina had to run to them but then run back because Nina felt like a bird falling and Comrade Jeni. Then Nina sat in a chair and said Wow again.

When Nina looked round Cas was writing and checking light switches and flushing the toilet and ticking boxes because Connect did a brilliant job but they were so fucking underfunded and lucky for Nina the last folk in here ran off to be homeless again. Not to worry, Nina wasn't going to be here for long and how weird was that, they left you a telly, pretty shit one, but hey. Then Cas opened the fridge and slammed it again. It smelled of the basement and Cas said, just as well I brought these then isn't it, and she sprayed Summer Breeze inside and put things not to be looked at in a black plastic bag.

There were many things Cas had to show Nina like bedding and the hot water but Nina couldn't take the eyes off the windows full of sky. Nina had some emotions because freedom is very wide and goes all the way to the end of the planet. Nina saw tiny roads and a thousand houses and each was full of people. There was a song in the street passing by and music through a wall and a big pattern of tiny birds flying far away. Nina stared and saw the tops of trees and Nina wanted to go to a real park and see real swans for the first time.

Nina said, It's like over the rainbow.

Cas set her phone down and said, What, Hackney? Yeah right.

Nina went close to the window and a swirling feeling came and Nina was not to look down again because it was the sixth floor and there were twenty-four self-contained flats with twenty-four-hour security. Cas checked the windows and said, Child locks, good, you can only open them an inch, best not to touch them anyway.

Nina saw a drawing of a little girl and a house and a bright sun and a black cat stuck to the fridge, and Nina asked, What was she called? Where did she go?

Cas didn't know and she put the picture in the black bag and she said, Right, Madam, I'm going to have to go now. There's an alarm cord in the bathroom, it's the red one, if you're scared or you have an accident you pull that and the warden will come and help you. Don't get it mixed up with the light switch, please, or you'll have him up and down all bleedin night.

Nina didn't understand so Cas showed. The bathroom had mould in one corner and would never have passed Comrade Chen's inspections. And inside every room was painted yellow.

Cas said, it's not perfect, but you'll be here three or four days max, I reckon. Now, I'll come get you again tomorrow for your next Doctors test, and we've got your PIP assessment coming up, now, I've left you some sandwiches and oranges and yoghurts and one sleeping pill and two pink pills. Then she ticked some boxes and she said, And you've got your phone and if you need anything you give me a call. Not Phil. Sonia will probably call as well. I'd imagine your phone'll be ringing off the hook, but remember if someone calls and you don't know who they are, hang up because they'll be hacks or ambulance chasers. Got that?

Nina said, Ambulance chasers and hacks.

And Cas said, Yeah, anyway, don't worry, no one knows where you are and they'll never find you and they're all swarmed round Sonia's now anyway.

Nina stared at the phone.

Cas said, Fucking hacks are after a scoop. First interview with you, could be worth a lot of money to them. Or to you. Silly me, shouldn't have said that, now you'll be wanting to sell your life-story and become a millionaire, eh.

Nina said, Nina would like to be rich.

Cas said, I'm just pulling your leg.

But Cas wasn't close to Nina.

Cas took Nina's phone and said, What have you got it turned off for? Bloody hell. You have to keep your bloody phone on, Nina, all the time! In case we need to get hold of you urgently.

Nina said, Sorry. And Cas sat up close on the wide chair and said, Look, Pet. It's not going to bite, is it? Here, give it me, I'll show you.

Nina knows if you stick to all your old behaviour patterns from the time when you were in the basement then you just keep on being in the basement forever so Nina agreed to a teaching time with Cas.

Cas said, You've only made one bleeding phone call since last time, and not even taken a photo. This thing's got gazillions of space on it, I'd be taking selfies left, right and centre. Are you kidding, never been on the net? And Cas showed what it was, and explained and her fingers moved very fast over hundreds of pictures.

Cas said, That's you on now, you get brilliant 4G up here and since the dole's paying for it you could be watching all sorts on this, TV series, YouTube, surfing, bit of porn even, only joking.

Nina felt tired and ashamed for being so ignorant.

Cas didn't look at Nina any more, only at the screen, and her fingers moved faster and the little squares of colour and people moved in her eyes.

Cas showed how to type a word and how to search and she said the answers for everything you can ever ask are all there, and she said nearly everyone in the world was on it now and it was signals that bounced through satellites and these are metal machines that fly round the earth.

Cas said you want a new pair of jeans you just click on it, or a song, or some food comes to your door. And you don't have to pay with paper money any more it's just numbers, you put the numbers into the phone. Nina saw jeans and wanted them and shoes with spikes and wanted them and a hat and wanted it and Nina said, Nina wants everything, is it really OK to be selfish all the time now?

Cas laughed and said, How should I know. Look, you can even get a bloke on it. And Nina asked what this was and it is a lover man so Nina asked how much is it for a lover man, and Cas laughed very much.

Cas said, I shouldn't really be telling you this, promise you won't tell, all right then. And Cas showed Nina a place on her own phone where there are millions of men who wanted to be the lover man of Cas, and how you swipe swipe swipe past the ones you don't fancy and you tick the ones you like, but the most important thing is to reject hundreds and Cas said sometimes when she's feeling a bit down she swipes them for a laugh and she swiped Jeremy and Dez and Tone and Bashir and Ross, saying Nuh, nuh, nuh, and she said, See makes you feel better doesn't it. God look at that loser, he's not getting near me. And she swipe, swipe, swiped.

Cas said, Here you are, Nina, you have a shot, and she put her own phone in Nina's hand and Nina looked at the faces of men and swiped and swiped, then Cas said, Wait. Don't want you telling Phil I set you up on a hot date, now do I! And she laughed and took her phone back and Nina stared at the place where the phone had been.

Cas said, What's wrong?

Nina said, It is just like Chen said.

Cas laughed and said, You're one of a kind, you are. Look at that, I've gone way over my time. If I don't get back to the office they'll have my guts for garters.

Nina looked at the place where Cas sat and said, Can you stay with me?

Cas said, Well, Nina, you know I can't do that. And she reminded Nina that Phil said Nina must pass tests for eating alone and shopping and washing alone.

Nina said, No one told me Freedom was like this. Do you get a prize? Do they say well done when you are an old woman and here is your prize for being alone.

Cas said, What you mean?

Nina said, Nina wants to get married and be a mistress and have children because being alone in Freedom is a waste.

Cas was silent and then she said, Well I'm single, Nina. I'm alone. And the things you say can be quite hurtful sometimes.

Nina said sorry.

Cas really had to go but Nina didn't want to be swiped and pulled the hand of Cas and said, Please stay. Are you my friend?

Cas said, You're getting really flippin weird, Nina. Stop grabbing people, OK, it's not appropriate. Let go. Let go!

Cas pulled away and went to the door and she sucked her hand and said, Look at that, you bloody scratched me. And Nina was very sorry but couldn't kiss it better.

Cas sighed and said, Look, just be a good girl eh, and sit down and eat your grub. Oh and Amraine from the Housing might call so don't hang up on her. And don't go wandering about the corridors neither, and if anyone knocks just say no thanks sunshine and lock your door. Got that? Just stay right here.

Then Cas looked at Nina and said, Here, and she turned on the TV.

Cas said when she is on her lonesome she always has the TV on and the stereo and her phone and it feels like people. Cas said, Right. Gotta go. Chin up, peeps.

Nina was emptier than before and sad for Cas. Nina thought of Cas swiping and swiping and swiping and Nina looked out the window. Hundreds of lights were coming on in little windows and people were far away and small. Nina thought of them all swiping and swiping and swiping each other so they could feel more wanted.

No one told Nina that Freedom was so lonely.

Nina had to have a rest but first Nina had to write down the time for eating and Nina couldn't lie so Nina had to eat as well.

Nina opened the fruit juice box and broke the six yoghurts into individual ones and read the flavours and the packet and it said, Help Support Your Body's Defences. Nina took the oranges out of the plastic packet and it said Try Something New Today. Nina took the sandwich out of the packet and it was ham salad and it said Be Good to Yourself. The Crisps just said Ready Salted. Nina put a crisp in the mouth but crunching was very loud in the empty room. Nina peeled an orange and sniffed it. Nina put a piece in the mouth and chewed it. It felt wrong, like people were staring into Nina's brain. Nina looked at the windows and it was too high for anyone to see in but then the dark window was turning into a mirror and Nina could see Nina's body and face and it was like a skeleton and it wouldn't go away because there was only one curtain and it only covered half the window when Nina pulled it.

All the city is watching Nina from all sides and the Wicked Witch in the sky is the eye of Comrade Chen and it made Nina run to the toilet and sick up the orange and the crisps.

Then Nina stared at Nina's food and sleep report:

Breakfast	Lunch	Dinner	Bathing	Sleep

Nina will have to lie to everyone. Nina can't eat when Nina is alone.

Even when Nina was starved in the basement Nina thought of nothing but food all day. The Comrades were upstairs and they worried about Nina and they talked to Nina through the door and Comrade Uma fed Nina under the door crack. Nina ate the crackers and pages like a Pig because Nina wasn't alone. But now that Nina is surrounded by all the delicious foods of capitalism and Citrus Delight from the fruits of thirty different countries, Nina has to run again to the bathroom to be sick.

Nina doesn't understand why people work to get money to eat to wash to sleep then wake up again just to work to get money to eat all over again. And why people in Freedom sit in cars all alone half the day and stare at screens with headphones on then go home all alone to sit and swipe.

Nina thought it might be a good idea to put the television on like Cas said and maybe then it would stop the echoing and the not-eating. Nina got the crisps.

Nina had to check the windows four times and Nina watched TV properly for the first time and it is safer with the sound off so the brainwashing won't work.

Nina watched pictures of clouds as if from flying. Then pictures of men dancing about under coloured lights and shouting to thousands of people below them who were all happy with hands in the air. And Nina changed the picture and there were cars going very fast in a circle round and round and not going anywhere else and this was a competition. Then Nina watched a haircut and then some men and women dancing and some other people held up numbers and this was a competition too. Then Nina watched some skinny women walking along a straight flat thing and then walking back and every time they had different clothes on and Nina thought they must be looking for a lover man but they did not have big breasts like Jeni and flashes came and this was a competition too.

It makes Nina sad but Nina has to learn. Freedom is just everyone trying to be winners and everything is a competition and everyone swipes everyone else but they have to keep on trying and this is called believing in yourself. Freedom is a bit disappointing and Comrade Chen was right about that but at least he was wrong about dogs eating dogs.

Because of the TV for company Nina had managed to eat all the crisps. Nina needed to eat the yoghurt next so there had to be more TV.

There was a man and a woman behind a desk and they had a square behind their heads and then it was a lie that things on the television are safe because there was a picture of a building burning, then it said, Headlines and then there was a picture of Comrade Chen, and the words Cult Killers. Then a picture came of Comrade Jeni when she was young that the Pigs had shown Nina. Then the picture went big and it showed a screaming woman and it was Comrade Ruth and two Pigs holding her arms and she was kicking them and being dragged from a doorway and it said Suspect Arrested. Then the picture was of a broken window and Nina didn't know how to turn the voices to hear, but then it moved inside and it was the Collective and it was covered with long thin plastic stripes that said Police Do Not Cross. They were carrying things out like the pots and pans and big black bags and there were flashes.

Nina hit the television to make Comrade Ruth stay away, but the picture kept coming so Nina hit it harder and it fell over and made a pop and when Nina pushed it over to see, it was black and the glass was cracked.

—

Nina had to make the curtains dark so Comrade Ruth couldn't find Nina but Nina pulled too hard and it fell down and Nina tried not to panic so Nina said, My current symptoms are just a conditioned response and they will lessen as I desensitise myself and Nina had to sit and count breaths and write.

Nina can't remember who said Comrade Ruth killed Comrade Jeni, if it was Comrade Chen or Charity Sonia. Nina knows the words are in the lost diaries but Nina is scared of them now and they are what Comrade Ruth and the Police are hunting for.

Nina knew it was bad but peed on the floor to make it safe and then it was OK to sleep but not under the sink because such behaviours are part of the Old Nina and Nina has to abolish of the old ways. Nina must soon take the pill for sleep.

Freedom is not about Doing after all. The list will have to wait until all the Don't have been sorted.

Don't speak to strangers on the phone only people you know.

Don't speak to the hacks because they will make you a millionaire.

Don't tell anyone where you or who you are.

Don't grab people or want them too much because this hurts them and makes them disappointed.

Don't forget to wake up because there are more tests tomorrow and don't be lonely and don't fail the tests or they won't let you stay.

Don't ever say Slaves. Or Pigs. Or Whores. Don't ever say I hurt other women. Don't ever say, I killed or We killed Comrade Jeni.

Don't think you are dying when you have a panic attack just take a pink pill.

Don't keep worrying about Comrade Uma and missing her.

Don't rock back and forwards and hum and hug yourself.

Don't keep picking off the arm-hole scab because it won't keep Comrade Ruth away.
Don't think you'd be better off in the basement.
Don't think Charity Sonia has betrayed you.
Don't think that everyone in the world is hunting for you.
Don't fall between the gaps.
Don't keep thinking about Comrade Jeni and her white eyes and the back door and the feathers falling.
Don't think nobody will ever give Nina gold stars now.
Don't break the child locks or touch the windows or you will fall six floors and die.
Don't take more than four sleeping pills or more than ten pink pills in one day or you could lower your heart rate and breathing rate and have a cardiac arrest and this means die.
Don't give up. Doctor Webber said Nina might get better. Nina will be normal soon. One hundred, ninety-nine, ninety-eight, ninety-seven, ninety-six, ninety-five.

This is more than enough for one day.

Jotter #69 2002

The Project had to hide in the wardrobe in case fascist pigs came to the Collective to interrogate. The Project was in the wardrobe from light to dark and fell asleep inside. The Project made the body very small with fingers in ears because the Pigs feed on the blood of others so don't make a sound.

Comrade Chen came to release The Project who had made a puddle in the wardrobe but this was understandable.

Comrade Chen makes The Project feel warm again and kisses the shivering head with his rough chin and says, Shh, it's OK now, they are all gone. The Project confesses to a wanting to kiss Comrade Chen then as other Comrades do, sometimes on his lips and sometimes in other places like Comrade Jeni and Comrade Zana do.

Then Comrade Uma went outside to see if Comrade Jeni would survive in a prison called Hospital and everyone in the Collective is fighting now.

Note from Comrade Ruth: We are pleased that Comrade Jeni has survived thus far but saddened that she has betrayed the address of the Collective. We are also very angry that the Comrade who promised to deal with the Jeni problem made such a bloody mess of it, placing us all in jeopardy.

We must stick to our narrative and remove all trace of Jeni from here. Comrade Ruth is concerned that if questioned The Project will tell anyone any of what she saw. She must be told, again and again that her memory is false and fed the better story. Comrade Ruth also raises a practical concern and that is while Comrade Jeni remains in intensive care she will be unable to make her weekly trip to the bank, we are already five months in arrears with the gas and electricity bills.

Note from Comrade Uma: Comrade Uma believes it is not surprising that The Project is in a state of distress and is herself distressed at how little the Comrades seem to care about Jeni. It is disgusting. The medical prognosis for Comrade Jeni is very poor. Comrade Uma asks permission to visit Comrade Jeni in St Leonard's Hospital. Comrade Uma is also very distressed by the state The Project is in and thinks it unwise that we keep feeding her so many sleeping tablets. Comrade Uma asks if there is advice from Comrade Mao on removing traumatic memories.

Comrade Chen has no notes.

The Project had a fright. At eight o'clock and thirty the door was knocking when The Project was in the bathroom and naked because it is the only place that is hot because we cannot pay the electricity bills and are on heat rations and it is shivering ice in the kitchen.

The Project did the wrong thing and ran down the stairs and dropped the towel and did not run the right way. The Project heard the front door's five locks and then saw the heads of two people at the bottom of the stairs come in and one had a black fascist hat. Comrade Ruth grabbed The Project and dragged me back up to the attic. The Project was very scared. Comrade Ruth quickly lifted all the heavy boxes of all the pamphlets from the

People's Liberation Bookshop which is bankrupt now because the stupid masses are too busy with opium and she started building a wall and she said, We're going to play a game together. But Comrade Ruth has never played with The Project before. The Project could hear a man's voice and a woman and Comrade Uma far below being like a rice mouse.

Here were the rules of the game that Comrade Ruth played with The Project.

1. Comrade Ruth builds the boxes all around The Project and The Project has to be silent and take two pills.
2. The Project has to hug the knees to be extra small as soon as the light goes off and the door is shut. And to breathe very quietly but not hold the breath as this might make The Project burst.
3. The Project was not to come out and shout surprise or here I am or to be scared if sounds of feet and voices come close or even open the door. Because if they find her the Pigs will take The Project away and eat her like they have done to Comrade Jeni.
4. The Project is not to hold her breath or pass out or have feet sticking out because the fascists will find me like that.

Halfway through Comrade Ruth stopped piling boxes round The Project like Emerald City and said, Shh, then Shit, then she ran to the bathroom and came back with a bundle of clothes that were The Project's from the floor. Comrade Ruth said, That was a close shave and Shh, they're down on the first floor. There were more rules:

1. The Project will not waste time asking why why why? Like bloody always and will be given all of Comrade Ruth's rations of rice for a whole two days and special bottle

of ketchup just for herself, if The Project shuts up and hurries up.
2. The Project is not allowed to sneeze or cough or shiver too loudly or call out for any further instructions because if the Pigs find The Project everyone will go to jail.
3. All of the reasons for this will be explained later but only if The Project fulfils the hiding test.
4. The Project is to feel very proud because all around The Project's body is the brain of our Glorious Leader, every single word he has ever written in thousands of copies of the Little Red Book that the foolish people of Britain will not even pay fifty pence for.

The Project tried not to hear but heavy boots came on the floorboards and strangers' voices, and Comrade Ruth's voice met them on the stairs and a stranger man said, We're speaking to all the neighbours. The woman at number forty-seven said she'd seen a woman fitting the description coming out of this house.

Comrade Ruth had a high voice saying, No, we haven't seen Jen for more than a year. She was just passing through. A friend of a friend. I didn't know she was back in London. Is she all right?

And the stranger woman said, Sorry, how many people live here? Can you give me the names? Why is there no door on the bathroom?

And Comrade Ruth said, Sorry, can you tell me what's happened to her?

The Project failed the test because of cold fears in the finger tips and The Project got confused about holding breath and nearly choked but then fell asleep. The words of the Glorious Leader made a safe home and The Project's feet didn't stick out when the strangers came into the room. The Project dreamed of being kissed by The Red Sun and some other things. The Project didn't make any sound when The Project heard the stranger woman say quite close to the boxes, So you're saying she never actually stayed here, is that correct?

When the Pigs were tricked and gone and The Project was let out, Comrade Chen said The Project has to stop ever talking about Comrade Jeni and is forbidden from looking out the attic window from now on or fascists will capture The Project like Flying Monkeys.

The Project is a failure because if someone says to you, Don't think about flapping wings, then all you think of is flapping wings for hours in the night and it is the same with Madonna and Ketchup.

The Project was banned from talking on and on about Comrade Jeni's white eyes rolling and her foaming mouth. And banned from asking Where is Jeni now? Comrade Ruth yelled to Just shut up in the kitchen, will someone shut her the fuck up before I go mad.

Comrade Uma told The Project very quietly that Comrade Jeni was very, very ill and she said, even though there was no such thing as miracles and she didn't care if Chen heard her say it, and we all know God is a vile lie but just this once, because no one else was going to help that poor woman, could we just all get down on our knees and pray for Jeni.

The Project is still stuck on that one day and has nothing to report of the other days after because The Project has to keep writing out what happened until The Project gets it right. The Project can't eat or sleep. The Project filled a kettle and forgot to put it on. The Project lay down on the floor to feel the face against the cold. The Project feels the hole inside is so big if you dropped the stone in it would just fall and never hit the bottom. The Project must write the report of Jeni and the birds again and hopes Comrade Ruth will not tear it out again.

Comrade Chen said the last writings are not of value and The

Project must stay awake and start again, because the Pigs will probably come back to interrogate everyone, because Comrade Uma made a grave mistake and Comrade Ruth gave a fake name. And we must send a powerful wish to Mao Zedong that they don't check our names and hope that Comrade Jeni did not register any bank accounts or bills in her name to this address. And if The Project is found The Project will be put in a white Pig room with radiation and made to answer questions till The Project dies.

The Project tries again.

This is what happened on the day of Comrade Jeni's incident. The Project was washing some stains from Comrade Jeni's sheet with Comrade Uma. Comrade Uma and The Project were nowhere near the attic book storage room and had not seen Comrade Jeni in many days.

Comrade Uma had the yellow gloves on and was very sad about how ill Comrade Jeni was with bipolars then there was shouting upstairs and The Project ran up and then a bird screamed and Comrade Jeni had been told before do not feed the birds. And she fell.

Correction: The Project did not see Comrade Jeni upstairs. The Project did not see any fighting. The Project was told to lie down and sleep.

The Project ran down the back steps to where the screaming was and saw. Comrade Ruth said, She needs a paramedic. Is she breathing? Get that child out of here.

The Project tried to cover the eyes but the hands didn't work. Comrade Uma said, For God sake if Jeni dies here by the back door? We have to move her.

Comrade Zana came and said, Stop feeding her pills. You're fuckin insane, the lot of you, I'm calling an ambulance.

And Comrade Chen yelled, No, I forbid it.

Comrade Uma said, I'll take care of it myself.

Comrade Jeni was lying with white eyes rolling and foam coming out of her mouth and her body jerking, on the back steps and the pigeons were flying scared above and she was lying where they poop.

The Project saw Comrade Uma trying to lift Comrade Jeni up and drag her and Comrade Jeni said one thing but it was up to the sky and she said it twice but very quiet and shivering and the floppy arm was reaching to The Project. She said, Nina.

Correction: The Project did not see any of this. Comrade Jeni was never a Comrade, she was just a visitor and no one was with her upstairs or out the back door.

Note from Comrade Chen: The Project's memory is completely confused. We should never have tried to erase the truth before she even formulated it. It is no good, her memory is scrambled now and we must erase it all.

She must not sleep until this is done.

This must be done quickly before the Pigs return. All Comrades must memorise the same sequence of events and where each person was at the time of the incident. All Comrades will be cross-examined by each other to ensure that the story is consistent and that we can withstand interrogation. Our enemies are looking for only one small error so they can tear us apart. This is the crisis they have sought. The future of the Collective depends upon this moment. Remember – Jeni never lived here.

Further to this, as both Comrade Jeni and Comrade Uma attempted to smuggle The Project to the outside, we can now deduce that it is The Project that is the corrupting influence. Because of this she must be kept under lock and key. Comrade Chen moves that The Project is to be kept in the small room on the third floor; the window will be boarded and a door put on with a lock and some kind of covering to conceal it.

Jotter #243 2018

There are so many Doctors in Freedom which must mean many people get sick from being free all the time. Cas gave Nina a tip that was to say Doctor and not say Comrade Webber or Comrade Kohli, because they'd probably give Nina a bad score because there weren't any real Comrades left in the world apart from them nut-jobs in what-you-call it, Korea. And Nina said, OK and thank you for your re-education, Cas, and Nina was nervous because Nina's emotions and other things were about to be tested.

Doctor Kohli was like Doctor Webber but with dark skin and soft black eyes. Nina had to follow him down a white corridor with people in green and blue clothes of the NHS and there were bigger rooms with grey metal machines and everything was white. And Cas had to wait on a red seat.

In the white room Nina was more nervous and Nina said everything was white in the Collective too. But the Doctor said nothing and Nina spotted a television and Nina made a joke about not bashing this one but Doctor Kohli didn't understand that either.

Nina had to sit in the big plastic chair and twelve sticky wires were put on Nina's head and these were going to draw a map of Nina's brain. A red eye was blinking on a camera on long legs and Nina was not to stare at it and just pretend it's not there. Nina had to hold a plastic grey thing with a wire and a red button on it, because this was a test to see if Nina could feel the pain of others.

Doctor Kohli said, OK, I'm going to flash images up and want you to push the button if you feel the picture is horrible or if it makes you feel sick or sad or sore. And if you feel nothing at all, don't press the button, OK?

Nina said OK and looked for a window but there wasn't one so it was like a basement but above ground and Doctor Kohli said, I know it's hard to focus in a new place but can you look at the pictures please?

The first picture was in a bright square surrounded by dark and it was of a girl with blonde hair laughing with a balloon.

And Nina asked, So if Nina feels a happy feeling Nina doesn't push the button. And Doctor Kohli said, That's correct.

And then there was a picture of a hand and a knife being poked into it but it didn't make Nina feel anything because Nina made my own cuts sometimes.

The next picture was a woman in a fairy costume and a man in black and then Nina remembered that it was like one in a magazine and was called wedding day. Then Nina thought it is selfishness and selfishness makes wars and children in deserts starving with flies in their eyes. So Nina pushed the button.

The next picture was of a child crying but the child was white-skinned and looked rich so Nina asked, Is it how Nina felt before or now that everything is the opposite?

And Doctor Kohli had a scrunched face and said, Just how you feel now, try not to analyse, just react please, Nina. And Nina said, Nina doesn't feel much about this one. And it was true because Nina had never seen the child before and it was just a picture. So Nina didn't push the button.

The next one was a white house with a mum a dad and two children, all smiling and a red car and a dog and Nina got head flashes of the dust and starving mothers and Nina pushed the button.

Doctor Kohli made a little cough noise and said, Fine, Fine, keep going.

The next was a fast silver car and Nina had to be honest and cars do still scare Nina so Nina pressed the button.

The next picture was a starving African child. And Nina said, Is this a trick?

And Doctor Kohli said, What do you mean Nina?

And Nina said, This was the picture already in Nina's head but a bit different.

And Doctor Kohli made a note and pressed a button and said, May I ask what you mean by this image was already shown? We haven't shown a picture of this child before.

And Nina said, Yes, but the wedding woman and the house made the starving child come.

Doctor Kohli said, Where, Nina, in your mind?

And Nina said, Nina had a test like this before.

And Doctor Kohli said, Where? With another psychologist? And Nina smiled and said, No, silly, in the Collective. Then Doctor Kohli had a confused face and so Nina tried to explain and said, If they hadn't got married there would not be starving children in the desert because the Patriarchal nuclear family makes the nuclear war come.

Doctor Kohli said, To clarify, the picture of the wedding made you feel ill or in pain.

And Nina nodded.

And Doctor Kohli said, And the picture of the family made you feel ill as well. These are what we grade as neutral or placebo pictures.

Nina said, Not ill but sick in my stomach. Yes. And then Nina said, But Nina knows that everything must be the opposite now, so if we do the test again Nina will give the right answers. Then there were fifty-three more pictures.

Nina had to wait on the corridor seats next to the waiting room of people with sick heads and Nina was very hungry because so many humans were around. So Nina ate the crisps in Support Worker Cas's bag and they were sour and called Cheesy Wotsits.

Nina was not to stare at the other people while Support Worker Cas was inside speaking to Doctor Webber and Doctor Kohli to get the facts about Nina's brain. Nina heard through the door and it was Cas saying, But maybe she found it hard to concentrate, Doctor, she's got a lot on her mind, Chen is in court today.

Then Nina had to wait more. Nina stared over at one waiting room man. He was very tall and young and handsome but had bandages on his wrists. There was also a fat woman in orange clothes and she was spilling over the edges of her chair and puffing loudly. And there was a woman who had pulled her hair out on one side, like Comrade Jeni.

Then Nina spotted the Bald Head Man again. The one who was in a silver car near Charity House. Being bald means you have a lot of testosterone and this makes babies and wars.

Bald Head Man had orange shiny skin like a man in a beach photo and is handsome with big shoulders. He had a blue shirt and a yellow piece of fabric hanging down from the neck so he is a man of business. He was looking round the waiting room for someone, then he caught Nina staring and he came over but not to give Nina a row.

Bald Head Man said, Hi, how you doing? Haven't I seen you before?

Nina was hot and shy because Nina had never had a tall man do this before and Nina knows from Cas if you fancy him you shouldn't swipe him.

Nina said, Did I see you at Charity House? Are you the man from the silver car?

He smiled and looked round the place and said, Nah, I think I saw you on the telly. That's what it is. You're famous you are. Is your name Nina?

And Nina felt hotter and more shy and said, Nina can't talk to strangers or men. And Nina looked round for Cas but Nina didn't really want her to come.

Bald Head Man put out his hand and said, My Name's Dave, Dave Pendergast. And then he looked round and said, I help people who've had horrible things happen to them, Nina, I go into battle for them, that's my job, and you've had some horrible things happen, haven't you?

Nina said, Are you a hack?

And Dave Pendergast laughed and said, No, no, no, I'm a solicitor and I specialise in abuse compensation and it was really lucky we bumped into each other.

Nina said, Is that like a lawyer? Then Nina said, Comrade Chen said the revolution would be complete when the last lawyer was hung by the entrails of the last capitalist.

Solicitor Dave Pendergast laughed and said, Wow, really, Wow. Then he looked over his shoulder and said, No. Actually, I protect my clients from lawyers. Lawyers will rip you off, they charge hundreds of pounds an hour. No, with me, I don't charge anything until you win. If you lose your court case, you don't pay a penny, so your risk is zero. No win, no fee, risk free, you see.

And he smiled and Nina laughed because it rhymed and because Nina remembered that when a man and a woman do this it is called flirting and this meant that No Fee Solicitor Dave Pendergast found Nina sexually attractive and Nina asked, Do you have a wife and children?

And No Fee Dave Pendergast said, Yes he did, and he saw Jeremy and Stacey at the weekends now because his ex-wife took him to the cleaners and he showed a picture of them in a park and they looked like him with big smiles in his wallet next to his money but they had hair. And Nina thought he is very fertile.

He took a bit of cardboard from his wallet and said, This is me here, you can call me anytime if you want me to go into the ring for you. And the cardboard said No Win, No Fee, Risk Free just like he had and it had numbers below and a picture of No Fee Pendergast smiling with his yellow tie, and below it said, Accident, Criminal Injury, Abuse – Don't Delay, Make Them Pay.

And he said, Now put that away in your pocket.

Then No Fee Pendergast was quiet and said, Can you keep a secret, Nina? And Nina leaned in to hear and he said, I know you've got a lot of people helping you but there are gaps, Nina. The one thing they can't get you is the compensation you need. Let me tell you, there was this woman I went into battle for, a normal everyday woman and her name was Karina, and Karina's boyfriend was a nut-job, and he went raving loony with a knife and cut off the end of her nose.

Nina felt pain in the nose and grabbed it.

No Fee Pendergast said, Well, the NHS and the social work, they got her a house, yes, and they got her bandages and some anti-depressants but could they fix her nose and compensate her for her terrible trauma? No. This was a very beautiful woman I should add.

Nina felt less pain in the nose and stared at No Fee Pendergast's nose and Nina said, Nothing is really happening but not out loud, but Nina's heart was beating fast.

No Fee Pendergast said, So she said to me, Dave, she said, the Social Work and the NHS have been no use to me at all, she said, Dave, she said, will you go into battle for me and I said, yes, of course I will, Karen, and I won her five hundred thousand pounds in court, and, Nina, that got her a new house and a new nose and now she's happily married with kids.

Nina was relieved but confused because before he said her name was Karina.

No Fee Pendergast said, Now, I could do that for you, Nina, I could get you even more. I did some calculations and, strictly between you and me, I'd say you could be looking at compensation of. And he stopped and then he said, Have a guess.

Nina said Nina didn't understand money yet.

And No Fee Pendergast said, A million pounds.

Nina said, Wow. Because being a millionaire was on Nina's list. And she wasn't allowed to get it from the hacks so maybe this was better. And No Fee Pendergast smiled and said, I tell you what, don't tell anyone yet, but if you want that money, which is yours by right, and I have to say, you're going to need it, because, maybe they're not telling you this yet but I've seen what happens, you get the social and the DHA and charities and they shunt you from one to another till you fall between the gaps. And as for sheltered housing, that costs fifty grand a year, and the government's not going to pay for that, are they? Money doesn't grow on trees, does it?

Nina shook the head.

No Fee Pendergast said, There's tons I can teach you about all this. Do you want to know more?

Nina was shy and nodded OK.

No Fee Pendergast smiled and said, Excellent, give me your phone for a min then? Don't worry, I won't nick it.

Nina gave it to him and Nina knew this was the bit called getting a girl's number and this meant he wanted to be in bed with Nina soon and it would be good to not be alone. Then he touched Nina's screen and his phone rang and he said, That's it, now I've got yours and you've got mine, and he wrote the word Dave and gave the phone back. Then he looked over his shoulder and said, Right, I have to go find my nippers. Remember, our little secret and he made his hand like a revolution fist but with the thumb up.

Nina felt warm and wet watching No Fee Pendergast walk away. He has very wide shoulders. Having secrets is good and so is being a millionaire and Nina could be on the cover of the magazines in the waiting room soon.

Then Nina felt a hand on the shoulder but not to panic because it was only Cas, and she said, Right, got all your results now and she was holding some paper.

Nina looked up and Cas had red eyes and was twitchy and sniffed and said, I'm all right, Pet. But Nina could tell something had happened in the Doctor room.

Cas said, Nina I have to call Sonia, we have to wait for a bit then go back in, because the Doctor has something to tell you.

Nina said OK, and thought Cas could do with some compensation.

Charity Sonia and Cas stood behind Nina and Nina had to sit in a Doctor room seat. Nina was tired and wanted to lie down but the bed was strange with wheels. Nina was worried about Charity Sonia because Charity Sonia felt very guilty about Nina being in the tower with people with complex needs and sometimes when people are feeling guilty they don't like you as much because you made them know they have failed.

Nina wanted to say, I forgive you Charity Sonia and I don't think your Charity made leaks to the hacks either, but Nina had to sit still and not keep turning round and just listen to what Doctor Webber had to say because he had results from Doctor Kohli, who wouldn't be coming back.

Doctor Webber's blue eyes went soft and he bent towards Nina and said, You see, Nina, in normal development a child cries and the mother comes and hugs the child, but you were denied that early intimate contact. Our first experiences are of a total bond with the mother, there is no I or You at that age, then later there is the separation from the mother and the self begins. I want. I need, and then the sense of doing right and wrong develops: I was bad and so on. In your case it appears that disruption occurred in this process.

And Nina thought he is very clever, and how did he know that I want and I have to be erased.

Doctor Webber talked to Nina but it was like he was talking to Charity Sonia. He said, There was no one person there to be your mother, Nina, so you learned not to react and not to trust. You would have had very high levels of the stress hormone Cortisol in the bloodstream, living in what we call the flight or fight state, and, well, these cut off growth in certain parts of the brain. When your parents should have been opening those doors towards love and learning, your brain was shouting Run and Hide, and high levels of Cortisol were shrinking the cells in your hippocampus, this is the part of the brain used for memories, emotion and stress regulation. On top of this you were subjected to an extraordinary degree of linguistic and behavioural modification, so you were robbed of your ability to express emotion, or to develop a stable self. And then, sadly, you were denied the chance to learn through play with other children as well as all this, so all social skills, the rough and tumble and leaps and bounds of healthy neurological development, well unfortunately there are entire corridors of your brain which were never opened and after time they have just disappeared. Am I making sense?

Nina nodded because when people talk about places Nina likes to see them in the head.

And Doctor Webber said, The doors were closed so you dug a tunnel around them and this could be in some situations considered a beneficial accidental side effect. You are exceptional at recording people, for example, but not at understanding their emotions.

He spoke to Charity Sonia and said, We first suspected Nina had Complex PTSD, but it turns out that Nina's development was frozen before what we call the concrete developmental stage.

Charity Sonia was chewing her lip and then she said, What does this mean in simple language, Doctor?

Doctor Webber said, Nina. And he looked into Nina's eyes, We have diagnosed you with brain damage.

Charity Sonia gasped but Nina wasn't to turn and hug her because Doctor Webber hadn't finished.

Doctor Webber said that this was sad news because it means Nina will never be like other people in Freedom. This is why Nina makes eye contact in unusual ways and why Nina hunches shoulders as if Nina is about to be attacked and why Nina stares out of windows and why Nina talks about herself as if she was someone else and why she must write everything down.

He said, One of the main problems is Nina's lack of affect and the inability to empathise. Nina is unable to tell whether she has committed acts that are harmful to others and she might feel no remorse over violent actions. Nina, therefore in a variety of contexts, is a danger to others and this raises care management issues.

Charity Sonia made a weep noise.

Doctor Webber said, Nina's lack of emotional reaction to this news is even more evidence that confirms the diagnosis.

Nina had to be brave and said, It's OK, Charity Sonia, Nina feels he is correct. Even when Nina tries to cry that door is locked.

Nina was more worried about Charity Sonia who was crying quite loudly and Cas who said she had to run to make a phone call but Nina knew she was crying too.

Charity Sonia kept saying, Nina, I'm sorry, I'm so, so sorry, and she touched Nina's head and sniffed. And Nina said, It's not your fault, you have only done good things and if I had gold stars I would give you six which is one more than the maximum.

And Charity Sonia covered her face and had movements of her shoulders.

Then there was the door and handing over of papers and some more pills and Doctor Webber shook Nina's hands and he said,

There's always some hope that the brain can forge new neural pathways and some tentative research has been done in Sweden. But by all means, get a second opinion.

Then he went down lower because Nina was sitting on the ground then and he said, What's really important, Nina, is that you're given peace to mend, don't let anyone force you into doing anything or acting in any way. Now, people might get frustrated with you, they might want to change the way you speak, they might tell you to say I. Well, You can't say I. Not yet. Maybe you never will. You certainly won't be able to till you have a breakthrough. It might be traumatic if and when it comes, because when you start to say I, you'll be taking on responsibility and blame. You'll be saying, Me, I did this. I am this. Forging a self, properly for the first time. And it can be scary to be an I. Do you understand?

Nina said, Don't let them make me say I things.

Then he said to Charity Sonia, It's really important that she's not dragged in front of the media and made to perform. If this happened she could be stuck in a cycle of re-traumatisation.

And Charity Sonia said, Of course, of course, our primary concerns are Nina's privacy and safety.

Then he said, Good luck and Nina kissed his knuckles and he didn't know what to say and Nina should not have done that because even Comrade Chen only allowed Nina to kiss on special days.

Nina had to sit in a corridor seat then and stared down the long corridor of many doors. There were people in green clothes with squeaky feet and bags and the people in white clothes are their bosses then they vanish again.

Nina listened to Charity Sonia and Doctor Webber whispering in the doorway. Charity Sonia whispered, You said this came from her not having maternal care, if we found her mother, could that help? There's a woman called Uma, who Nina seems to have some kind of maternal attachment with, or even Comrade Ruth, she was caught by the Police yesterday. We could have them both DNA tested by law. Do you think that could make a difference, Doctor, if she knew who her real mother was?

Doctor Webber shook his head and touched Charity Sonia's shoulder and he said, I'm sorry, it's much too late for her to form that kind of attachment to a parent.

And then it was time to go.

Nina was back in the high tower for vulnerable people and alone again. Nina had to find a clean place to write and it was hard because of the kitchen splatters and toilet splatters left by the last people.

It took a long time to do the report of today.

Charity Sonia said in the car, Maybe you're in shock, Nina, maybe that's why you're not upset. And Cas said, She's been snarfing those Beta blockers like they're sweeties, you know for the panic attacks. You think we should have told the Doctor before the test? Maybe they gave a false result?

And Charity Sonia said, God, I really hope Webber is wrong.

Nina has decided to do a test, to prove that Doctor Webber was incorrect. Nina is sure that Nina has empathy. Millions of it. Nina just gets it too strong and then has to hide it and sometimes it is delayed, like with Karina-Karen and the nose cut off that was still making Nina feel sad and sick for her after five hours.

Nina decided to do one test of Nina's own in the bathroom.

Nina had heard Charity Sonia whispering in the car to Cas when Nina closed the eyes and lay flat on the back seat. Charity Sonia said to not talk to Nina about Chen's court appearance today and don't mention cults or Maoism because if Nina realises she was part of something much bigger it might be too much for her.

So that is Nina's test. Nina will find out about Mao since he was the man who Comrade Chen said was the greatest man in the world. This will make Nina feel something big. And if Nina did evil things too maybe Nina will feel it and that will be good because it will prove Doctor Webber is wrong, and the shock will make Nina remember everything.

Nina has always liked science and prepared for the test by eating two yoghurts and being naked so there can be no contaminants in the experiment.

Nina remembered that if you put your finger on the top bit of the phone some letters appear for making words and if you make a word, it searches the sky for it.

Nina did a preliminary test. Nina typed FREE. And it said From alco-pops to espresso makers, designer sofas to zed-beds, hundreds of top-quality goodies are available every day across the country for free. And there were three hundred and seventy-four thousand million places to go where people knew what free was.

The Project was created on the specific instruction of the Chairman Mao Zedong himself so he was the test. Nina put his name into the net and there were pictures of his glorious face against red and three million one hundred and ten places Nina could find him.

Nina touched the first one so the test began and it was a story with grey pictures and a man's voice.

In the grey pictures there were metal boxes in China on street corners held on with string and they have hand-painted Mao symbols and the voice of the man said this was The Cultural Revolution. There was a slot in every box because what you have to do is write down the name of a person who you denounce as a traitor and put it in and it is a secret. Everyone has to do this. And if you don't people will think you are a traitor first, so most people just tell lies and accuse someone they don't like very much, maybe over a little thing or a jealousy, or because someone has a nice voice or is prettiest or beat them at cards, even though they are innocent, and sometimes just because you are scared that if you don't tell on someone, they will tell on you first.

Then Nina saw the little skinny China man with shaking face in colours and he said, We were just children, we didn't know, we just wanted to get a red star because we were Red Guards and to make our Great Leader proud of us, so we had a competition to inform on the most people, and that was when I informed on my mother. One day she was in the kitchen and she took down the picture of Chairman Mao because she said, people were starving. And I told her, Mother, you are a counter-revolutionary, put the picture back or I will have to report you. And she refused and so I did and the next day they came to take her away and she was put in prison for a month then they took her out in the street and she was like a skeleton and all the children hit her and the guards shot her through the head.

The wrinkled Chinese man started crying. He said, I am so ashamed, I cannot forgive myself, we were only children, children.

Nina wrote this down because Nina had many times whispered the crimes of Comrade Uma and Zana and Jeni and Ruth to Comrade Chen like, She has not cleaned the dishes. She smells of chocolate. She did not turn her light off. She was crying in the toilet. But Nina did not feel anything.

Nina watched more moving pictures and the little children marched up and down the streets with their red scarfs and their sticks, poking the adults, dragging the teachers out of the schools, making them stand up straight and wear pointed hats with their crimes written on them, making sure they stood for hours and if any of them fell over they were reported as traitors in a circle and the children hit the grown-ups with their sticks and with their little red books and they burned many big old books in a great fire.

And Nina wrote this down too because of erasures.

Then Nina felt the hollow begin, because Nina saw an old woman being dragged and beaten by the little children and Nina remembered Comrade Chen didn't force Nina to inform and hit. Nina volunteered, and it made Nina proud, reporting everything the grown-ups said. Nina loved it and Nina loved hitting. And it wasn't just one bit of paper, it was a hundred hundred pages of Nina's diaries.

Nina had to stop because of sick feelings but still no crying came and no empathy, just the numb.

Nina put the head in the corner to make it very tight and dark because Nina had failed the many tests and has no empathy and it was too much for one day.

Nina could not sleep because Nina could not stop thinking about Comrade Jeni. Nina remembered the torn edge and choking on pills. And Comrade Ruth saying, No good, write it again. Again. Erase. Swallow the pill don't spit it out. No, you can't go to sleep. Write it again, different. Erase that. Say this. Again. Comrade Uma saying, Drink the coffee, please, Nina stay awake, if you love Comrade Chen please do this.

Nina closes the eyes and picks off the arm scab to make blood come and the diaries come back to the eyes of memory. Nina can't see words but Nina remembers pages and pages of the diary were torn out. The torn edges are like feathers. Nine in total and seven from the next diary, number 68 and 69. Nina must remember what was written before and who tore them out but the pain in the scab is too tired now and Nina won't be able.

Nina doesn't know if the hollow is a lack of feeling or the biggest feeling of all, sucking all the others into its big hole. It is like the hungry feeling after five days with no food but it is a hollow growing so there is no room for lungs, so breath is like gasps and sore. Nina once heard Comrade Uma howl with tears and mouth wide open and it was so low, the sound of all her hollow coming out.

Nina remembers all sitting in the circle the night after they said Comrade Jeni was in the Hospital. Comrade Ruth rubbed out the words and tore out a page and the Comrades read the next one over and over to get all the words right. Two nights or three and no sleep allowed going through all the versions of the story by candle. Then taking turns interrogating each other.

Where were you when she did it? What room?

What time was this?

No, it did not happen here, we cannot let the spies of the State in.

Who touched her? Who moved her?

Why is she talking about birds?

Nina sees the diary but it is getting dim. Sixteen pages are torn out. Nina remembers in the basement, putting pages in the mouth.

Nina stared at the new jotter. Comrade Chen said, Destroy all diaries, there can be no evidence linking Jeni to us. If they interrogate us we will all say that we thought she moved to Scotland.

The scab was finished and there was blood on the pages and Nina remembered this is proof, Doctor Webber said, that you can't feel.

Nina has failed two tests now. Nina is not stupid. Nina knows what Doctor Webber means when he said, Nina is a danger to others.

And No Fee Pendergast said, You'll fall into gaps and the government's not going to pay for that, are they? And Comrade Chen was right, Nina will be put into jail.

Nina looked out of the window and saw thousands of lights in the city and in the reflection there were a thousand little window people inside Nina's naked skeleton body. Nina is too alone and wants No Fee Pendergast to come.

Nina went back to the phone and pressed Dave and there was ringing and then the voice was a woman and it said, Hello, who is this?

And Nina said Nina. Then there was a fumble and another

voice was loud and happy and it was No Fee Pendergast and he said, Nina, hello there, I'm so glad you called. Then his voice was quieter and Nina heard him say, It's the girl from London Fields, like he was talking to someone else.

Nina got shy and said, Can you help me, please?

And No Fee Pendergast said, Of course, Nina, absolutely, where are you, and I'll pop over, we can chat one to one, much better.

Nina looked out of the window and the city was so big and dark. Nina was not scared of radiation as much, but Nina was afraid of the littleness and everything so far away and the hollow and the alone.

Nina remembered the name of the tower and told him but then No Fee Pendergast said in the phone, Aw, right, what the hell they stick you in there for? We can sue the social work for negligence on that as well. Right, excellent. But getting in to see you, in that building, well, that's not ideal, Nina, yeah.

Then he said, I tell you what. I can drop by and meet you in the car outside the tower would that be easier, Nina? I tell you what, if you can meet me on the corner at De Beauvoir Road, that's just a couple of hundred yards from you. How's that, twelve o'clock tomorrow morning. I'll bring some paperwork and we can get started on fighting for what you need.

Nina has been told not to get into rooms and cars with men by Charity Sonia but No Fee Pendergast said he could win Nina a million pounds and it would take away all of Charity Sonia's problems. So Nina said, OK. I will meet you in your car.

Nina heard him say, Great. I'm so glad you called, Nina. You've made a wise choice, Nina. I'm going to go into the ring for you, Nina, and we're going to win, all right, excellent, cheers.

He said Nina's name many times and it made Nina feel good. Then his voice went away and he was just the name Dave on the glass of the phone.

Nina felt proud to have been independent because this is the goal of Charity Sonia. Nina stared out the window. Nina went close and Nina's face in the glass had dark holes where the eyes should be and inside were window lights full of little people. Then they vanished because of steam from the mouth.

Nina looked and tried to think of Nina out in the streets alone like a normal person and Nina saw the trees in the bit after the roofs. Nina felt a growl and Nina had eaten the three oranges already and did well to have eaten all alone with no TV or humans. Nina had a good idea.

Test two. Nina will go outside and walk all alone as a practice for meeting No Fee Pendergast. Test three. Nina will buy some food because Cas said the corner shop is called this because it is on the corner near Nina. Nina was hungry for bread and it would be good to feed to birds. If Nina can buy food for the first time it is more proof that Doctor Webber is wrong and Nina does not have brain damage. Nina will have to pass many cars and not be scared but Nina has many techniques now.

Nina took two pink pills to stop panic in the metal elevator of graffiti and Nina said in the head, nothing is happening in this moment, see, you are under no threat. The doors opened, and Nina saw the man of security in his window and walked past but he said, Where are you going, miss?

Nina knows Nina is not supposed to be outside because of hacks and Comrade Ruth. Nina looked at the metal door and the camera ball. Nina said, Let me out and the secure man did not. Nina thought of Comrade Chen and his front door. And if Nina didn't get out now Nina would always be stuck. And Doctor Webber said the doors in Nina's head had all disappeared but Nina had to prove he was wrong.

Nina looked outside and two men were smoking then they stopped and rang a bell then the door went buzz and Nina squeezed past the smelly smoke men and closing metal door and the security man shouted but Nina was out and the air was cold and black and orange with lights from the tower.

Nina said in the head, Nina has to walk two hundred yards and buy bread and then come back and then two tests will be done. Nina said, walk now, and Nina counted, one hundred, ninety-nine, ninety-eight, ninety-seven and kept walking and breathing but then there was a big black car.

Nina froze. And it did not kill. And Nina said, nothing is happening, there is no danger and Nina counted the breaths and said My current symptoms are just a conditioned response and they will lessen as I desensitise myself when Nina made it sixty backwards Nina was calmer and Nina said in the head, cars are just passing by, they don't know who Nina is, and look how far Nina has come all by herself.

Nina looked and the buildings were a kind Nina hadn't seen before with no windows. Nina said in the head, when I get to the corner shop it will be done. And Nina sang, Follow the Yellow Brick Road and made it to the end but the shop on the corner for food had metal on the windows. Then Nina heard more cars and Nina clicked the heels together and said, Nina will run and there will be another shop on the next corner and no one will see Nina and Nina was excited about Nina's progress.

Nina took a breath and ran. Then Nina was three streets away but then Nina was confused because the road had a bend and Nina could not see the tower any more because of other high buildings. Nina said be brave and go only to the corner but then a truck came and it chased Nina. Nina ran over another street and a car skidded and Nina ran harder and hid behind bins and the truck did not kill Nina and Nina counted breaths, one hundred, ninety-nine, ninety-eight. Nothing is happening. Ninety-one, ninety, eighty-nine but it couldn't stop. So Nina had to go back, but then the going back street was two hundred and seventy in counts and Nina could not see any towers in the sky so it was the wrong street.

Breath came very fast and Nina took two more pink pills but Nina was choking and the pills came back out with sick. Then loud men were coming down the road and closer and they were singing and a big silver car came faster and Nina ran. Nina saw a man in a dirty sheet in a doorway and his eyes were down and his skin was grey and smelly and he was a hack because he wanted things from Nina.

Nina saw a tower and ran to it and cars made horns. But it was the wrong tower with only fifteen windows up in a row. Nina's head was hot and eyes sore and car lights were faster and radiation started. And Comrade Chen said, if you leave here you will die in the gutter like Comrade Jeni. Then Nina was at some place where three roads come to one and Nina was lost and the lights were buzzing hard. Saying Nothing is Happening, I am safe, didn't work any more and Nina couldn't breathe and Nina found a dark place of big bins and crawled in beside for a shadow and curled up small and put the head in the dark corner. Many feet were passing and loud and not seeing Nina and not helping Nina because Nina was clicking the heels to make Nina invisible and Nina put the finger in the scab to make the thousand cars of the city go away and Nina said My current symptoms are just a conditioned response and they will lessen as I desensitise myself over and over but Comrade Chen was right, Nina should never go outside and Nina had failed all the tests. One hundred, ninety-nine, ninety-eight and our Glorious Leader made children kill their parents and Nina was lost in the shivering streets and the sky opened and radiation poured down and Nina could not breathe.

Jotters #71/#72 2003

The Project is so happy to have an own room and is not sure why it is OK to have private property now but is very grateful. The Project loves all the special things that The Project has been given. I love the hairbrush and the doll and the plastic flower in the pot and the Observer Book of Trees and the Tampax and the lampshade and the watercolours and the picture frame and The Project hopes this is not making me greedy and materialistic and understands that even though all these things are locked in here with me, they are communal.

The Project is also very grateful for the new bra and the slippers and the lifting weights. The Project loves the record player and the headphones and the five records of the Songs of the People's Republic. There Is a Clear Sun in Peking is The Project's favourite. And so is Song of the Factory Men. The Project loves all the songs equally but wants to know if it's OK to have favourites now or if this is still incorrect since things seem to be changing since Comrade Jeni.

The Project has tried very hard to get the name Nina out of my head and the face of Jeni. The Project would like to know if

Comrade Jeni made a mistake calling The Project Nina or if The Project was called Nina long before The Project could speak and write and was a baby.

Most of all The Project is grateful for my door because The Project knows that in these teenage years there is greater danger from the outside spies and rapists and fascist pigs and The Project is locked with the key for my own protection. The Project is also very grateful that wise Comrade Chen boarded up the one window with metal screws to assist The Project from not wasting hours just staring out for pigeons and passing hair and hats above the walls. The Project knows this is to save me from the same fate as Comrade Jeni who always looked out and never within.

The Project is sorry for not erasing Comrade Jeni yet.

The Project will stop asking about what happened to Comrade Jeni because all who betray the Collective are dead to us.

The Project requests more jotters as there are so many hours now that The Project is not labouring at the photocopier or cleaning and The Project has nothing else to do but write the report. The Project is not lonely and will stop saying that I am and trying to grab Comrade Uma when it is time to take out the bucket of pee or in the ten minutes to get out to poo.

The Project knows it takes a lot of effort to take the big flat bit of wood on and off the door and is grateful that the Comrades have hidden The Project so The Project doesn't have to be taken away to an orphanage even though The Project is practically a grown-up now. The Project loves the free hour and to hear all your stories of the outside and please come to the door more and talk through it because I like that a lot.

The Project runs out of things to write about and must stop going on about missing the kitchen and the hall and Comrade Jeni and Comrades Uma and Zana. The Project will stop asking for a report on Cornflake and Rosa Luxemburg and the others but is very worried that the baby egg chick might have hatched and fallen like the ones before. The Project would welcome a report on whether poor one leg Gramsci is still there because some bad black beaked birds were circling around. The Project asks if it would be possible to just have one hour at the old window to gather all this information.

The Project also wants to know if anyone is reading the diaries now or if The Project is of the age to correct all of my words by myself as the last four weeks had no correction in them and no comments.

The Project has now memorised all the books by Chairman Mao and Comrade Lenin and is very grateful for these in the room and would like to discuss what I have learned. Let a Thousand Flowers Bloom.

The Project will now make a list of the things that I would like to be changed and will edit them and then put them under my door like always. Most is the smelly bucket. The Project is sorry for having to pee so much and for spilling some and can I have some bathroom Pine Fresh air freshener spray please and for Comrades to come running when I bang hard if there is another spillage.

The Project will ask for no more now because this has already been too capitalist.

Notes from Comrade Uma: Comrade Uma expresses concern that The Project is stooped in her posture and has begun talking to herself. It is practically solitary confinement in that room and she often whimpers and whispers to herself and clings to me and to the others when she is let out for her shower. She paces about in there all day. Her self-harming has not ceased although she hides it well. Comrade Uma would like to raise the possibility that The Project may suffer from the hereditary condition that afflicted her mother.

Comrade Uma also requests that we call The Project Comrade Nina from now on, as she knows the name and cannot delete it.

Notes from Comrade Ruth: Comrade Ruth commends The Project on accepting her new conditions. In terms of the noise issue, the singing is not so bad, but The Project also does not understand that masturbation is not acceptable and we can hear her doing it through the door. She needs more activities to keep her occupied. Comrade Ruth would also like to correct Comrade Uma. It is for The Project's good that she does not run wild round the house, we all know she was nearly caught on two occasions in the aftermath. Comrade Ruth would also like to correct Comrade Uma as there is no such thing as Normal healthy needs and desires, all gendered behaviour is a social construct.

Notes from Comrade Chen: Comrade Chen apologises for his recent absence. World events have overtaken the matters of the Collective. A great betrayal of the pure ideals of our Great Helmsman is taking place in China and the cause of Socialism is in danger. Without Comrade Jeni's money we shall all have to work more in the outside. Comrade Chen is concerned that all requests from The Project and fellow Comrades are for more things, always more things. You must work, work harder. We are fighting for our survival.

Comrade Chen refuses the proposed name change. To regress to the use of birth names is an admission of defeat. Comrade Chen asks that other Comrades edit The Project's diaries as he no longer has the time.

The hole of lonely is overtaking the belly and is crawling along the arms. The Project feels it round the throat and then can't breathe.

The Project wants to get punished because that would at least be something.

The only way to make the boring empty and sore legs go away is the window. It is my biggest secret yet. I can write this because no one even reads it and they want to forget I am here. Last time The Project gave a jotter under the door to

Comrade Zana and she said, Don't bother we are far too busy with important shit.

The Project is proud of a secret. Last week I stole a metal nail cutter thing I found in the shower room and then smuggled it back to the room and used it like a screwdriver to take the screws out of the board Comrade Chen fastened to the window. The Project took off the board to make no noise and looked out of the window for one minute in the dark but could see no birds and hear no cooing and The Project worried they had all flown away because they had not seen The Project in many days.

There is more. In the time before morning The Project jams the wood back in place. Comrade Ruth came in to spray with Pine freshener and she looked at the boarded-up window and didn't even notice the missing screws. The Project is sawing through the screws very slowly to stick the ends back in to make it look like they are not missing.

A knock on the door and shadow under then a square note slipped through. Then footsteps went away. It said,

Your real name is NINA.

Underneath it said, *Sorry*. Then there was a space and it said, *Erase this.*

The hand writing was like little fat sneaky Comrade Uma.

The Project felt very angry then and bashed the door. But no one came. Then, The Project sat on the floor and looked at the note and felt like a need to cry but all crying has been buried with Comrade Jeni.

Nina.

And thinking of Comrade Jeni, saying it. Nina.

The more it is said, the more it is like it had been known a long time ago in the body when The Project was another person, outgrown like the skin of a snake from National Geographic.

Nina Nina Nina.

The Project is not The Project any more. The Project is now Nina and secrets are the best of all.

The Project has decided to make a special diary for Nina, The Project needed a friend and this was very kind because now there is The Project and Nina. Nina will start on a fresh page for Nina Nina Nina.

Nina feels dizzy quite a lot of the time from wanting and sneaking at the window and Nina saw an old lady with a bag by the bins and she dumped it then pigeons came so she is a good person. And Nina saw Gramsci again so he has not died and only needs one leg anyway. This made Nina too excited and Nina waved at the old lady but she was far away and the size of a thumb nail and didn't see Nina. Then there was no sleeping and Nina tried to make the old woman come back by wanting it very hard but it didn't work.

Nina is quite brave. The Project does everything the Comrades say but Nina doesn't. Nina hates them.

There was a crashing in the night and footsteps, and Comrade Uma whispered through the door that it was OK, it was just Comrade Chen had got a bit drunk. This was confusing. Comrade Chen said alcohol was the enemy of the revolution and Mao's cure for alcoholism is to put a gun to your head with your family there and say if you drink again we will shoot you and it is one hundred per cent effective. So if he was drunk then he is becoming the enemy of the revolution.

Nina has dug a hole in the wall with the plastic spoon that Comrade Uma brought with rice, not to escape but to hear the talking about Nina better. It is hidden behind the bed and it is proof that Comrade Chen does not have an all-seeing eye because no one knows it is there and no one says, Hey You! Stop digging. Nina had to stop because the spoon was plastic and snapped but it is a good secret to know it's there.

Comrade Chen came back and Nina knows the sound of drunk people because there are stumbles and Comrade Chen shouted that Comrade Zana had to be re-educated again and Nina listened very hard through the wall. There was whispering, then a sound of a heavy body landing, then breathing very fast, then him saying, You slut, then Nina heard footsteps and more moaning.

Nina has made a proper lying diary for them as if The Project still exists.

Nina's head empties when Nina thinks of all of this because every single thing The Project was told could be lies as well.

For a special treat Nina was allowed to eat with them downstairs because Comrade Chen was out working at the Cashing Carry and he had granted a benevolent small indulgence for how correct he says the Comrades have been and so they included Nina too. So we had extra rice with fish fingers and two rations of ketchup and Comrade Ruth hid her eyes from Nina. Comrade Uma kept touching Nina and saying, I'm so glad and I'm so sorry. And, You need to eat more, and she called Nina Love. And Comrade Ruth blushed more.

Then the front door had key noise and he was standing there and stormed in and yelled, What is this? The Project should not be here!

The women stood at table with heads lowered and Comrade Uma said, She has been in that horrible room for too long. And Comrade Chen slapped her, but he staggered. His words were blurred and he yelled, What is going on here? But all the women looked to each other and Nina said nothing.

Comrade Chen yelled, A conspiracy of silence?

Then Nina said, Leave us alone, you are a bully.

Comrade Chen's face turned dark and he yelled at the others.

He said, Who put these words in her mouth?

He went round each person. Was it you? Was it you?

Comrade Zana said, I haven't said a word to her in bloody yonks. Comrade Ruth gritted her teeth. Comrade Chen shouted at Nina, Your tone of voice is sarcasm and bitching, who taught you this?

Comrade Chen said Nina should have ten beatings of the kitchen spoon on the wrists and he went and got it from the drawer. Then he stopped and stared at Comrades Ruth, Zana and Uma and yelled, You would not betray me like this if you had lived through the atrocities of the British Military Imperialism as I have. While you were fat little babies they were beheading the children of Asia.

He handed the wooden spoon to Comrade Ruth. He said, You will now correct The Project with twenty hits on the wrist.

Comrade Ruth shook her head. Comrade Chen grabbed her by the throat. She is taller than he is and she has muscles from cleaning but she did not fight back.

Comrade Chen said, Maybe I will contact the police, Comrade Ruth, and tell them you are hiding here. I'm sure they are still curious about your past activities.

Comrade Zana shouted Stop! Please.

Comrade Chen dropped Comrade Ruth and went to Comrade Zana. He said, What have you to say? She shook her head so he said, I could turn you out, back to your drug-dealer boyfriend. I am sure he would be very happy to have you back whoring for him. Maybe you should whore for us, we need the money.

Comrade Chen handed her the spoon and said, Will you correct The Project?

Comrade Zana looked at Nina and at Ruth still gasping and refused the spoon.

Comrade Chen shouted, Is this a plot against me? Do you not know what the beloved Mao did to traitors?

Comrade Chen spun round, looking at each of us. He shouted, Ingrates and bitches, have you any idea how much I have sacrificed for you?

Nina looked at Comrade Ruth and she stared at Nina and a thought came from her eyes – if we had all attacked him at the same moment we could have overpowered him. But Comrade Ruth lowered her eyes and said, I am sorry, Comrade, it was my idea to let The Project out for one meal.

Comrade Chen grabbed her arm and marched her to the front door and we all followed. The Project was not allowed to go near and Nina has never stood close to it but he unlocked the five locks and pushed her into the light.

He yelled, Go! And pushed her. You think you will survive out there then go! When I tell the police what you did to Jeni!

Nina felt hot and Comrade Ruth was frozen in the door and for a second Nina thought Nina would run too if Comrade Ruth went, even though electricity would strike Nina, Nina would still have been free for one minute.

Comrade Uma gripped Comrade Chen's shirt and begged him to let Comrade Ruth stay, and shut the door, please, because neighbours will see and Pigs will come. There was a sound of a car machine out past the door and Comrade Chen pulled them both inside and slammed the door.

Comrade Chen shouted, You stay only out of fear, but not out of belief. He pointed his finger at Comrade Zana. Do you not see how you are all as wretched as this poor whore? Do you truly believe in socialism or is the only thing that keeps you here fear of the police and fear of failure?

He said, It is not good enough. It is not what I wanted. I wanted you to free yourselves not be more wretched! You have understood nothing, re-education must begin again.

Comrade Chen dragged Comrade Ruth by the arm, along the corridor to the bathroom. She did not resist. Comrade Uma led

Nina past so as not to have to see but Nina pulled free of Comrade Uma's hand and crouched in the dark and peeked round the doorframe and saw Comrade Ruth on her knees before him. Comrade Chen said, You will be grateful.

Comrade Uma tried to whisper and drag Nina away to the room but Nina refused and watched harder and saw Comrade Ruth bowing and then removing her shirt. Comrade Ruth tried to cover her breasts, they were pale and thin with large dark pinks and her skin was prickled like chicken. Her eyes looked up at Comrade Chen and he unfastened his trousers and he grabbed her head. Her eyes shot past him and out into the dark, like she knew Nina was there, like she was praying for Nina to make it stop.

For the first time Nina felt great sorrow for Comrade Ruth and soon she was making the choking noises that Nina recognised from through the wall with Comrade Zana. Nina could not look at her head but could still hear Comrade Ruth being forced again and again and the noise.

Nina was locked back in. Nina could not sleep and Nina waited then looked out of the secret window for the old bird lady but she did not come. Rosa Luxemburg and Cornflake are nowhere to be seen and the nest is empty with only a little broken shell but there is no baby bird anywhere so it must have fallen and be a skeleton now but Nina never wants to look down to see and this is so cruel and why does it have to happen again and again?

Nina put the board back on the window and lay in the bed and peeled the big scab to make the room vanish.

Nina needs a weapon to fight the evil Witch and the evil Chen. Nina will make a secret hole in the trousers for the broken plastic spoon and if Chen touches Nina like he touched Comrade Ruth, Nina will stab him in the eye because even fat Mao says war is the central task and the highest form of revolution.

If Nina can blind the leader of the Global People's Liberation Army, then this means one of two things. Either Nina is even more powerful than Comrade Chen or Chen is a liar and not the leader of the Global revolution at all. What if nothing in the world outside is like Comrade Chen had told us?

One thing is sad and one thing is good. The sad is that Comrade Uma is sick and has to stay in bed so she will not bring Nina the food. The good is that Nina has written three different letters to the fascist oppressors who cannot be worse than evil Chen, and Nina has seen them at the window when the light comes up and they take the bins away then there is a strange noise of machine then they come back empty.

Nina has written, Help us and don't tell the police and told them how they can rescue Nina. They have to climb up the pipes to Nina's window.

The first letter, Nina scrunched up and threw through the gap in the window glass but it did not get very far. The second one Nina made into a paper aeroplane with a paper clip for weight but it did not fly very far either and it was dark and hard to see.

The third one was a paper swan because Nina thought, if the fascists men of bins were to see it they would think it special then pick it up and read it but it did not go far through the air either and then Nina was scared because if fascist men were to follow Nina's instructions they would climb high to Nina's window but it does not open more than one inch and jams and then they would fall like Comrade Jeni.

It seems a long time since she died. Nina feels some contradictions about Comrade Jeni.

Nina makes bigger scabs with the plastic spoon and waits by the window for the fascists to come and find the secret messages and then Nina is very afraid because what if Comrade Chen is the one to find them first. Nina went up on the window ledge and looked down and the paper bird was near the path and Comrade Chen comes back through the back path when he is drunk and if he finds it and reads, Please come and help me, I am held hostage, he will kill Nina, by poison in the food or electricity or doing what he does to Zana and Ruth.

Nina stared at the paper bird below and got very afraid and praying does not help and then Nina heard the back door.

Jotter #243 2018

They asked, What's your name? Has somebody hurt you? Why are you lying in the street in the rain? Who are you hiding from? Why are you hitting the constable? Do you want to be restrained?

Nina had to write it down because the Pig officer did not understand the way Nina speaks and Nina was too scared in the doorway when they pulled Nina out and Nina scratched the female one in the face by accident and couldn't breathe in the Pig car.

They asked, How long have you been homeless? Are you on any drugs? Are you running from someone? Have you got a home?

And Nina told them that first it was Charity House then the high tower. Nina didn't understand when they said which tower and postcode. Nina knew Nina was in trouble. They said, Are you all right, miss? Do you have Mental Health issues? Nina said Nina had to call Charity Sonia but the phone was back in the tower or lost like Nina in the street.

Nina could not breathe being so close to two Pig officers in the hot car with the red and blue spinning, because there were too many towers round here and they couldn't try every one of them, they said and Nina had to rock back and forwards and sing very loud and the Pigs did not like Nina and this is why Nina had to call them Pigs again.

There were many in the Pig station and some were tall and two had a brown face and the female Pig held Nina's arm tight and there was a sitting man with blood on his head and a woman with spike feet shouting that they had no fucking right to arrest her.

Nina was next to be interrogated and the man at the desk got angry when Nina had no surname and he said, I'll ask you one more time. And Nina said, Call Charity Sonia, please, and there was a picture on the wall that said Murder, and a picture of a man with a black mask with pointed ears and it said, Be A Crime Stopping Superhero. And the male Police said, Which Charity? And, Can you calm down please, miss, no one is going to hurt you. Are you a drug or substance user? What are these pills? Can you tell us how you came to be on the street? How long have you been homeless?

Nina hugged the knees and was cold and wet from radiation and said, Call Charity Sonia six times, and the female Pig officer with the short hair said, Is this someone who cares for you or a family member? Can you remember who this Sonia works for? Then Nina did and Nina said Sanctuary and the Police female said, That's a women's aid centre. Has someone hurt you recently, Nina? And Nina shook the head.

The male Pig officer who was very low behind the high desk said, It's just ringing out. They're closed for tonight. Have you got a second name for your carer?

And Nina was confused, then the female Pig touched Nina's arm again and said, Nina, look, I'm sorry, but it's after midnight and unless you've got names or numbers, we might have to hold you here overnight. You're not in any trouble, it's just that the homeless shelter is shut already and we can't find a way to contact the people who care for you now.

Nina asked, What is hold overnight?

And the female Police said, Well, in a cell, just so you can get some rest.

And Nina was scared because Comrade Chen said, if you ever go outside the Pigs put you in a prison cell like Comrade Meinhof and hang your neck and this was where Comrade Uma would end up if she ever ran and Nina became more scared.

Then a male Pig came and they left Nina in the room of the table and the two chairs of plastic alone and Comrade Chen was right. Nina should never have betrayed the Collective and Nina was sorry and put the finger in the scab to the make warm pain come.

Then the female Pig was back and she said, Nina, Was that you in the newspapers?

Nina nodded and said, Hacks came and stole Nina's face.

Then the female Police said, OK, OK, can you lift your head and stop singing please, no one is going to hurt you. Can you think hard and remember any of the names of the Police officers that you've met before, because if we can locate them then they might know how to reach Sonia's mobile?

And Nina remembered Officer Alia Jusef who was nice and not a Pig.

Then there was two and they said, Can you come with us please, and they took Nina down a narrow corridor with many doors of metal and behind one a man was shouting and banging and the female Pig opened the special door at the end with the two holes in it, one for food and one for spying and inside it had a plastic mattress and a metal toilet of bleach and worse smells and the female Police said, Don't panic you're not being charged or anything, but we can't let you have your shoes or shoelaces in case you harm yourself, and we've left the door open, see, so you're free but please don't wander about like you did before. Nina said, One hundred, ninety-nine, ninety-eight, ninety-seven, ninety-six and gave them the trainers and the ground was cold in the cell.

Under Charity Sonia's long coat was a pretty white dress with flowers and this was called a nighty because Charity Sonia had raced out and didn't have time to change. Nina was very sorry and pleased to be rescued by Charity Sonia again and sitting in her car outside the Pig station and not driving just breathing.

Charity Sonia said, You're impossible! Thank God the Police traced me, Nina. Why the hell were you outside in the middle of the night, anyway? What if they hadn't got through to me and they'd sent you off to a homeless shelter, it could have taken days to even find you. What if they'd arrested you, you'd have been in that bloody cell all night and court this morning. God, Nina. You could have got lost and got mugged or raped or hit by a truck.

And Charity Sonia bashed the inside wheel and said, Fuck, Fuck, this is all my fault. Sorry, sorry, I should never have let Phil put you in that bloody flat, you weren't ready.

And Charity Sonia lit one of her cancer sticks which is also a cigarette like Zana had before she was Purified and the smell made Nina think Comrade Zana would be on drugs and on the streets again now without her perfect Chen. Charity Sonia blew smoke out of the car window and she said, This is all my fault. I should have demanded you stay in the Women's Refuge. Whether you liked it or not. I was negligent. I'm so sorry. I'm fucking sorry.

Then Nina saw Charity Sonia was wet in the eyes and Nina took Charity Sonia's hand and said, You are like Comrade Uma.

Rain drops made shadows drip on Charity Sonia's face and she said, I really wish this hadn't happened, Nina, because there'll be a Police incident report now and that goes into your risk assessment file and Phil will say you're a danger to yourself. Please tell me you didn't hit a police officer.

Nina stayed quiet and Charity Sonia blew smoke out and said words to herself. One was Stupid and another was Bloody and she meant herself.

Charity Sonia's hand was warm and she didn't take it away. Nina squeezed and said, I am sorry Nina has brain damage and makes problems. Nina won't ever go out of doors again.

Charity Sonia said, No, Nina, please, that's not what I mean. I want you to be outdoors and to get better and have your own life and be fully independent, it's just, you can't run before you can walk. It's my fault for wanting you to.

Then she let go of Nina's hand and smashed her cigarette in the mirror in the rain and she put mint gum in her mouth and Mint Fresh spray in the car and she said, Four in the bloody morning. Where do we go now? I'd put you up in my flat if it wasn't breaking every single rule.

And Charity Sonia started the car and Nina would like to drive with Charity Sonia all night and sleep since Nina is not scared of Charity Sonia's car any more and Nina likes looking at the side of Charity Sonia's face with all the lights moving through her curly hair and she is beautiful and to rest the head on her shoulder.

Nina knows Nina doesn't have empathy but Charity Sonia makes the hollow fill up quite a bit and this is an improvement from when Nina was made to sit in the cold jail for hours because then Nina hated Charity Sonia quite a bit and the hollow was the size of the whole room.

Charity Sonia opened the charity building offices in the dark and made beeps and lights happen and she said, It's far too late to get you into any hotels or hostels, you'll have to spend the night here. I'll do some emails. That'll give us a head start. What a mess.

And she made Nina follow her through the place where the forty women with headphones had been but were gone now and empty desks but lights turned on when Charity Sonia moved and there were some people but it was just Charity Sonia and Nina's reflection in the glass and not Comrade Ruth.

Charity Sonia took Nina to a red sofa and said, Stay there, don't touch anything. Just sleep. OK. And Nina said, But Nina needs a pill to sleep and they're at the tower and Charity Sonia went into her bag and said, All right, here's some Ambien but just take one and she was in a hurry.

Nina couldn't sleep on the sofa with the bubbling water machine and Nina's wet clothes still on so Nina took them off and tried to make the jeans like a cover but Nina's eye kept being seduced to all the magazines that said, Jennifer Haunted by Her Baby Loss and Look Hotter Naked and Sexy Hair Hell Yeah. So Nina had to pick one up and look for information to make Doctor Webber be more in love with Nina.

Nina found 12 Steps to Make Him Fall in Love and Nina had already done some of them like Ask for His Help and Laugh at his Jokes and Disappear Mysteriously but number seven said, Feed Him Grapes, the way to a man's heart is through his stomach and Number twelve said Love Yourself, he will find it hard to fall in love with you if you don't love yourself first.

Then Nina was cross because Doctor Webber said Nina didn't have a self yet and it might be painful to get one, so Nina tore the pages out and made some swans to make the angry go away. Nina made forty-one and the paper was not the best and the Swans had bits of female eyes and hair and chest and legs on them.

Nina went to get normal paper and found Charity Sonia asleep across a desk and her shoes off and a hole in her tights so Nina tiptoed and took some paper with less writing on it and didn't stare at Charity Sonia too long because staring makes people wake up and Nina saw Nina in the glass and Nina was naked. Nina took a pen too because there was too much to catch up on and a knife just in case and Nina had to work out if the last days were a punishment for not enough self-criticism.

Nina felt the eye of Comrade Chen seeing all and making bad things happen and remembers Comrade Chen said, Nina had to be locked up for Nina's own protection and that of others.

Nina wrote for a long time and wrote this, and now it is up to date but Nina still can't sleep. Nina will make more birds and think of Doctor Webber's curling eyebrows.

Nina had to wake up and put clothes on for God sake and hurry the staff are coming and Nina got shouted at for using up all the admission forms and all those paper birds were put in a bin. Nina saw in Charity Sonia's eyes that she was disappointed like everyone is and if you disappoint people for too long they have to erase you.

Stranger women walked past with paper cups and stared at Nina when the jeans and socks were put on. Then there was shouting at the place of the desk at the front door and the man of security couldn't stop the hacks and flashes went off and Nina tried to cover the face and a woman shouted, Would you like to comment on the arrest of Uma Schwartz? Then there were pushing hacks and the man of Security held them back and Charity Sonia was grabbing Nina into a room with no windows and just a white plastic board that said Self Esteem and some erased words but Nina could still hear the shouting.

Social Work Phil pushed through with newspapers in his hand and a phone in his ear and Charity Sonia said to him, You said she'd be safe in Trinity Court.

Social Work Phil said, There you are, Nina, thank God. And then he said, Look, Sonia, there's no point pointing fingers here. This can't go on like this, slinging blame, we have to make a definitive decision on Nina's care plan today. Nina doesn't fit in any of the boxes, we know this now. You know what'll happen if Nina keeps getting pushed from agency to agency. She'll end up in a blind spot, getting seriously injured or harming someone else, then she'll be off our hands completely, and in the care of Hospital or in the prison system.

Charity Sonia said, That's rich, you're the one who put Nina at risk.

Social Work Phil said, Enough. Right, I've managed to get everyone together for a Multi-Agency Risk Assessment Conference for four. Can you attend? We need to get this done, for Nina's sake.

Then he stepped away with his phone on his ear and the noise from the hacks at the door was very loud. Then Support Worker Cas pushed through. She yelled at Nina and said, There you fucking are, I've been all over the bloody place, you didn't half give us a scare. Here's your phone, you dafty, you left it in the bloody flat. What are we going to do with you, eh?

And she wasn't really angry because she ruffled Nina's hair.

The hacks at the door were very loud and Charity Sonia said, what the bloody hell is going on out there. Please tell me they didn't find out Nina went missing last night?

Cas showed her phone and said, Nah, it's that Comrade, what's her name. Uma, she's at Shacklewell Police station, it's all over the news.

And she showed the phone to Charity Sonia.

Nina felt a warm feeling and a hole for Uma and Nina said, Is Comrade Uma coming to see me? And Nina was excited.

Cas said, She tried to sneak into the Collective but Police were there and forensics and they nabbed her.

Charity Sonia touched Nina's shoulder and said, Was she looking for Nina?

Cas said, Dunno, but they said it was like she wanted to get caught. She came quietly, they said. Well, as quietly as you can when there's twelve fucking hacks on you like flies on shit.

Nina had a feeling of ache and said, Can I see Comrade Uma?

Social Work Phil came back and he was reading his phone, and he told Charity Sonia that she had to see it too. Then he said, Uma Schwartz is saying she's going to make a statement to the police about the death in the cult, but she'll only make it if Nina is present.

Then he spoke to Nina with a gentle voice, Looks like she has also implied that she knows who your mother is, Nina.

The ache in Nina became the emptiest one.

Social Work Phil said, Says here Uma's being DNA tested.

Charity Sonia put her hand to her mouth and said, My God, so Uma is Nina's mother?

Social Work Phil said, We don't know. She'll only speak with Nina present.

Nina said, No.

Social Work Phil said, Well one good thing about it is it'll get Nina off the list of suspects and get these hacks off our backs.

Cas interrupted and said, Excuse me, but didn't the Doctor say keep Nina away from upsetting things and the bloody media?

Charity Sonia said, But it should be up to Nina.

And she bent down and said, Nina don't you want to find out who your mother is and who hurt Jeni? It could help us move past this violence issue and get you faster up the housing lists. Remember what the Doctor said, it might even help you have a breakthrough and get better.

Nina said, No, No, liar. Comrade Uma is a liar, liar. Nina doesn't have a mother erase, erase.

Nina was very angry and had to sit and wait and then the Pigs came and moved the hacks away and Nina remembered about No Fee Pendergast because the phone was shaking with the name of Dave. Nina pressed the button and heard his voice but it was far away and hissy.

No Fee Pendergast said, Nina, where are you? I've been waiting here outside your flat for half an hour. I hope you're not having second thoughts.

And Nina told him about the police station and being lost and Comrade Uma and he said, Listen, Nina, I'm not a criminal lawyer, and it looks like there's a hell of a case brewing against this Chen character and that's going to be on our side with the press, Nina. So, it's really important, right now, that we prepare a civil case for damages. As I've said, Nina, when I go in the ring for you, with the level of physical, sexual and psychological abuse you suffered, you'll be looking at a massive payout from the Criminal Injuries Compensation Authority, the maximum award, Nina, and I need you to sign a contract with me today. We need to start documenting all this negligence you're going through right now. We'll be making a case, not just against Chen, but against the social services and the police, who should have actually found you in 2002. And the NHS, we'll sue them too. And your neighbours, twenty-odd years and not one of those fuckers reported the boarded-up windows, the sounds of screaming. Surely one of them must have seen you. It's shocking. And these people who say they're helping you, Sonia and Sanctuary, they're making a balls of it, like they always do, and they won't be telling you when their aid runs out and no doubt they're setting you up for some substandard care package sticking you in some stinking nursing home with nut-jobs and vegetables because it's the cheapest option. I've seen it happen, Nina. Are you listening, what I can and will do is seek substantial damages from the Social Work department and the Charity for all their cock-ups, Nina, because I want to turn your pain into your gain so you'll be comfortable for the rest of your life, so we need you to write down everything they're doing to you and sign with me today.

Nina thought about all the lists Nina had to do now. Nina had to write down all the times Nina was hurt by Comrade Chen and all the times Nina ate and went to sleep and washed and so Nina asked if it was OK to skip writing down all the mistakes of Charity Sonia and Social Work Phil because it was too many lists.

A voice said, Nina, who the hell are you speaking to? And it was Cas standing over with cross face and reaching for the phone. And Nina said, He is called Dave Pendergast and he has no fee and he makes your pain your gain, and Cas yelled, Bloody fucking hell, Nina. And she grabbed the phone, and yelled into it, Fuck off, you scum, leave her alone!

Then she yelled for Social Work Phil and she shouted at Nina and said, You never talk to those people, they're sharks, they'll rip you off. Please tell me he hasn't made you sign anything, has he? Please. Did you give him a verbal agreement? Nina!

And Nina hugged the knees because everyone is angry with Nina now and hummed the Yellow Brick Road.

Nina had to go in Social Work Phil's car with Cas but two male hacks ran after with flashes. Then it was roads and another grey building like a brick but with dark big windows and Nina had to wait and not worry on a plastic chair with thirty empty ones and a big box machine for coffee and tea.

The people called MARAC are the kindest because R stands for risk and A for assessment and they are everyone who Nina has ever met in Freedom and some more who know about Nina's case, but no hacks. And two Police, female and male went in to the special meeting room, and Doctor Webber and Charity Sonia and Support Worker Cas and Social Work Phil and the housing woman Amraine and Sheera who is an Independent Domestic Violence Advisor, and they were to all be inside for two hours and they would not come out of the room until they had made a package for Nina so that no accidents could ever happen again.

Nina was alone and nobody had given Nina food. Nina looked out of the thick windows and there was a street of many people walking, and all of them had their phones near their faces and sometimes they nearly bumped into each other and all looked a bit scared of each other but were all happy because it is progress.

Nina was glad to have the phone back from Cas because it had The Wizard of Oz film. Nina doesn't want to get to the end because then it will be over. So Nina listened again to when Dorothy put the water over the Wicked Witch and this made Nina feel better and turned into a steam and then the people sang the song.

Then it was over and time was still long and only one person walked past and they had a phone to their face and didn't smile. No birds came to the window no matter how much Nina tried.

Nina pushed the picture on the phone and had an idea. Nina typed Mao Zedong again and lots of pictures came up and one had birds in the sky and Chinese words. Nina thought that will cheer Nina up, so Nina touched the screen and it started. Nina held it close to make it secret. In the waiting room was only empty chairs and Comrade Chen had his spies in the sky trying to find Nina, so Nina hid the phone inside the coat.

In the phone the Chinese men in the past are out in the dusty fields and they bash their pans and the women wave their sheets and birds fly away from them into trees and then a man shoots them and some fly again. The woman's voice said it is called The Four Pests and Doctor Webber was right because Nina remembered when Chen bought the mousetraps and banned the birds from windows too.

The woman's voice said, The Four Pests Campaign was one of the first actions taken in the Great Leap Forward between 1958 and 1962. The Four Pests to be eradicated were rats, flies, mosquitos and sparrows. And Nina had never heard of two of these and put the hand at the mouth at the picture of a dying sparrow in dirt.

Then there are a hundred and then a thousand people all grey with caps on in a field and all have long poles and the Chinese voice said, We were so busy. The trees were very high and hard to shake but everyone did their best so the sparrows couldn't land and they flew and flew and some died from exhaustion.

Then two children with Mao scarves spring their catapults, then a small black bird fell from a tree. Then there were pictures of birds on their backs in the dust, twitching, and little children hit them with sticks and pans, and Nina bit the hand and couldn't look but Nina had to.

Then poor people walk in a line with dead sparrows threaded onto a rope and they hand them over to children with stars on their caps who sit behind a table covered in a thousand dead sparrows with big painted signs behind them and the voice says, The citizens who killed the most sparrows were given rewards. Then a line of hundreds comes and they all empty buckets filled with sparrow bodies into a huge tub and all are smiling and just children and they are handed cards with stars on. The voice says, Those who caught fewer were criticised. Then there are three people with a box as big as a washing machine and they dump it into a hole as big as a car and it is full of a hundred thousand dead sparrows.

Nina was sick and caught it in Nina's hand and wiped it on the back of the chair but no one came.

Nina could not move and stared and then there was the great famine that was caused because the killing of sparrows, the woman said, because there were no birds to eat the locusts and bugs and the next year insects came in a plague and wiped out the crops and thirty million people starved to death and there were pictures of skeletons in the dust and one was a baby lying in a road like a dead sparrow and it said it was the largest man-made disaster in the history of the world and all because Chairman Mao had made the most terrible mistake.

Nina felt the hole inside get very huge but could not cry.

The voice said this was the horrific outcome of human engineering on a mass scale and how Mao had to get Stalin to loan him ten million new birds to eat the bugs and they were sent by train. But even that failed because it was too late and poor people died from trying to eat grass and mud and they said Mao shut off the province of Sichuan and let the people starve and there was widespread cannibalism but no images remained because Mao shot the photographers and erased all trace.

But Nina still could not cry.

Then the voice said, Mao Zedong said that if it took 300 million deaths to bring about communism then he would kill 300 million people. The pictures ended and some words came up and they said, Communist genocide:

China: 65 million deaths
USSR: 20 million deaths
Vietnam: 1 million deaths
Cambodia: 2 million deaths
North Korea: 2 million deaths
Eastern Europe: 1 million deaths

This took the breathing from Nina but still it did not make Nina cry.

Then Nina looked out of the big windows and saw some birds far away flying in a pattern over a roof.

Nina went very small against the wall and closed the eyes but couldn't stop seeing pigeons on the roof and dead sparrows in the buckets of smiling children and a wetness came on the face, but it was not a proper cry.

And Nina knew then that Doctor Webber was correct. Nina had failed the last test and was broken and not human because dead birds make a tear come but not a single tear for a million dead Jenis.

Nina put the head in the corner to make it very tight because it was too much for one day. But it was only morning still and then Charity Sonia was walking slowly to Nina and all the others were leaving their meeting.

Charity Sonia's eyes stared and Nina had to take the head out of the corner and Charity Sonia's eyes were red and her face was full of things not to say, and a smile that was to be brave and Nina knows when this happens it means someone has died and you are just a child.

Charity Sonia drove her car and said, The decision of the MARAC wasn't unanimous but we'd need to bring in new evidence to overrule it. I'm sorry. Will you please stop chanting those numbers, please, Nina. And Nina said, Seventy-four, seventy-three, seventy-two but the magic of Doctor Webber had gone.

Charity Sonia said, Now I know you were scared of the Women's Hostel and you don't want to go back to the Hospital either, I don't want to take you back to square one.

And Nina thought Comrade Jeni died in Hospital and everything is happening again. And Nina will never have the skill to have empathy and no one will ever love Nina because Nina's only friends were pigeons.

And Charity Sonia said, Well, the new place the team have for you is very different.

Nina said, There is no radiation in the sky, there is no radiation in the sky, but Nina could feel it through the car window and Nina was getting worse and the magic of saying My current symptoms are just a conditioned response and they will lessen as I desensitise myself, wasn't working any more.

Charity Sonia said, I tried to argue your case, but after the Police report and Doctor Webber's results and this new incident, I couldn't overrule their vote. So we're trying another strategy. This is one of the best places in the city for people with complex needs, Nina. And Cas will be back to get you tomorrow to take you to see Uma, so just try it for one night and see how you fit in. OK?

Charity Sonia stopped the car after the longest time and Nina's fingers were numb and many pictures were stuck in Nina's head of the dead sparrows. Charity Sonia had a smile that looked sore and she said, Maybe I was wrong to try to segregate you as well and maybe if you're in with a mixed crowd of women and men with different abilities, you might make new friends but the main things is you'll be one hundred per cent safe now.

Charity Sonia opened the doors and said, Please just pick up your stuff and don't yell when we go in, just try to be.

And then she stopped and she said, Just come now and don't count out loud.

There was a little garden round the car park and small trees and flowers and a sound of birds because it was very far of a drive and a sign said Horizon House.

Nina didn't want to go to Horizon House and a bigger man of security was at the door and Nina went back in the middle of the road but a car came and Charity Sonia grabbed Nina hard and said, Enough! Come on! Please! And Nina said, No, but Charity Sonia wouldn't let go. Nina yelled. I hate you. But Sonia's grip was strong and the man of Security took Nina's other arm. And a voice yelled from inside Nina at Charity Sonia and it was like The Project and it shouted, Traitor!

Inside two locked metal doors there were women staring and Nina looked at the floor and counted in secret and Nina felt Charity Sonia's grip and she said, Here we are at reception, look it's nice and clean, we just wait here a minute.

And Nina looked and there were wall pictures of an old woman with a young woman helping her drink, and a brown-faced man and a woman was helping him walk and there was a child picture of a rainbow and the words on a sign said Care For Life and a smiling fat woman came and she said her name was Becca and she said, This must be Nina, we've heard so much about you. And her smile was wide but her eyes were small and looking Nina from hair to trainers, and she said, Thank you so much, Sonia, do you want to wait here, I know you're busy, we can take it from here. Then she said, Is this your only bag, Nina? I can carry that for you. But Nina gripped it tight and Nina made the eyes shoot at Charity Sonia the traitor who was going out the second door with the buzz lock and walking, and she said, Goodbye, Nina, but she did not turn back, then she was running with her hand to her face.

Horizon House Becca said, OK. Great, and she said to the woman behind the desk, A pass card for zone three please, then she said, we have it all prepared, see. Well, just follow me. And she slid the card into a plastic machine and the light went green and the third metal doors opened and she walked past a man in a chair with wheels and stripes and a tube in his nose and a woman with a head like a ball and she said, Just follow me, Nina, and we'll take care of you.

Nina followed Horizon House Becca and she said, There are men and women from diverse backgrounds and mixed abilities here and this is one of our care workers, Lisbit. And a woman with papers passed with a phone on her ear and then Horizon House Becca said, She's busy just now, and this room is our first meeting room and we meet with our clients here which means people with needs like yours and we like to talk about the special needs that you have and you'll have a meeting here with Lisbit later and you'll interact and talk about what services we can provide to suit your abilities.

Nina's body became very stiff and cold and walking was like going back into the time before.

Then Horizon House Becca put the card in another door and pushed beeping buttons and it buzzed and the doors opened and she said, No one who isn't staff is allowed in or out, so you've nothing to fear and we have special excursion days once a month, OK, Nina? By the way can you hand over your mobile phone please, that's also part of our security and this is our recreation room.

Nina looked and the windows were small and the chairs were

all of different kinds and covered with bright coloured rugs and pictures by children of many coloured huge faces. And Nina had the shiver feeling of no power, like Comrade Chen was making this happen too.

Nina saw through the window and there were three cars in the car park and one was Charity Sonia's not very far away and there were clouds in her car window and she was bent over as if to cough with her fingers in her eyes and her body shaking.

Horizon House Becca said, OK, well, I can see you're keen to get to your room, Nina. And she walked past other open doors and she said, This is the basic needs room, and you can get soap and a toothbrush and deodorant and tampons and conditioner, did you bring these things? No problem, they're all for free and you just sign in the book and take what you need. OK. You can come back and get what you need, after the tour.

Then she led Nina on past locked doors and Nina heard Doctor Webber say your brain is like a corridor with locked doors and Horizon House Becca said, All the doors are locked in the evening for privacy.

Horizon House Becca said, And through the back there are the specialist care clinics and we have a practice nurse, a pharmacist and a psychiatrist nurse on site twice a week. And this is the communal kitchen, and every client has the opportunity to cook and clean with plastic tools, nothing sharp, and there's CCTV here too, so you're safe at all times and for those who are able, there's a cleaning rota.

And Nina heard Comrade Uma saying these words to Comrade Zana.

And Nina saw three women in the kitchen and one had a mop like Uma and one had a rag tied round her neck and was being fed by another woman with a spoon and there was a picture on the wall of children in a sunset like the one with Chairman Mao and Nina felt a buzzing begin.

Then Horizon House Becca slid the plastic and a door beeped and Horizon House Becca said, OK, so now we're going to the client rooms, this is the ladies wing. Our clients like to share together so we have bunk beds. We also have special spaces for clients who're finding it hard to transition, so let's take a look at where you'll be sleeping, Nina, the ladies will be so happy to meet you, come on with me.

The door beeped and hissed and Nina had a smell of bleach and the sound of a woman yelling and running like a memory and Nina felt dizzy and had to stop after walking past three doors, all like copies of the same doors and all full of women sitting on beds and staring back and a woman with arm sores like Comrade Zana had and food on her sweatshirt and pictures coming of strings of dead birds, one after another after another. And Horizon House Becca was talking and smiling and Nina couldn't breathe and Horizon House Becca said, OK, Nina, here's your room, you'll be sharing with Tina and Amira and, sorry what was your name again, and then a woman spoke from inside, and Horizon House Becca turned and said, Halina. Halina has been with us nine months and today she went on her first excursion to a shop, isn't that right, Halina?

Nina put the arm out because of not breathing and Horizon House Becca said, Are you all right, Nina? And Nina looked past and saw one woman hitting herself in the head again and again and another with a picture in her skin of her face in a spider web and one had the hair of Jeni but grey and a T-shirt with a picture of Comrade Guevara and Nina fell down and hugged the knees and Uma touched her and Nina said, Stay away. And Nina lay the head on the ground and rocked back and forwards and Horizon House Becca called to a beeping machine, saying, We need assistance in section 3C, and Nina was going down the steps and Jeni whispered, there's not much time if we're going to run, and Nina was counting ninety-nine, ninety-eight, ninety-seven and Doctor

Webber was right, you don't pass out and you don't die, but the shivering doesn't stop and the choking and you can't leave the basement because all of the doors have gone. And you think you are out of the basement but the basement is everywhere.

They made Nina take a blue pill and it made Nina feel floppy for a sleep but Nina still couldn't go into the room with the staring women so when Nina stopped scratching and hitting Nina was allowed to go to a quiet place and it was called the observation room.

Nina lay on the ground until the breathing came and there was a camera on a stick like at Doctor Kohli's, not pointed at Nina, but at the toy area. And there were red and yellow balls and one was a doll of a girl and another was a shrunken house but Nina had not heard or seen any children anywhere. And a table like at Doctor Webber's with a mirror wall.

They had gone a long time and Nina got up and touched the pocket alone and felt the newest jotter inside and Nina knew what was wrong most of all. Nina needed to make a new diary page. It had been too long and that's why everything had become incorrect.

Nina crept out for a place to write and the corridor was empty but a roof eyeball looked down and Nina went fast to the doors and tried them but they were all locked and Nina hid from noise of women together then found a door with a picture of a woman on it and under it said Staff Only.

Nina was in a room of desks and Nina took the far one and sat and there was still the pencil in Nina's joggy bottoms and Nina took out the jotter and it was nearly full.

Nina repeated the words over and more pain came. Mother. Uma. Uma. Mum.

But no tears came and no I and Nina was still Nina.

Then Nina stood up and looked round and Nina saw a sign in a frame with a gold star and it said:

> Horizon House has four-star accreditation under the Golden Standards Framework, offering high quality residential care services in the following specialist categories: Asperger Syndrome – Challenging Behaviour – Drug Dependence – Epilepsy – Head/Brain Injury – Profound & Multiple Learning Difficulties – Speech Impairment – Stroke – Schizophrenia – End of Life Care. Staff and managers pride themselves in keeping staff and residents happy, motivated and feeling loved.

And Nina made a shiver because the toys in Horizon House are not for children but grown-ups with child minds and Nina must be in a big mistake.

Then Nina was out in the second corridor looking for a door to get out but Horizon House Becca came fast with a man of security and said, There you are, Nina, we've been looking all over, where did you get to? And Nina said, I need to speak to Charity Sonia, and tell her this is a mistake and Nina needs to go, please. And Horizon House Becca said, Well, we're just trying to get settled for the night, how are you feeling after your pill, are you calmer now, we're just serving ice cream and jelly.

And Nina said, Please, Nina has to go to Jail, now. Nina has to speak to Comrade Uma. And Horizon House Becca put her hand on Nina's arm and said, You won't be going to any Jail, Nina, and don't you worry, there are no Comrades anywhere, you're safe here now and there's no rush to do anything or go anywhere. You've been very unwell and it's important that all you do from now on is rest.

Jotter #73 2003

Nina heard the downstairs door lock and had to put the secret wood back in the window very quick. Nina kept a little crack to peer out and glimpsed a shadow going out into the night lane and prayed it wasn't Comrade Chen. Nina went cold and hoped very much he wouldn't look back and see the wood moving or Nina's crack of light or find Nina's secret paper messages. Nina waited for the longest time and then heard footsteps creeping on the stairs and Nina hid in the corner. The wood cover over the door moved and there was the sound of the heavy boxes being lifted and Nina called out, I am deeply sorry Comrade Chen, forgive me.

Comrade Ruth's shaved head came through the door and she had only T-shirt and pants. Comrade Ruth said, Stop hiding, are you in that damn corner again?

Comrade Ruth was very tense. She would not stand or sit still. She said, You have been very foolish, I found this, and she handed Nina the paper aeroplane letter and it had mud on it.

Nina couldn't speak and stayed under the sink.

Comrade Ruth read from it, Dear man or old bird lady, please come, I am in the window and they have locked me in the Collective. I do not know the number or the name of the street, but I can wave and then you will know what to do.

Comrade Ruth shook her head and said, You're fucking lucky I found this and not the bin men or the Pigs. You have no bloody idea, do you?

Comrade Ruth stared at Nina very hard. She had just shaved her head again and it was like a ball with no bristles and the white scar bump. She smelled of bleach.

Comrade Ruth scrunched up the paper and said, If Chen had found this.

Nina stared at the paper ball on the floor. Comrade Ruth said, You think you're safe, do you? You've no birth certificate. No national insurance number or passport. Do you know how easy it would be to make you disappear? Huh?

Comrade Ruth muttered, So like your fucking mother.

Nina asked, What do you mean. Who is she?

Comrade Ruth stood and checked the door. She said, Look, I know this is hard but I have to ask you something personal.

Nina told her the personal is political, just in case it was a test.

Comrade Ruth whispered, Forget that. What I need to know is. And she stopped. Has he touched you?

Nina shrugged because Nina didn't know where on the body and was embarrassed. Comrade Ruth said, I don't mean hitting you with the spoon or the ruler or grabbing your hair, I mean. And she stopped.

Nina said, Do you mean like on the chest and the vagina and other private property places?

Comrade Ruth nodded and said, Keep your voice down.

Nina said, Do you mean like he makes Comrade Zana do on her knees and Comrade Uma and then you in the mouth.

Comrade Ruth put her head in her hands. She said, You saw that?

Nina said, Only one time but I heard it through the wall another two times and I knew it was you because the crying noise was different.

Comrade Ruth's face was red. She said, You'd think we'd stick up for each other wouldn't you. But every time it happens to one of the others we tell ourselves, at least it's not me, let him take my sister instead. Let him take Zana I think. I want them to suffer in my place. It's sick. Disgusting even thinking these things.

Comrade Ruth looked hard at Nina. She said, I'm sorry.

She took Nina's hand and put it on her chest. She said, Next time, when he touches your breast tell yourself, this is not me, this is a bag of fat. Feel it.

Nina felt it.

Comrade Ruth said, These are not for men's pleasure. Understand. Below, feel the ribs. The ribs are the skeleton. Think of your skeleton when he touches you. It won't even be yours any more.

Comrade Ruth moved Nina's hand to her belly. She said, Inside here are the small intestines and the ovaries and the womb, a man will get pleasure from putting his penis inside and moving back and forwards. After a hundred moves he will ejaculate his seed and fertilise a woman's eggs. When Chen does this to you, think of dead animals. This is how you survive, you cut off from all feeling. You picture your body as the skeleton it will be one day. You tell yourself, You sick fool, thinking you can cheat death, you're fucking a corpse. You look at his face as he gets lost in his own pleasure and you make yourself see the bone structure of his skull and remind yourself, every skull has the same smile. You may think you are fucking me but there is no Me. There is, in the end, just bones. Do you understand? Next time he violates you, think of him like that and you'll get through it, then after, you and me and maybe the others, we'll work out how to put a stop to this for good.

Nina began shivering, because of too many pictures of skeletons and deserts.

Comrade Ruth knelt beside Nina, took Nina's head from Nina's hands and put her arm around Nina's back. Comrade Ruth said, I know I've not been a good friend to you, but I swear, if he's touched you, I'll stab him.

Nina saw a picture of blood and a knife and was breathing fast, so as not to vomit.

Comrade Ruth said, So tell me, how many times has he touched you and where on your body?

Nina was so confused. Nina shook the head and said, Never.

Comrade Ruth said, Don't be shy. It's not your fault if he rapes you.

Nina shook the head and said, Never, he hasn't done it to me, ever. No times.

Comrade Ruth said, Not once?

Nina shook the head and said, Nothing. Never. Not even kissed me any more on the nose when I want him to.

Comrade Ruth said, Comrade Zana is pregnant. Do you understand what that means?

Nina nodded then shook her head.

Comrade Ruth said, I need you to tell me if Chen raped you. Why was your shirt torn the other day?

Nina said, No, he hasn't touched me, he only hits me with the ruler, he wouldn't put his thing in me.

Comrade Ruth said, Is that the truth? And her eyes turned away.

Nina said, You think I'm just saying no, so I can be better than the rest of you?

Comrade Ruth said, You are sure he's not done anything to you, when you're asleep even?

Nina told her, Of course I am sure.

Comrade Ruth stood and looked confused and went silent. She said, Why the fuck? She rubbed her bare skull. Finally she said like it was an answer to a secret question, Uma.

Nina said, What about Uma?

Comrade Ruth muttered, So many fucking secrets in this place. Never mind. And she got up and she looked angry.

Nina said, What, please tell me, was it about me or Uma or who?

But Comrade Ruth was already at the door with the keys, whispering, Shut up. Keep quiet and don't tell anyone about any of this. Promise me.

Nina nodded and Comrade Ruth locked the door behind her, and put the big wood and heavy boxes back over it to hide it again, leaving Nina in a long quiet time.

Nina was sad for Comrade Ruth again that night because Nina heard Comrade Chen's thumping feet return then later Comrade Ruth moaning and crying through the walls. Nina knows Comrade Ruth did not fight but submitted, because Comrade Ruth knows she is middle class and privileged and is guilty and needs to be re-educated.

Plus Comrade Ruth forgot to empty the pee bucket.

Nina moved everything around. The lamp and the table and the chair and the picture frame and the plastic plant and the bleach, to make it like a different room. Then the bed too, but then worried about them finding the little wall hole and all the paper birds under the bed. So Nina moved the bed back and counted the paper birds and there were three hundred and seventy-one and that must have been like the days.

Nina pretended Nina was sick by rubbing the head skin very hard to make it feel hot and by putting dust from behind the bed up my nose to make it sneeze. Nina put fingers in Nina's throat and made vomit come and made sure it was smeared on my sweatshirt when Comrade Zana came with the rice.

Comrade Zana said Nina had the flu and it was contagious.

This was very cunning of Nina as they gave some pills and some slices of lemons for vitamin C which Comrade Uma cut up with a knife. Comrade Uma said we can't come back for two days until you're not contagious any more and seemed glad Nina was sick because she stroked Nina's hair and had that sad face of hers. And when Nina had her eyes closed Nina took the knife and Nina tried to give Comrade Uma a hug, but she ran away and forgot all about the knife then. Nina thinks Comrade Uma is a silly weak person and she wants to make other people as sick as she is. Weak people can't rise up, so they want to bring everyone else down.

Nina listened very carefully at the door for the sound of Comrade Chen going out because he has to work at the cash and carrying place now like a slave because the revolution didn't come and they have changed the rules for the dole. Nina lifted the wood off the window then Nina took out the knife and put it in the sides of the window to wiggle it free so that Nina can get more than just a hand out and push it up higher. The old white paint made it stick and Nina scraped it thirty times and little bits came off and a cut on the finger came.

Then the window was a bit more loose. And Nina put a whole hand out, all the way to the elbow. Then the thing happened.

Nina saw something moving and it was the old fascist bird feeding lady with a hunchback and a black bag that made a sound of bottles near the bins and she was staring up but not at Nina no matter how hard Nina waved but at something in the sky.

Nina went to shout but got afraid because if any Comrades saw the woman staring they would guess that Nina was at the window and say Halt, Comrade, you are trying to escape.

So Nina stopped and put the flat wood back and picked up the hundred and two bits of white paint and hid them with the knife inside the plant pot underneath the plastic flower. Nina sat on the bed and breathed and waited for one of the Comrades to come up the stairs and punish Nina with the ruler.

But no one came. Nina took the wood down again and looked out at the lane of escape. Nina looked to find the place the fascist men of bins come from, but it was hard to tell in the daytime and nobody came.

Nina forgot the finger blood and puke smell and Nina counted seventy-two windows and saw metal dishes fastened to wires for catching radiation from the sky and every third window had one and the dishes must follow you and zap you if you try to escape. Nina took a breath and tried to look for things that proved that Chen had lied and this is what Nina discovered.

Some of the faraway windows are like Nina's window and have wood on them and no glass and some have flat metal on them so there must be other women locked inside. Nina counted twenty-seven windows boarded up. Nina had no idea there were so many other collectives. There was also a very high building above the roofs and it was like one big flat brick but giant and many of its windows had sky in them. Some of the walls were covered in writings like Zana tattoos but they weren't pictures or words apart from one that said A with a circle round it. Then Nina saw the pigeons again at black bin bags and Nina got excited.

Nina had never ever looked for so long at the outside in the light of day. But the bright was too hard and Nina was getting radiation burns from all the wires.

Nina heard feet coming and Nina's eyes were very sore, but it added to the effect of being sick. Comrade Zana unlocked the door and Nina got the flat wood back on the window just in time but couldn't make it all the way back to the bed so Nina lay on the floor and pretended to be dead like a bird. Comrade Zana shouted for help and Comrade Uma came to feel Nina's head and to take away the poo bucket and to whisper, What have we done to you? Then we were alone and Comrade Uma said, I'm sorry, I'm sorry but then she locked the door again anyway, so she was not really sorry and only crying for herself. And Nina didn't care anyway because Nina had to get back to window looking.

—

When Nina woke and took the board down the high brick tower had vanished because it was blackness.

Nina waited and every time a light came on in the building over there Nina got a buzz, but never saw anyone at a window. Then the light went on in a yellow room. Nina touched the cold glass and saw a faraway man throw down his coat and he drank from a can.

Nina waved to him. He couldn't see Nina because Nina was stupid and in the dark, so Nina put the lamp on and ran back to see him but he didn't look up. Nina waved again and he looked down at something not up.

Nina pushed the window up all the way and the air was cold but there was nothing Nina could do just with one whole arm out. Then Nina had an idea, like when Dorothy oiled the Tin Man.

Nina took the lamp and pulled the wire and it almost reached all the way and Nina shone it out to the man's direction. Then Nina turned it off, then on, then off then on like a fire then waited.

The man looked up. Then Nina flashed again.

He leaned close to his window and put his hand up to look out and it made Nina breathe very fast and the chest very empty and full feeling at the same time.

He looked out but all he would see was the light so Nina turned it up to the face to show him and Nina had made it go off and on off and on.

The far window man kept on drinking with another can and turned away. But Nina hopes he has seen me. He must have. This is what the voice said as Nina hid with the light off behind the curtain and was happy.

He will come and break Nina's window and protect from the radiation when we climb down and run. This is Nina's plan and having this is the best private property of all.

—

Nina had to sleep all day and it made it better for pretending to have flu. Nina was excited and Nina made a sign on paper that said Help Me with crayons and had feelings of flying in the whirlwind out of Kansas. Then Nina thought the words were incorrect so did another and listening at the door just in case Comrades came and sometimes Nina made a cough noise to make them fear contagion. Nina did a sign that said, Rescue Me, then Nina thought Hello would be better first, then one that said Come Here and an X because it also means kiss. Then Nina waited for the night time and there was much time so Nina wrote and is writing.

Nina is waiting now.

The Project is very sorry. The Project must write a full confession. The Project jeopardised the safety of the entire Collective and the future of communism. The Project is sick in the mind from ideological contamination from looking outside.

The Project lied to all Comrades about sickness and said, Please let me sleep, the flu is much worse, then after Comrade Uma went away, The Project took the sweatshirt off to be more appealing and got the lamp ready on the table by the window and went to take down the window board. The Project has been conspiring against Comrade Chen and all other Comrades for weeks and in thoughts for a year.

The Project is grateful that foolish Nina dropped the board of wood and that Nina screamed and alerted Comrade Chen to the attempt at sabotage from within.

The Project confesses to being found with not all clothes on and with signs of paper on the floor made with the intention to alert the authorities and to betray. The Project confesses to desiring male attention and of making hidden diaries with forbidden words to overthrow the peaceful Collective. The Project confesses that she hates Comrades Zana, Ruth and Uma and that she wishes Comrade Chen to be dead like Comrade Jeni who The

Project cannot erase. The Project was found with a secret diary of the traitor who calls herself Nina.

The Project asks to be punished by slaps of the ruler on the wrist and fingers and buttocks but please not the face again. The Project admits to saying terrible things to Comrade Chen when he bashed into The Project's room in the middle of the night and caught The Project with red hands.

The Project confesses to fighting on the floor with Comrade Chen, and screaming when Comrade Chen said, Put your top on. What the hell are you doing?

The Project confesses that when Comrade Chen saw the three other Comrades at the door all with faces of fear that The Project was very afraid when Comrade Chen shouted at them to leave with The Project and he slammed the door.

The Project confesses that she thought Comrade Chen was going to touch her breasts as The Project has seen through keyholes and doors left a bit open. The Project feared that Comrade Chen was going to make The Project go on knees and that he would open his trousers like to take a pee but then to make The Project move her head on it fast like The Project has seen him make other Comrades do.

The Project confesses that she went down on her knees and said, OK, I will do it, Comrade Chen, please forgive me, and closed the eyes and opened the mouth and waited. The Project admits that The Project was confused when Comrade Chen said, No! Get up. What are you thinking, please, cover yourself up.

The Project confesses to using reactionary female techniques of manipulation to try to make Comrade Chen feel bad, when The Project said, Why not me? Why do you make all the other women do it but not me? Put it in then you won't hate me any more.

The Project confesses to being scared when Comrade Chen stared hard and then suddenly cried. The Project has never seen Comrade Chen cry before. And he made a hollow sound. The

Project tried to calm him and said, It's OK, you can put it in and it will be over quick, and I can show you I am sorry and will obey you from now on then we can all be equals.

The Project confesses to being scared when Comrade Chen said, Never, I could never. Christ, you have no idea what you're saying.

And The Project said, But that's favouritism. That's why the other Comrades don't like me any more. Why won't you do it to me? I want you to.

The Project confesses to feeling a strange feeling then, because Comrade Chen shouted, Never, my God, what are you? And seeing a look of great terror on his face. And he said, What the hell have we done to you?

The Project tried to touch him but he said, Take your hands off me. Then he tried to get out of the door fast but it was jammed and he was scared of The Project and he yelled, Let me out! And was like a scared child.

The Project is very sorry to have become so evil and repulsive and doesn't understand. A re-education of the greatest severity must be given to The Project and The Project accepts this gratefully but please not to be locked in the basement because it made Comrade Jeni mad and dead and it is not true that The Project is like Comrade Jeni in many ways.

The Project doesn't know how many days ago it was. The Project had nights and days without sleeping and being sick when trying to eat. The Project reports that Comrade Ruth came to the room and locked herself in and said to whisper only. The Project told her to stay away or I would stab her but The Project only had a pencil. She held The Project's hands and said, Listen, listen, listen, things are very bad. You have a choice, you have to be quick. Chen is going to lock you in the basement. It is decided. He's out at Pound Stretcher right now. You can run now, or he'll do it. He's buying locks and a chain. Please, Nina, go now.

The Project said, But where will I go?

Comrade Ruth said, I don't know, anywhere.

The Project said, Will you come with me and show me how?

Comrade Ruth shook her head.

The Project submits this report to Comrade Chen and hopes this will make him not angry with The Project any more. The Project accepts being in the basement now and hopes that Comrade Chen will talk to The Project again and not say, Keep her away from me, I never want to see her again. The Project will erase that The Project heard him weep, It's over, I've failed, I've failed you all. The Project hopes that one day he will tell The Project what The Project has done wrong for all of life and promises that The Project can be a good experiment again and not a failure that makes everyone even Comrade Uma so ashamed.

Jotter #244 2018

Nina has learned many things of the tricks of Charity Sonia and her conspirators. Nina was awake at five a.m. and Nina was told by the man of Security that Nina cannot walk in the car park or walk to a park or leave Horizon House at all. He won't ever let Nina out unless someone in authority signs for Nina and this made Nina angry and Nina sat at the door and said, You are a fascist and Nina will never grow new doors in the brain now! And Nina refused to eat breakfast or to lie down or to reply to Horizon House Becca who has the teeth smile of the Capitalist wolf.

Nina was angry with Charity Sonia when she came at ten minutes past nine because Nina will only be allowed to be in freedom for three hours this one time before being locked back up again forever. Nina refused to speak to Charity Sonia in the car because of her lies or to hear lies from stupid Comrade Uma in her jail. Nina wanted to slap Charity Sonia when she was driving and then to kiss her hand and beg for forgiveness but you cannot do either.

Charity Sonia said, Nina, please, I know you're very angry but please try to trust me, I can see how much you hate it there but

I'm doing my best to get you a place that's more flexible. I'm also trying to get you a second psychiatric assessment so I can launch an appeal. But look, today I'm really hoping what Uma has to tell you will help and that the Police will drop you from their investigation. Because part of the reason the committee had you sectioned.

And then she stopped.

Nina said, What is sectioned?

Charity Sonia chewed her lip and said, Well, it means you've been detained under the Mental Health Act, Nina, because they made a mistake, the Doctors and the Police and Phil, and they think you're a risk to yourself and others, but you have to know, Nina, I fought really hard against them but I was overruled.

Nina looked at the road. Charity Sonia says Nina's name too often, like No Fee Pendergast did. Charity Sonia wants Nina to forgive her for having good intentions. Mao Zedong had good intentions and he killed 65 million people and some had to eat each other. People try to hide dead bodies by telling you they had ideals.

Charity Sonia tried to make a happy face to make Nina trust her again and she said, But aren't you excited to hear what Uma has to say, Nina? Maybe it'll help you get better, remember what the Doctor said.

Nina had the churning inside and burps and Nina asked for another calming pill and slept nearly all the way of stops and starts of green lights and red in the stupid Charity car for forty-two minutes because the jail of Comrade Uma is far away, just like Nina feels from Charity Sonia.

The female Police took Nina and Charity Sonia through many doors with beeps and locks and she said Nina had no obligation to speak to Comrade Uma but that the Police were very grateful that Nina had agreed and she said, If you, for any reason, don't want to listen to Uma or you hit her or cancel this meeting, Uma will not give that evidence. So, please do not strike her, do not use a pencil as a weapon. Do not in any way jeopardise this meeting. This crucial evidence may be what we need to present to the CPS to prosecute Chen. If we can get a conviction, that may in the long run be in your interests, should you choose to file a civil compensation case once he is convicted.

Then she stopped at a metal door and Nina couldn't look in her face and she said very quietly, Just to let you know, there's been a substantial amount of counter-evidence this last week as a second member of the Collective has now come forward to defend Chen.

Charity Sonia said, No! As well as Ruth? Is it Zana?

The female Police nodded and said, Yes, she handed herself in, she's claiming that Chen saved her life and that your witness is making false claims for cash.

Charity Sonia swore.

The female Police said, So you see, if for any reason, due to anything you might do or say in there, Uma changes her mind and refuses to testify, then Chen could walk free. Do you understand, Nina? Please nod if you do.

Nina nodded to the female Police and she said, No physical contact and no whispering because it is all being recorded and if you cry someone will bring you a tissue box.

And Nina thought it was rude to be told how to talk to the person who taught you how to sing and smile and fold swans for twenty years. The Police had incorrect ideas of Comrade Uma so Nina decided they would be Pigs forever now.

Then Nina and Charity Sonia were led down echo corridors past many locked doors and Charity Sonia walked behind and then into a room and it did not have metal bars like San Quentin in National Geographic but was just like the canteen in the Charity Office but with green walls and small windows high up and seven empty tables and fourteen red seats and on one was sat Comrade Uma in a sweatshirt that was too big and behind her was a woman who was called Solicitor Ellen and a male Pig standing and another Pig woman sitting.

Comrade Uma didn't look like a comrade any more but just a small old woman.

The sight of little Uma made feeling come and Nina said, I'm sorry, Uma, and wanted to run and hug her. But a male Pig held Nina back and Nina could see wet in Uma's eyes but Uma was smiling. Nina said, Is it OK if I just call you Uma now, because we are on the outside and there are no Comrades left here. And Uma nodded and her smile was the same as her tears and she said, I'm so glad you're safe, Nina, I was so worried.

Nina said, Why are you so shrunk, Uma, like a doll of yourself? And Uma said, Maybe it is just a big room, Nina. You must have been in lots of new rooms, I hope they've not scared you too much.

Nina said sorry for being so far away even though Nina was so close that Nina could just reach and touch her as Nina sat down, but the male Pig said, No contact please. Charity Sonia nodded and she stayed very far away with a female Pig.

Solicitor Ellen said she would sometimes speak on behalf of Uma and the next male Pig pushed a button on the black machine on the table and said, Time is eleven fifty-two and he said the names of everyone and said that all were present and said, Recording.

Nina sat at the Uma table. Nina just stared down at Nina's bad hand in the shadow underneath and up at Uma's face, then Nina had a hundred questions and they spun too fast. And then Comrade Uma's eyes got wider and Nina knew Uma was going to keep crying.

Please, Uma said. Can't I just hold her hand? Please, Nina is scared.

Solicitor Ellen whispered to the first Pig and then he nodded and said, If it's all right with Nina. And Nina nodded.

Uma's hand was out and it was so thin and wrinkled but the

grip was strong and Nina felt the empty growing inside like a warning.

Uma said, So, Nina, I thought about you all the time out in the world. I know you must be very, very confused and scared and many of the things they've said in the newspapers about you and me and Chen, they are lies. Like one said I was your mother, now, I want you to know that that's not true.

Nina said OK, and the empty got bigger because if Nina was ever to have a mother it would be best if it was Uma.

Then Uma cried all alone but her hand squeezed very tight across the table. Then Uma whispered, OK, Nina, listen to me please and try to understand. I had myself arrested so I could find you again and tell you the truth. Will you stay focused on what I'm saying? Will you write it all down afterwards? Will you promise not to judge me?

Nina felt a coldness coming but nodded and Uma said, You remember Jeni, then she coughed and her body shook, then she started again and said, When Comrade Jeni first joined the Collective, before you were born, I was not pleased. I thought she was a foolish, immature girl, a decadent. Comrade Ruth called her a Guru Groupie. She was not like us, she was rich, her father was in business, a millionaire and doing deals with the Saudis, and I said to Chen, You know it is always like this, the spoiled daughters of the rich, she is taking drugs and on the pill and now she wants to play at soldiers, this is all just a game to her, she is not a true revolutionary. She'll go back to the upper class when she thinks the adventure is over and she will betray us.

Nina had the hollow, like someone was scraping Nina out. And a metal taste in the mouth came.

Uma said, But Chen told me we needed Jeni's money, he said, it was good to steal money from the capitalist Pigs and use it for the revolution. We would exploit the exploiter class he said, and use Jeni.

Uma held Nina's hand tight and Uma's skin looked yellow and her bones showed through the tightness as she squeezed.

Uma said, After just a short while I knew something was going on. Jeni brought many men into the Collective, runaways, drop-outs and drug dealers too and I was very against their ways. These people were promiscuous, they said sex was liberation. There were thirty in the Collective then and she was always having sex with the men, I told Comrade Chen, we cannot have this place turn into a brothel.

Nina wanted to stop listening now or Nina would be too hollow but Uma's hand gripped tighter.

Uma said, Jeni was loud and she used to wear those big kaftans and capes, she hid it from us at first and maybe even from herself, she had been doing a lot of drugs maybe she thought the baby would never carry to full term.

Nina felt a bad thing coming and Uma said, Yes, Jeni was pregnant.

Uma said, Maybe she was confused. It was a very strong belief in the Collective that no one should reproduce, that it would get in the way of our revolutionary work, and that this was no world to bring a child into. At that time, we told ourselves the nuclear family must be destroyed, that overpopulation was destroying the planet. It was said we should be throwing bombs not changing nappies. It was agreed that any woman who fell pregnant in the Collective was being inconsiderate and selfish. I myself had a termination to keep to these rules.

Uma's hand felt wet and Nina could feel Uma's pulse.

Uma said, There were thirteen million abortions a year in China at that time.

Nina's hollow feeling shifted and started to ache.

Uma said, In truth, I would have loved to have had a baby, just one, not many, but the Comrades said this would make me an enemy of progress.

Nina felt a stab in the belly and watched Uma's eyes but they had gone far away.

Uma said, Jeni ran away for months. But she had nowhere else to go, and we were the only place she could come back to. Maybe we should have pushed her away back then, maybe I was weak and Chen was too generous, but she was heavily pregnant, you see, and it was just days before she went into labour. She was laid out, on the table in the kitchen. It was a long and difficult labour but Comrade Chen forbade the Hospital of course, no doctors. The umbilical cord was tangled round the baby's neck. I didn't know what I was doing but I put my hand inside her and pulled out the baby and I cut the cord from round her neck. I brought you into the world.

A shock went through Nina. Nina couldn't speak. Nina touched the neck and felt the eyes of Charity Sonia from the back wall and the Pigs, all on Nina.

Nina pulled away the hand and Uma's face was emptied. Uma said, Please, Nina, I know this is hard to take in. I know we are being watched and I know you have lots of questions now, but just whisper to me and I will say yes or no. OK? Just ask me.

And Nina said, Why are you lying? Jeni was not my mother.

Uma said, Yes, she was. I swear on my life.

Nina shouted, Lies, bourgeois lies. Why are they coming from your mouth?

Uma said, You can't see it, can you?

Nina shouted to Charity Sonia and the Pigs, Don't listen to her. Uma is a liar.

Uma said, You look so like her now.

Nina put fingers in the ears but Uma's voice was too strong and she said, She must have been the same age as you when she first came to the Collective. You have her eyes, her hair, her mouth.

Nina yelled, Lies, lies!

Uma's face was red. Uma said, Please let me tell you it all,

Nina, let me finish my self-criticism. There are things that are much worse.

All the Pig faces around Nina looked to each other. Nina felt cold and shivery.

Uma said, I am sorry, but I wanted her and you gone. I hated you, little one. Because she was allowed to have a baby and I was not. And the things she said. She said the baby was Comrade Chen's. That he loved her more than me and all of it was lies. Chen was mine, like a husband. I know all possession is bad, people are not objects to be owned and I told myself this day after day.

Nina felt a stab of cold. Nina said, So Chen is my father?

Uma said, No, that was what Jeni said, but it was almost certainly a lie. Jeni had no idea who your father really was, a drummer or a squatter. He was most likely a drug dealer from Brixton who she often slept with in exchange for weed. She said it was Chen just to manipulate us. To make Comrade Chen feel guilty and sorry for her.

Nina needed it to stop.

Uma said, Chen saw the fighting between me and Jeni and I said that you must be put up for adoption, but he decided that we would keep you. He said that every Comrade should share the burden and be your parent. Chen is such a noble man. You have no idea how much he has sacrificed for us all. He wanted to save you. When you were older, I went along with that lie, to make him think he was your father so he wouldn't touch you. I know this is hard, Nina, and I am sorry that we lied to you for so long, but please, please listen.

Nina had sickness in the throat and the female Pig said, Are you all right, Nina? Do you want to stop? But Nina swallowed and shook the head.

Uma said, One day, Nina, when you were very tiny, you were in your cot and your mother was talking to the neighbours, breaking the rules, flirting with some man, she disgusted me. She was not fit to be a mother. She'd go off and leave you for days on end. It was me that cleaned you and bottle-fed you. I put you to bed, held you to my breast, you even started calling me mama.

And Uma got to her feet to reach for Nina but Nina stepped back and Nina's chair fell with a bang and Nina said, This is all lies. I have no mother. My mother died in the revolution.

And Pigs stepped in to restrain Uma and pushed Uma back down into her chair. Then Uma breathed and nodded to Solicitor Ellen and Solicitor Ellen went into a bag and took out a plastic thing and she said to the Pigs, As per our agreement, Uma would now like to provide the substantiating evidence.

She took a piece of paper out and Nina recognised it because of the writing and it was The Project's. And Nina felt anger filling up the hollow.

Solicitor Ellen said, This is written evidence that shows that my client accepts full responsibility for the death of Genevieve Lamberton. With this evidence she exonerates Comrade Chen and asks that all further charges against Comrade Chen be dropped and that Nina be released from all further investigations. The evidence demonstrates that Nina knew nothing of the events around the death of Genevieve Lamberton, and neither saw anything or acted in any way that contributed to her death. Uma takes full responsibility. And volunteers a confession of culpable homicide.

And solicitor Ellen pushed the page of the diary forward on the table towards Nina and Nina stared at Uma because Uma had become the worst of all traitors.

Nina couldn't touch the page. It was old and dirty and evil and torn with many words rubbed out. Nina remembered the diary it came from and Nina felt hot in the head. Uma said, Please, Nina, read it. You must stop blaming yourself. I know we damaged you. I did.

Then Uma spoke to the Pigs and Solicitor Ellen and she said, Nina became very disorientated after Jeni died, caught in a loop, she kept saying over and over that she killed Jeni. We tried to erase that. This was the start of Nina's mental problems. This was all my fault too.

Then Uma spoke to Nina and said, I'm sorry, Nina. I know you don't want to know it, but trying to protect you from the truth has caused you so much damage already. Maybe once you know it you can heal. I hope you can.

Then she made a big breath and said, I killed your mother, Nina. When she overdosed I was supposed to take her to the Hospital, but I was so scared. I think she died because no one found her in time. Please, read it.

Nina was scared. All the pages of those diaries were burned by Comrade Chen. It was a ghost page. Not real.

A Pig leaned in and said, The suspect has submitted a piece of torn paper, from a diary. Filing as evidence nine B. And he took out a plastic bag and picked up the page and Uma yelled, Take your hands off it, it's for Nina only, she has to read it first. Nina, there are other diaries too, Nina, remember, I saved some and your pages.

Nina watched and little Uma struggled in the grip of the Pigs and she kicked them, screaming, Pigs, fucking Pigs. Uma was dragged away and she yelled back,

I'm sorry, Nina, I'm sorry.

There were echoes then quiet then Charity Sonia came and touched Nina's shoulder and she said, Are you OK, Nina? And a male Pig took the page and said, Copies will be made now and made available to all involved. Thank you.

Nina stared at the empty room where Uma had been, and the chair she had knocked over, on its side on the floor. Then another Pig picked it up and put it back at the table to make it look like nothing had ever happened and then it was just Nina breathing.

—

In the long grey corridor Charity Sonia kept saying, Nina, you must be in a state of shock. She said, Your fists are clenched so tight, Nina, here, please take a Beta blocker.

And Charity Sonia took two for herself and gave one to Nina and a Pig got a cup of water but Nina couldn't swallow.

It was all too much for one day but then they got a room for Nina to be alone with the photocopy. Nina had to sit and shiver with one black table and one bright light and three chairs and grey walls and one mirror and one camera and a metal smell. Nina felt like The Project was watching from the corner and The Project said, Don't read it. It is lies. Erase it. Eat it.

Nina had to confirm the page was real and true. The photocopy didn't feel right. It had a picture of the torn edge but it didn't feel like the torn edge but Nina knew it came from the diaries of the number 60s because of all the rubbing-out and Nina remembered that Comrade Ruth had torn out many pages, so Uma must have stolen and hidden them, for seventeen years.

Nina knew Uma must have been brainwashed by the Pigs and made to say false and cruel things. Nina said over and over, Uma did not kill Nina's mother. Jeni was not Nina's mother.

Nina saw all the forbidden words and was tight inside and it said,

> Comrade Jeni was in The Project's special attic. Comrade Jeni is still unwell and should have been in the basement with cold Turkey. Comrade Jeni is so selfish, why does she think she is allowed to do nothing but be depressed while others slave for her. Comrade Jeni was not wearing proper clothes and she had bruises on her face and her chest was showing and The Project felt sick in the belly for her. Her hair with some bits missing stinks like soup and her breath was sweet like sick and she kept begging for The Project to take her hand and made The Project afraid.

This is The Project's tenth report and The Project has to erase Comrade Jeni because Comrade Jeni is dead now. The Project can't stop thinking of Comrade Jeni and the window and the shouting. There were birds flapping, then Jeni grabbed at The Project. Then Comrade Uma yelled and pushed and Comrade Jeni fell back. Then The Project saw Jeni outside lying on the ground far below in pigeon poo. The Project did something bad and it must be erased. Comrade Jeni was lying outside and her eyes were white and foam was in her mouth and blood on her head.

The Project sees Comrade Jeni falling and the Comrades say this is just dreams planted there by the enemy and The Project must stop waking up and screaming and waking everyone. The Project must erase. The Project has never seen Comrade Jeni. The Project repeated this one thousand times today. Comrade Jeni has never existed and was not a member of the Collective.

The Project pushed Comrade Jeni hard upstairs. And she fell against the window.

This is not true this was done by Comrade Uma. There is no such thing as Comrade Jeni. The Project never knew Comrade Jeni.

Note from Comrade Uma: This is terrible. We have made things much worse by trying to hide the truth from The Project. She is putting together the day when we fought with Jeni upstairs and then next morning when Jeni overdosed. The child blames herself because our attempts to modify her memories have scrambled her mind.

We must tell the child the simple truth. Please. I am ready to confess. My list of errors is long. Yes, I gave Jeni the pills. I should have done something about it when I saw her convulsing but I was so angry with Jeni, I left her. I thought it would make things easier if she was just gone. I closed the door on her and left her there for an hour and when I came back she'd been sick and passed out. I borrowed the car as we agreed to drive her to Hospital but I panicked and dumped her on the street outside, in the dark, in the frost. I didn't check if she was OK, I dumped her as near to the Hospital as I dared and I drove off because I was scared of being questioned at the Hospital. I'm sorry, I did it to protect us all, but I did wrong. These pages must now be destroyed.

The paper felt heavy in Nina's hand. Nina stared for a long time. There were no notes from Comrade Chen, or any other Comrades, they were missing. Something more was missing.

Two Pigs came in with Charity Sonia and she said, You must feel terrible Nina, this must be a shock to you. Oh, Nina. Poor Nina.

Over and over.

Nina felt like hands held in freezing water.

The Pigs asked Nina to confirm that this evidence was the actual handwriting of Nina and Comrade Uma and Nina did and had to sign a page and Nina wrote Nina and an X where they pointed.

Charity Sonia stared at Nina and Nina looked at the prison room and Nina had only an hour to get back to Horizon House and you cannot escape from a car so prison, car and Horizon House are the same thing in a row.

In Charity Sonia's car Nina stared at the roads moving. Charity Sonia kept saying, Nina, please speak to me, are you all right? Is there anything I can do?

Then she said she was worried that Nina didn't feel any different and why didn't Nina cry? She said it would be OK to do it, it might do Nina a lot of good.

And Nina said, Nina has brain damage and is a danger to herself. Remember.

Charity Sonia went silent and smoked out the window. Nina tried to hate Charity Sonia to see if it would make feelings come.

Charity Sonia drove fast and said, I know you're angry with me, Nina, but listen, one good thing has come out of this, and it's more evidence that Uma was telling the truth. I had this confirmed by email by morning, but I didn't want to say, but I have some more news.

Nina said nothing. Charity Sonia said, Nina, we have the results of your paternity test.

Nina said, This is enough for one day, this is enough for one day. Nina held the knees and rocked. Charity Sonia waited for Nina to stop, then she said, I was concerned, we all were, that it might upset you, if it turned out that your father was Chen. So that's the good news. The DNA tests show that he isn't related to you at all.

Charity Sonia said, Are you relieved or— And she stopped. Then she said, I suppose, we still don't know who your father was. But maybe he'll turn up. So that could be good news as well.

Nina said nothing.

Then Nina said, People don't care for other people in Freedom.

Charity Sonia said, Well, that's not true. Lots of people care about you, Nina.

Then she sighed and said, I'm sorry. For all the horrible things you've learned today. I really am sorry.

It made Nina angry. People say sorry too much. They just look at Nina and say I'm sorry, I'm so sorry, Nina, we're so sorry, we all are. Sorry.

Nina's brain is nothing to do with them. They didn't put a sperm into an egg to make The Project, they didn't rescue The Project or rescue Nina. Charity Sonia and Social Work Phil and Uma. It is just a phrase they say so they can pretend they are good people. I'm sorry. Sorry. So sorry. Sorry. Sorry. Sorry, as they lock you away.

Nina stared at many cars coming fast towards and always just missing and Nina wanted to push Charity Sonia hard to make a smash.

Charity Sonia said, Are you OK, Nina? Nina. And Charity Sonia said, I know the Doctor said you don't have empathy, Nina, but I don't think it's true. You have so much, maybe even too much and maybe that's what that hollow feeling is.

And her voice cracked and she said, Can you hear me? Oh, Nina. Where have you gone?

Nina's head was on the window and Nina could see Comrade Jeni and her eyes rolled back all white but it felt very far away, like the words for the banned song Uma used to sing, Poppa's going to buy you a diamond ring, and if that diamond ring turns brass, Poppa's going to buy you a looking glass.

Charity Sonia said, I know you feel very angry and everyone seems to have let you down, but please, Nina, please speak to me.

Nina closed the eyes and rolled the head hard on the cold glass and felt the wheels vibrating.

Then the car got slow and Nina saw it was the circle road of Horizon House.

Charity Sonia said, OK, well here we are. Now, please try and rest and I'll be back on Friday.

Nina stared at her very hard. Charity Sonia couldn't look back at Nina. Nina wanted to punch Charity Sonia very hard in the face and scratch her eyes till blood came. Nina wanted to grab her and beg her and scream, Please don't lock me in there. Please. Please.

But the car was full of only breath and then Nina was holding Charity Sonia's face very tight and kissing her on the lips, very hard, and Charity Sonia's lips were soft and wet but her arms were struggling and she was trying to yell. But Nina kept kissing her and sucking air from inside her and Nina used all the muscles and bit on Charity Sonia's lip so she couldn't push Nina away because there was big feelings in Charity Sonia and Nina needed to feel but Charity Sonia grabbed Nina's face and pushed Nina very hard and screamed and Nina fell against the door and Charity Sonia was gasping and yelled, What the hell are you doing? Are you fucking insane? Fuck, that was not appropriate, Nina. I did not consent to that! You never do that to anyone, ever again, you hear me?

Nina has learned what you are supposed to say when you feel a big feeling with someone and it is, I love you. So Nina said it to Charity Sonia.

Charity Sonia looked terrified and wiped her mouth. And Nina knew Nina should feel guilty, but Nina didn't and this was more proof that Nina had no empathy and was a danger to herself and others. Nina felt only the taste of Charity Sonia's mouth and it was sweet and salty and of a little blood.

Then Nina got out of Charity Sonia's car and said, Goodbye.

Smiling Horizon House Becca led Nina inside the second security door and she nodded to the Security man, and she said, Don't worry, Nina, I've heard all the news. We've made a special space just for you, put a single bed in the observation room. Just for a few days, and we understand now, sorry for the misunderstandings before. You need some rest at this hard time, and it'll be good for you to have some peace and quiet.

Nina was walked down the corridor with pictures of stick men and rainbows and smiling animals. Then a corridor of closed doors had been walked down and Nina was stopped in front of one and then Horizon House Becca pushed in a beeping number and turned the handle and had her hand on Nina's back and said, Maybe you can tell us all about how you're feeling in the gathering in the communal room on corridor B, after supper.

Nina was breath and footsteps but not feeling the ground. Nina was stuck with the eyes of Jeni. Her hand reaching out.

Her face and the word can never live together.

Mother.

Erase.

—

Nina was in the observation room on the bed and Nina unpacked all the things Nina had got for free in Freedom. Nina laid them out.

The pants Charity Sonia gave in the pack of three from Marks and Spencer.

The four T-shirts from Pound Land of yellow and pink. And the four plastic cups of red, yellow, green and blue.

The trainers Charity Sonia brought and the microwaved Egg Foo Young and the pink jumper and the purple puffer coat Cas brought.

The five pack of socks with the words Sports Direct on them. The wrappers of fifteen Cheese and Onion and Prawn Cocktail crisp packets. The Vaseline intensive care deodorant. The eleven magazines for how to be a woman. The set of plastic cutlery. The empty jotters and the twelve pack of Bic pens.

Nina looked at the stupid list Nina had made that first week.

Get Married. Fly an aeroplane.

Nina made the stack and Nina thought, they have been very kind but Nina has to give all these things back. Then Nina had to write down everything to make things connect but Nina's writing hand feels incorrect.

Nina knows this feeling of not being in your body and looking at yourself from far and Doctor Webber said it is bad.

Nina sat in the window with the curtains drawn apart from a slash to peek through. There is a garden and five women on the grass. Nina looked at the grass and thought of The Project. The Project had never been allowed to play on grass.

One of the women had a squashed face and one had an arm that was too short and they were all doing the same exercises and a woman shouted at them, Raise your left leg, reach for the sky, now lie on your back and kick. Nina stared at the women doing what they were told. And Comrade Ruth was shouting, Raise your foot, stand on one leg, hold it there and hop.

Then Nina saw Nina's reflection and it wasn't Nina's face looking back.

Then Nina took off the T-shirt over the head and it wasn't sweat Nina smelled, not the sourness, or sweetness but something old. It was smell of the learning bathroom and washing the body with Uma. It was the smell of The Project.

Nina held the T-shirt to the nose and smelled it in deeply. The child was in it. Nina tried to bring her back, but then The Project and the smell were gone.

A candle with perfume from it. Five women and a man sat in a circle and Horizon House Becca said, Thank you all for coming to the group sharing session. There are some first timers here today. Tamara and Nina. Let's welcome them.

And they all spoke with the same smile and said, Hello Tamara, Hello Nina.

Nina watched the sitting Nina from the doorway. Nina looked very weak. Nina walked round the room and stared at the other Nina. Nina felt sorry for Nina.

Nina stared at the picture on the wall. It was of the planet and all the countries in green and the seas in blue and round it, in a bigger circle, were a woman with a black face, a woman with a yellow face, a woman with a red face, and women with many different colours and kinds of clothing, all smiling and all holding hands around the world.

Uma said, Nina did nothing, she wasn't involved, Nina saw nothing.

But The Project saw.

Horizon House Becca said, Now, we'd like each of you in turn to just talk about your health experiences, some of you have lived here for some time and know each other quite well. We all have a variety of conditions, some hereditary, some due to injury, and some of you are combatting addiction, but let's try not to criticise or judge others. Let us look inside ourselves first and foremost and try to share our experiences of today. Who would like to go first?

Nina closed her eyes and saw Ruth in the middle of the circle of women punching herself in the face. Again, harder, Comrade, again, erase the self, prove that you can criticise yourself. Harder. Share for the benefit of all. The drops of blood falling on the floor.

Jeni screaming, Stop, this is madness.

Nina looked up, all the women and the one man were staring at Nina. Their faces looked scared. The words echoed and Nina realised they had come from not from Jeni but from the mouth of the other Nina.

Nina was told to sleep in the room with the staring women and given a pill but Nina spat it out and waited till everyone was asleep then crept out. Nina had to escape by going invisible again but clicking the heels was just stupid so Nina needed to find another way. Nina found the little office room again with the Staff Only sign and the other one that said Our staff and managers pride themselves in keeping staff and residents happy, motivated and feeling loved. And Nina went into drawers and did searching because Nina is the best finder of hidden things. And there was lots of tape and pens and some chewing gum, then Nina found some scissors and Nina locked the door.

All the locked doors are in Nina's head so they follow Nina wherever Nina goes. Nina knows why Jeni took the pills now and it is because you try to run away but everywhere is just the Collective.

Nina found the best corner and picked the arm scab to make warm pain come and it made the room spin and go away but only for a little time because there were still head pictures of Uma.

Nina remembered Uma saying, if Jeni sneaks up here at night and takes more pills and doesn't tell us, she could overdose and we wouldn't know till we found her in the morning, we can't take the risk, we have to lock her up.

Nina knows Charity Sonia will not come on Friday like she says.

Nina knows this wanting to empty everything is not a new feeling. It is just a different layer of the same hollow. It is under the skin, in the sighing and the weight feeling dragging. This feeling is ten years long. In the basement Nina was like this, and it took muscles to fight it, days and days and years and so angry and hoping for escape and that was how Nina fought the feeling. But now the angry energy is gone and the same feeling is there underneath like a dampness in the floor that never goes away or the piss smell in the concrete. It takes too much energy to put on Charity Sonia's smile, to eat and sleep and eat and wash and hope.

Nina still cannot cry and that is final evidence that all doors are closed. Nina's neck feels numb now. The bad hand is a spider of bones with shiny skin stretched over. It is not Nina any more. Nina put the scissors onto the skin to see if empathy would come. Nina told Nina a sad thing to see if Nina could cry. Nina said, Jeni was The Project's mother and she is dead. And Nina pulled the scissors over the bad hand until lines came. Nina said, Chen thought he was The Project's father. Then Nina cut harder. Nina said, Uma loved The Project.

It was very sore but no tears came and Nina stared at the new holes filling with blood but they were not Nina.

Nina has to write it all down with the good hand.

Nina had hoped that Freedom would be a lot better then Nina had thought there was a problem with Freedom but the problem is really Nina. Nina was never meant to be free.

Nina thought about the photocopy and about all the diaries Chen destroyed and when he said, erase The Project's memory, he didn't realise what he really meant. Nina hated Chen a great amount but still wanted him to give Nina gold stars and forgive Nina and Nina doesn't know why.

Nina never got to see the end of the Wizard of Oz and Nina is scared of finishing it because then there will be no more. Nina must lie down on the carpet.

Nina feels very light, like Nina is missing something and then Nina knew it is The Project. Nina misses The Project.

Nina will make a big cut in the arm to make The Project come back. And The Project will be scared so Nina will sing her the Uma song. Poppa's going to buy you a mockingbird.

Then Nina will take The Project's hand and tell her, Now, be good so we can vanish out of here with the scissors and that will be a good experiment. And Nina will tell The Project, It's OK, we were just an experiment too, but it failed, so it's best for us to go now. And Nina will say, it's OK, don't be scared of some silly blood, the last time this happened Nina vanished out of the basement and woke up in Hospital but maybe this time it will be somewhere better.

Hush little baby, don't say a word.

Nina is writing this now and then will make a deep cut so Nina and The Project can go invisible and escape.

Jotter #135 Date unknown

The Project would like permission to draw a window on the dark wall with chalk. The window is not to dream but to remember about birds which are not counter-revolutionary creatures but doves of world peace.

The Project would like to have light bulbs and not to have to wait for the upstairs committee to decide on the distribution quota and the committee is always right. The Project is always grateful to be permitted to write requests now that The Project is still locked in the basement till further notice for grateful re-education.

The Project would like to see outside, just for once, to the back area where it is safe. The Project would like to be reminded of colours and the sky. If you do not trust me then I can be put on a long rope.

If this is not possible then The Project please requests a report to make sure Gramsci has not been eaten and can you please make sure Rosa Luxemburg makes no more eggs, but please don't chase her away like happened to Ho.

The Project would like to know how long it will be until The

Project is better and would it be fine if The Project just went very quietly to the toilet just to empty the bucket without any help. This would eradicate the smell that other Comrades have complained about as the bucket would be emptied every day, and if you give The Project the keys The Project will lock The Project back in again every time.

The Project knows it is a great indulgence but asks to see a picture box, even if it is just for a little bit each day. The Project can hear that there is one upstairs now and Comrade Uma when she visits tells about programmes like Strictly Come Dancing.

The Project would like there to be some new Comrades or for the old Comrades to visit more even though they are very ashamed of The Project.

The Project would like to know the truth about Comrade Jeni so every bit of her that remains can be erased.

The Project asks if it's OK to reduce the number of sit-ups each day to two hundred. The Project has already surpassed the quota for press-ups and squat jumps but finds sit-ups very hard on the concrete floor.

The Project asks permission to have a bath upstairs. The Project can be watched while this happens and will not try to escape or to hit anybody like before.

The Project would like some things in the basement that are not for a child as The Project has had these things for many years and the eye is tired and The Project has no need of the doll or the plastic flower.

The Project is sad to hear that Comrade Zana has returned to taking the opium of the masses. The Project asks if it is possible to have the Wizard of Oz comics back. And can The Project have some white paint please because the basement is so black.

The Project would like for there to be peace in the world so that the people outside will not hate us and try to kill us and then we can open our doors and teach them how to be good like us.

The Project promises not to cut The Project's arm again and asks for a metal spoon as the plastic one is rubbish and broken.

The Project knows it is selfish to have so many wants. If they cannot be answered then The Project still is happy and bows to the greater wisdom of the committee.

The Project will erase all memory of being Nina, and the name.

The Project is very glad to have been allowed to re-read some of the old diaries. The Project asks Comrade Chen not to destroy any more, please. The Project has been studying them every day to see where The Project made the wrong turn.

The Project will stop pacing about and singing as it disturbs the upstairs Comrades.

The Project requests more jotters so that self-examination can be improved. And some more pencils and a sharpener. The Project understands that a knife will not be allowed and thanks the Comrades for this kindness.

The Project is grateful that the beatings are regular and not at unexpected times and that they are of regular number with the stick and belt mostly.

The Project has no criticisms of Comrade Chen and thanks him again for his generosity in tolerating The Project. The Project knows why she was called The Project now. The Project has not seen his face for a year now and would like to.

The Project asks if it is OK to have to sit on the hands for only two hours every day.

The Project is deeply sorry to have disappointed everyone. The Project does not think we should give up on the hope of the socialist revolution and the coming of the perfect person. But maybe you can try again with another child who will be better.

—

Nina is a good liar. They have not destroyed Nina. Nina hates all the begging to keep pretending she is The Project. Nina spits at their shadows. Nina doesn't care if they hit me any more. They are only hitting The Project, they cannot touch Nina. Nina gives them their stupid fake diary every week about The Project and hides this one.

Nina puts my fingers down my throat and pukes up everything they force into me. Nina vomits up their words into their faces.

Rice rice rice righteous rice.

Revolutionary rice.

Nina hoarded sugar lumps before they locked me away.

Nina hid one secretly every day.

Nina has blackmailed Uma into giving me more, under the door.

Nina has hidden the sugar lumps in a dark corner in a secret place.

One each day is all Nina eats.

Nina looks up and the night is so dark there seem to be no walls, but there are. Nina finds them with her face when she walks into them. Every day the light runs in and out of the place like water, coming in through the crack under the door, and shadows over the cracks in the roof and Nina can hear the water flowing upstairs.

Against the cold wall Nina hears footsteps in the street above.

The pipes Nina can nearly reach to touch, the plastic and the metal ones and the kitchen taps beyond the wooden rafters and Comrade Uma's noise of little fat feet and Comrade Ruth's big slower feet. And the filling and spinning washing machine above and the gurgle and choke through the pipes into Nina's place below.

Nina lies here and just stares at the sounds. Nina can't do anything, can't even concentrate, and the mind spins just like the clothes in the machine. Nina writes. Nina is so tired and smells of sick.

Nina can hardly stay awake and bites the lips for the taste of blood.

Nina's ribs are like the ones in the pictures, even the dead in the war were piled together, but when Nina dies they will hide her somewhere, alone, maybe just dig a hole in the basement, right here, cover it over with concrete. There is a bag of it and it is burst and it tastes of grey dust and choking and maybe that is what it is for.

Nina still has pencils. Uma sneaks them under the door.

Nina made secret notes in the secret pages. Nina makes plans and lists. Nina hides words in birds or eats them.

It's too late now. If you watch a pigeon half their lives they just aren't thinking about anything at all. They make their nest, they lay the eggs, they get the food for their babies, the babies fly or they die and there are times in the day when they just walk back and forwards thinking of nothing but food and babies.

Nina is like this. Nina knows the birds are the reason it's OK for Nina to die because some eggs will live and some will not and Nina doesn't care. Uma said there is nowhere to go out there. Nina watches the light dripping in under the door and crawling back out when it's night and the sounds, always of water in pipes like the house is a body and it was veins and the scratch of the mice and the pencil on pointless paper.

When you write, Nina is locked down here, it doesn't feel as bad as when you write I am locked down here.

It is like an unpeeling and erasing. A memory of Uma teaching The Project how to put on a sanitary towel. Erase. A picture of Uma pointing to the trees and talking of the great fire. Erase. Everything has to be erased. Nina reads the pages and tears them out and eats them. Nina has eaten the first seven diaries of when The Project was only six years old and one said,

We had some rice and it was nice, then it was bath time with Comrade Uma and she said turnips are growing in The Project's ears and this was a joke and laughing is allowed and this was a lot for one day.

There are many faces in the walls and Nina stared at them because they are there and then not there and your mind can bring them back.

There is an old man with a big beard looking over Nina's bed. By the high vent there is a woman with horns and fat cheeks. By the place where Nina piles her clothes there is a woman with a large chest and one arm and in the speckled plaster above the door there are children with a ball. Along the roof crack there are footprints of birds with claws. On the floor there is an old face that smiles at Nina all the time. Nina tries to make it go away and Nina stomps on it and covers it with stinky clothes but Nina knows it is still there.

The only place where there are no faces is in Nina's corner. It is very flat and with no texture and it is always having Nina's shadow because of the way the lightbulb is. Nina's shadow is lower than Nina and it might be a child. Nina asks it about its life because it can travel through time and walls. Nina knows this because when Nina stands up and goes under the light bulb Nina's shadow goes back in time and becomes a tiny fetus and when the light is turned off Nina's shadow escapes and runs through the lane.

Nina is not sure if it was a dream, Nina woke and there was a hanging shadow above. Nina did not know if it was a ghost. It felt like a man. The shadow was just weeping and staring. Nina waited for it to strangle her and tried not to twitch. Nina knew that if Nina did anything or opened the eyes, the strangling would start. Nina's skin went prickly but then there was nothing, just the weeping man, and a whisper, that sounded like Sorry, then footsteps then the sound of the door being locked again.

—

Nina's corner is the warmest and when Nina's shadow goes Nina wedges the shoulders into it and hugs the knees but Nina is full grown now. Nina likes to suck and rock back and forwards and hum the hummingbird and when Nina tries to see very hard in the dark little sparks of silver flash and Nina chases them across the eye. The more Nina chases them the faster they go.

The face on the floor is The Wizard of Oz and he is Chen. Nina knows now that the reason he let Nina be locked down here with all these books for years was to prepare Nina for the truth. Dorothy was fooled. The Wizard sent her on a voyage to get the broomstick of the Wicked Witch because he knew she would fail and die.

Nina's corner smells of Nina and Nina. Nina does a little piss there before Nina does the bucket, just enough to dry each day and Nina takes the collections from the nose and puts them there too in a little pile to bring back The Project.

The Project comes back to tell things if Nina goes inside and asks the right questions.

The Project has told Nina that death is fine because it is the greatest thing to die for equality because all the dead are equal. The Project says to eat the disgusting food but Nina knows it is poisoned and The Project is tricking her because The Project is dead and lonely and wants to be together.

Sometimes Nina puts the other pair of clothes on the ground and does the arms of the jumper round Nina and the leg of the trousers around the legs, and it is a bit like hugging a person and mostly Nina thinks of Uma.

Other times Nina turns round and sits in the corner with Nina's body jammed in and the basement grows bigger and bigger the more Nina looks, till it's all just dots of silver fuzz and Nina's stomach growls from trying to eat itself. Nina's breath smells of sour and Nina's teeth are sore. Pain in the back helps Nina to focus, and Nina has saved my two fallen teeth in a safe place where no one will find them because they are Nina's private property. Nina hides the diary pages too in the secret place.

When there are no more Little Red Books left to chew and no more paper to make swans Nina will stop eating. Nina won't eat any more of their stupid mouse rice. Apart from the sugar lumps.

Nina hates Chen eighty-seven per cent and the rest of the hate is just for Nina.

Nina tears out more pages from the diaries to save them from Chen and the purifying fire. Nina hides one at a time in the crack in the plasterboard wall, and listens to them fall behind in the hollow where the teeth live now and some sick.

The hole is not big enough to dig Nina's way out and the plastic spoons break so fast. When Nina stuck fingers down the throat the good Comrades knew that Nina had not eaten because the vomit was in the bucket and they saw it when they emptied it and it was black. The wall hole is where Nina hides rice too. The smell was bad and in Nina's hair and the clothes and they gagged when they came in to search Nina. The wall is becoming mouldy and it makes Nina cough. Nina can see things in the air like feathers but very small. They have reduced the number of press-ups Nina has to do because they found Nina asleep on the floor and not on the mattress.

Nina will not let them try to feed Nina again and Nina will not let them take Nina upstairs to pretend, even though they say Chen has gone away for five days and please come up and talk to us, we miss you so much, we'll leave the door open.

Nina does not trust them any more.

The birds have come alive in the wall. Nina can hear them scratching.

—

Some days Nina hears weeping behind the door and a thump and a scuffling mouse sound and Nina knows it is Comrade Uma. Nina does not care how much Uma cries for Nina or how much Ruth apologises. Uma passes stupid notes under asking Nina to forgive her. Then one saying, Please will you listen to me I would like to confess. Then another saying, Please hide my all notes.

It might be Chen trying to test Nina and make Nina write confessions.

They say that when Comrade Chen is out working and Comrade Zana is out selling her body to pay for the Collective, they are going to let Nina come upstairs and watch television with them once a day, if I would like that, but Nina is sure that is a trick too and said No.

The hole is full of swans now and it makes insects crawl. Nina is putting on both sets of clothes at the same time to look fatter so they won't know and because of the cold even though it is summer.

Soon Nina will be with Comrade Jeni. Nina knows what happened to Jeni in the basement because everything is the same. When Nina sees her Nina will say now we are equal and there will be no more arguing.

If Nina could stop the lungs going in and out Nina would but they keep on going by themselves, in and out like a stupid machine. Who is breathing then? If it is not Nina then it must be someone else. What is this person called?

Keep Nina alive, for the sake of someone else.

Nina is suddenly hungry. Nina will eat.

You have to be written very, very tiny and be hidden in the special place inside the wall but Nina will move you later once a safer place is found. Nina is sorry because Nina will not be able to write in you very often.

They say Chen works like a slave now and drinks like a fish and is rarely here, they whisper through the door and say slowly they are convincing him to forgive Nina, but his shame is great.

They think Nina is so faithful but Nina is making a plan.

Secrets make Nina strong. And rice. Nina is going to try to get strong again to escape. Nina will make a hole to escape or Nina will be put in a hole like Jeni.

The only one Nina worries about is Comrade Uma who has become very skinny with eyes sunk in her head like the trapped way Comrade Jeni was before. Nina doesn't think she can be taken when Nina runs. Because Nina is going to. Even if it takes years and years and years. Nina will pretend to be the obedient little Project but Nina is going to escape. Nina has a secret piece of metal. Nina will trick weak Comrade Uma, Nina will pretend she is dying and Uma will take pity and then Nina will fool her and cut her and be out. Nina just has to wait for the right time.

Nina is breathing and waiting. And breathing.

If Nina can't escape Nina will stop breathing and that will be the way.

Unnumbered

Nina walks in bare feet and there are no cars and no people and dust is deep and everywhere. A sound was in the air and it is most beautiful. It is a million birds all singing and all so many different songs.

Nina looks but there are no birds flying and no birds sitting on the wires or on the ledges of windows or on the trees, just dust. The branches are white like bones with their skin stripped off. There are no pigeons or sparrows and Nina knows why, it is because the Glorious Leader told the little children with catapults to kill them all and Nina saw the millions dumped in the big hole and the children smiling because they got a gold star but these things are hidden now under the ground of the dust street.

Nina thinks, This must be the dream of Chen and his radiation sky or the heaven of the man on the wood.

And a voice says, Three eights circular and a number two.

But Nina could not find the man behind the trees.

The singing birds got louder and Nina was pulled to their music like by a string. Nina looks everywhere and Nina found a paddy field but it was all dry with cracked earth and Nina recognised the place from the picture of the Glorious Leader.

And the dust stings and wind nips the skin and Nina can't breathe or find the man or the birds. Nina finds only rusted machines and shoes scattered and the noise changes. The bird song is really children, a million, and they sing, Heaven and earth are big, but not as big as the Party's kindness, and it is one of The Project's favourite songs and Nina wishes to be holding The Project's hand.

Nina looks through the hanging doors of the empty houses and on the road and Nina finds a torn red necktie in the dust but no children even though Nina can hear their voices sweet and louder now singing, Mother and Father are dear But Chairman Mao is dearer. And a man said, Systolic BP is under ninety.

Nina walks into the stinging dust to look for the voices and sees a deep pit and a shadow dash around it and it is a little girl running in a torn grey dress and hiding. Nina shouts out, Come back, don't be scared.

The little girl cannot run fast because she is too thin and Nina grabs her arm like a bone and she is The Project and she looks at Nina with an angry face and kicks and shouts, Let go of me. Who are you?

Nina says, I am Nina.

The Project shouts, You're a liar.

Nina says, I am not, I used to be you.

The Project shouts, You said I, you said I. I is incorrect. You need to be corrected. And she pushed Nina and shouted, Go away, traitor!

Nina said, How can I go away?

The Project said, Click your heels together, stupid, and make a wish. Then The Project looked behind and there was a loud wind and The Project was scared and said, Hurry up! He'll be back soon.

And Nina said, But, we have to go together, no one needs us anyway.

And Nina grabbed the little hand of The Project but The Project yelped and whimpered, Please, don't eat me.

And The Project pushed Nina again and Nina screamed and fell back and down and a man's voice said, Type B, four-fifty.

And a woman said, Can she hear us?

And Nina was in the pit and The Project stood at the top looking down. Nina tried to get up but the ground moved and a pink stink of sweetness came and mould smell everywhere, then Nina tried to stand but sank into a wetness like meat bits in soup and Nina was sinking and grabbing but the grabbing stone was a skull with hair and wet and the gripping place for fingers was eye holes and Nina screamed and the heart went very fast like to burst and hot wetness came up Nina's face and Nina was sinking with nothing to get a hold of but a hundred slimy ribs, all chewed and broken feet and torn wet clothes and leg bones all falling in from a hundred rotting bodies and stinks of old excrement and scabs and the walls were too steep and a woman's voice said, Her eyes are moving, is that a good sign?

And Nina heard Charity Sonia say, But why won't she wake up?

But Nina couldn't speak.

Nina hit the bottom and all air forced out and Nina jolted up but Nina couldn't see and then there was choking and many hands and something was on the face but Nina couldn't move to take it off. Nina said, this isn't happening, ninety-nine, ninety-eight, ninety-seven. And woman voice said BP, one ten. Then it was black and Nina heard pages turning and someone eating. But Nina couldn't open the eyes.

Nina woke and had gone back in time. It was Hospital and it was the first day of Freedom so it was twenty-five days before. Nina didn't want to time travel because Nina didn't want to be lost in

London again and be locked in Horizon House. But one thing was different, it was night and someone was sitting in the chair and it was Charity Sonia asleep with her shoes off and a hole in her toe stocking with her coat on the floor and some grapes in a box, all eaten apart from three.

Nina was pleased to see her but Nina felt a cold wetness in the bed and a smell and was shivering and Nina tried to speak but no words came and something big was in Nina's mouth and Nina felt heavy but the arms could not move.

Then Nina was pulling at a choking thing on the face and it was bright and sore and then an itchy feeling came all over the burning skin and a tube with blood was in Nina's sore arm and Nina screamed and tried to pull it out, and a woman came in running in white clothes saying, It's OK, it's OK, you've just had a reaction to the drip, you'll be fine, please calm down. Then a woman in green came and said, She's awake but she's in distress. And there was no Charity Sonia in the corner only machines. Then a man put a needle in the hole in Nina's sore arm and all shouting stopped, and he leaned down and said, It's OK, Nina, can you try to stay awake now? Can you hear me? Can you speak? And a warm piss came in the sheets and heavy eyes.

Nina woke and Charity Sonia was there and reading in the corner and Nina raised a hand and then Charity Sonia dropped the jotter and came over and she shouted, Nina, Nina! How are you feeling? And Nina said, Sore but the voice was like an old person.

And then Charity Sonia started crying and Nina asked why and Charity Sonia could only say, You can speak. Then she said, We thought you weren't coming back. Then she said thank God, many times, and stroked Nina's face and Nina was confused. And

Charity Sonia cried and held Nina's hand very tight and leaned and kissed Nina on the head for a long time and you are not supposed to kiss people without their consent, especially women. But it must be OK if Charity Sonia did it because it was her rule and it felt warm.

Then a man in a suit and a woman in white came and Charity Sonia just waited and smiled from the corner of the beeping room and the man was called Doctor Fraser. Nina shivered and the teeth rattled and Doctor Fraser said that Nina had been unconscious for four days and Nina's body had suffered major blood-loss and been in shock. Then he said, You had a close shave, Nina, at one point we lost your pulse and we had to use a machine to help you breathe.

Nina felt sore like blood cramps but all over and said, Sorry.

He shone a bright light in the eyes and asked a lot of questions and Nina didn't know the date or the name of the Queen, but Nina said he was holding up seven fingers. Nina could read his name from his badge out loud and Nina could stand up and walk and showed him and Nina asked, Is this one of the tests to see if Nina has empathy because there is no point. The Doctor was confused, but Charity Sonia laughed and said, It's OK, Doctor, it means she's back to normal. Then the Doctor laughed but Nina didn't.

Nina said, Do I have to write a report?

And nobody understood when Nina said about the dust and bones but Charity Sonia said, Only if you feel up to it, Nina. And Charity Sonia said to the Doctor, It's something Nina does to help her make sense of things.

Then Charity Sonia said, Maybe you can write in your journal tomorrow Nina, there's something I have to share with you first. But, why don't you get up and have a wash and something to eat? I have to go and make some phone calls now and get someone to stand in for me today but I'll be straight back.

Then Nina was alone in the beeping room and wires still on the body and shivering and Nina could smell something in the room that was old, like the stink of the Collective.

Nina ate porridge and an apple and had two boxes of orange juice and three yoghurts and the green nurse called Phyllis said, You're putting that away like it's nobody's business. Then Nina had a pee and a shower and Nina was aching and weak all over and Nina is not to touch the big net on the wrist called gauze because of the itchy stitches underneath. Then there was pain in the arm from the tube hole and Nina had to go everywhere with the stand for drips and if the tube gets blocked your blood goes into it but don't panic and you have to pull the red cord and then Margaret comes again to flush it and give you a little row but she doesn't really mean it. And she said, Oh, you've had another accident, Pet, let's wash your legs and get you a towel.

Charity Sonia came back with big pink and yellow flowers and Nina was scrubbed and Charity Sonia had a surprise and it was a black bin bag, very heavy with stretched bits.

Charity Sonia said, Can you sit down on the bed please, Nina, I have something very important to share with you.

Nina sat and the smell of the Collective was strong and Nina became scared.

Charity Sonia sat on the edge of the bed and she said, When you were unconscious I kept thinking about things you said. So I went to ask Comrade Uma, she's awaiting trial, and she was very worried about you and generous and she made a list of where to find the things you need.

Nina stared at the bags on the floor and the heart went faster.

Charity Sonia took Nina's hand and she said, So I went to the Collective. The Police let me in. Nina, that place, it's more horrible than you told me, all the walls and floors painted white like a prison and no private places, and those rooms with no doors, and that basement so dark, it made me sick. And I saw your little attic room too, Nina, they've packed up most of it now, for evidence, and I saw your special window and looked out, and a lot of things you'd said before made sense.

Nina said, Were there birds?

Charity Sonia's voice cracked and she squeezed Nina's hand and she said, Yes, Nina. Little birds. And Nina squeezed Charity Sonia's hand back but the stitches and tube of blood made it sore and Nina's chest was filling up.

But Nina was still scared of the black bag.

Charity Sonia said, Nina, you remember you said the diaries were destroyed by Chen and Ruth? Well, Uma saved some of them, not many, about thirty and many other pages, and she hid them, in all the places you used to search when you were Chen's top searcher.

Nina thought of the places and asked, Where?

Charity Sonia said, Inside the shower base, behind the cistern, inside the split wood beside the window – the Police helped me. So I have them now. I have them here for a little while before they get used in the court case.

Nina felt pain in the chest. Charity Sonia lifted up the bag on to the bed and it was the whole weight of a person and it stank of dust. Nina didn't want Charity Sonia to open it, Nina was scared and Nina shook the head.

Charity Sonia said, I know, it must be like going back. I understand if you want me to take them away.

Nina nodded and stared at the bag. Nina said, Please. Erase them. They are bad.

Charity Sonia stood and said, OK, OK, but don't worry and she went into the bag and took one out. See, it's not harming you.

It was very old and creased and had child's writing on the front.

Charity Sonia said, When you were asleep, Nina, I hope you don't mind. I didn't know if you were coming back and I sat here and I started to read some, then I couldn't stop.

Nina shook the head, no one must read the diaries, ever. Nina said, No, no, erase them. The Project was very bad.

Charity Sonia said, Yes, exactly, you keep saying The Project was bad and you feel some kind of guilt, Nina, and according to the Doctor's diagnosis, you should not be feeling these things because he said your brain damage occurred early before you could develop a sense of self or a conscience.

Charity Sonia became strong in the face and she said, But your dairies, Nina, from when you were seven years old to eleven, all the time, you said, I, I, me, me, me. On every page there's this needy, bossy, greedy little girl, struggling to get out. See. You used to say I all the time. I want chocolate, I want to play, I love Uma, I hate Ruth. You were a normal little girl once.

And Charity Sonia put her hand to her mouth and held out the jotter and said, See.

Nina didn't like to touch it but Nina read where Charity Sonia pointed and it was in the scratchy writing of when Nina was The Project and it said,

> I wanted to have Comrade Uma as my only teacher but then Comrade Jeni accused Comrade Uma of going behind backs and favouritism and the committee argued. So now Comrade Uma only comes to my little attic room under the dirty roof one time a week even though the other Comrades forget to teach me at all.

Charity Sonia said, Look, at that age you were perfectly mentally healthy. Every page is full of I and me and my. Look, I want, I feel, I worry. See. And Nina looked and it said, the pigeons do funny dances and I did a copying dance sticking out your head and anus to make the other Comrades laugh. Comrade Ruth never laughs because she is like a Daddy Long Legs and always cross and I had to stop dancing because it made Comrade Jeni giggle.

Nina was confused. Nina could not remember ever writing I did, or I am. Charity Sonia said, It's possible that Doctor Webber was wrong.

Nina said, Do you mean the doors in the head haven't gone away?

Charity Sonia said, I don't know, I'm not a brain specialist, but I think they made mistakes in your assessment. They said you were frozen before the mental age of five and have no empathy, but this is rubbish, it's just the way to express it is so different. Nina, some of that little girl who rubbed out her words is still here, she's in the dairies and I see her sometimes in your face. And that hollow feeling you get all the time, I think I understand it now. I got it too when I thought you weren't coming back.

Charity Sonia gulped with crying and Nina's wideness was expanding again.

Nina said, So Nina doesn't have brain damage?

Charity Sonia hugged Nina and said, No, I really don't think you do.

Nina had to breathe out or Nina would burst.

Then Charity Sonia went into the bag and took out more diaries. Some were torn and had stains and some had mould and made a choking feeling come in the throat. And Nina was not so scared and Charity Sonia read them out and on all the pages there were the words I and me, and me and me and I, and all rubbed out. And Charity Sonia said, They made you call yourself The Project but that wasn't you at all, Nina.

Nina looked at the words in the writing of The Project and

a strange feeling came of wide and expanding, like all the bits in Nina's body were separating, arms and legs and atoms. And Nina felt dizzy as if to faint and Nina said, But if Nina wasn't The Project then who was I?

Charity Sonia got off the bed and said, Well, why don't I leave you to read about yourself for a bit?

Nina said OK, and breathed a slow breath and Charity Sonia said she was just making some calls down the corridor.

Nina read diary #72 and it was all about rice rations and the need for ketchup and hitting Comrade Ruth. And #73 was about getting a period and another was about feeling sorry for Comrade Uma.

Nina read one bit and it was about Comrade Chen and it said,

> he gave me his special smile. These words of Comrade Chen fill us with tears of joy. I love the curly hairs in his eyebrows and his chin. Comrade Uma always cries but I don't because I am The Project and I have new kinds of emotions.

Nina said out loud, I wrote this. I did this. Nina felt very sorry for the little I that once loved Chen's eyebrows.

A feeling rushed then from the chest. Nina thought, Is this a cardiac arrest? And then it burst out and the eyes were wet and streaming and a low moan came. Nina tried to make the tears stop but they were coming from a machine inside or another person.

Then a nurse with red hair came and she said, Are you all right, Pet? And Nina told her, Yes, I am thank you, because crying is a good sign that Nina has doorways.

And then there was laughing mixed with crying that made hiccups come but Nina felt stuck, because Nina has lots more inside and they need to come out.

Then Charity Sonia was back and worried about Nina's hiccup

but Nina remembered something and it made everything stop and Nina felt guilty again.

Something was missing. Something very bad and shiver making.

Charity Sonia had to ask four times, What's wrong, Nina?

And Nina said, Nina feels bad. The birds with words on them.

Charity Sonia was confused so Nina explained.

Ruth tore the pages out and said, These are the very worst ever, every word is lies and badness, and Ruth said, They must be destroyed, I'll take those away and burn them, but The Project said, No, I'll eat them. And Ruth said, Please yourself.

But The Project hadn't eaten the scary pages, The Project made them into birds and they were in the secret place, hidden in the cracks, that The Project had to try to forget but Nina never could.

They were birds behind the wall.

Nina looked out the big Hospital window and it was on the fifth floor and it was all too much for one day but then Nina saw over the roof and past the car park was a round shape of sky in the ground and it was water with trees and a thing flew and it was white.

Nina said to the nurse, Can Nina go to that park?

And Nurse Margaret said, What park? And she came over to see Nina pointing and she laughed and said, Oh, that dirty old pond, that's just where the smokers go.

Nina said, Can I go? Because a park is on Nina's list.

Nina had to get out of the beeping room because Nina was still expanding. But Nurse Margaret said, You should be resting, Love. Here, it's time I changed your IV.

But Nina knew the feeling would stop if Nina stayed in the room and it had to keep growing and it did when Nina thought of I, so Nina said I said Want. And then I and Need.

I need to go there.

And Nurse Margaret said, All right, all right, keep your hair on, I'll call the porter and we'll see.

Nina was pushed in a chair with wheels with the drip bag on a hook and a paper coat and the porter was called Abdul and he was handsome and one of the people who blame the system because he was not happy about pushing people, but he said it was an excuse for him to have a fag and check his grinder.

He pushed Nina through a gate and stopped next to a metal sofa before the pond and he told Nina not to get up and to stay in the chair of wheels or his neck would be on a line. And then he went away to be on his phone.

The wind was blowing leaves on the water and Nina looked and saw many kinds of birds. A bit away an old woman threw things of food and birds came all around her with their cooing. There were pigeons and it made Nina feel good and some small black birds and then sparrows and Nina was glad they had escaped from Mao's children.

Nina watched them feed and Nina thought of the millions of dead sparrows and how millions of Chinese people died too. Then Nina thought of the humans Nina knew and how they made a mistake too like Mao and didn't mean to really hurt Nina because they just wanted to change the world and they didn't realise that to want to change the whole world means you despise everything in it including all humans and wanting to change everyone does not make you a good person.

Then Nina thought, once you nearly die, and you fail at that then it was OK to feel sorry for everyone because no one would have existed any more if you did die.

Nina felt sorry for Comrade Ruth and Zana and Comrade Uma and Comrade mother Jeni and even felt sorry for Comrade Chen with his big dead belief and his little gold stars. The Project was always asking Uma, Why do you cry so much?

Now Nina knows. Nina felt sorry for Uma. Then Nina thought of The Project and felt sorry for her too. Then Nina remembered Nina was The Project.

And emotions came again.

Nina will never understand humans and birds are better.

The pigeons fed close to Nina's feet and Nina felt a wide feeling looking over the pond. A voice said, Excuse me, do you have any bread?

It was an old man who Nina was not to call a slave, staring and he was sitting on the other metal sofa and he said in a too loud voice, Hope you don't mind. I came without. Forgot it. Then he said, Sorry. Do you have any bread? For the birds.

Nina told him that Nina was trying to get better from massive blood loss but he didn't seem to hear and got up with shaking legs and came closer and he had lumps of pink plastic in his ears and he pointed and said, Sorry if I'm shouting, batteries. Then he went over to the other lady and she gave him something and it was bread and he came back. He tore it up slowly like his hands were sore from the big ball knuckles and Nina watched him. Then he threw the crumbs at his feet and the pigeons ran to him. One of them had a burned foot like Gramsci.

The old man looked at Nina and nodded and he handed some bread and something told Nina that he meant Nina should throw crumbs too. Nina did and felt a sharpness so was extra careful of the stitches and three more pigeons landed and then four sparrows and Nina threw some more and they all swarmed round the feet and one was very huge and white with wings as wide as a person and it came gliding over the pond and Nina was amazed and scared because its wings were so wide. And Nina wanted to ask the old man the name of this bird but realised he would think Nina had severe learning challenges and would ask Nina why Nina didn't know such simple things and Nina would have to tell him about the Collective.

The big white bird flew off and Nina thought maybe it is a swan. But it looks nothing like the ones made of paper. Nina stared at it and it was strong and beautiful and scary and that made it more beautiful.

The old man threw his last piece and said, I don't much care for them myself. She used to feed them. Nina wondered who but didn't ask.

He said, Sorry – Peggy, my wife.

Nina wondered why Peggy didn't feed the birds any more then realised Peggy was probably dead like Jeni because this was a Hospital.

And he was done throwing bread and the bird that might be a swan flew away with a huge noise of wings on water and then little pigeons ran to Nina, but Nina was in shock.

Nina looked at the pigeons and their dance and the old man's wrinkled face and he didn't even like birds and Nina thought, Why do you even come? Your wife is not in Hospital any more and she's not in Heaven watching over you and making sure you feed birds, because Heaven is a lie.

Then Nina thought it might be cruel to say this to the man and it was better to let the man live with his lie. Then Nina remembered that was something Uma said, not once, but three times. Uma said it of Jeni. She said it of Chen. Kinder to let him live the lie. She said it about The Project.

Nina threw the last crumb and the old man smiled and got to his wobbly feet and he said, See you tomorrow then. And he said it not like a question but like he knew it would happen and his eyes were very serious like he was saying you just have to keep being here, like birds just have to keep eating bread, so don't take forty-one pills again.

Nina watched the old man limp away with his walking stick.

And Nina thought of live and lie and how they are just one letter different, and Nina tried to stroke a pigeon but it got a fright and flew and from nowhere the big feeling came again and Nina began to cry and took in deep gulps of sky.

Then Abdul came back and he said, Right, that's me got a hot date for tonight, let's get you back inside. Then he said, What's wrong, darling, you all right? But Nina couldn't speak because Nina has twenty years of tears to catch up on and some of them do not even belong to Nina.

Nina was in bed when Charity Sonia came back and she was very serious and she had another bag and it rustled and she was shaking with red eyes. She slumped in the chair by the window and the nurse came in and said visiting time is over and Charity Sonia said sorry but she was not leaving.

Nina was more scared of the bag because Nina knew from the sound that it had the birds in it. Charity Sonia was not touching or kissing Nina any more and not saying Nina would get better. The sun had gone over the roofs and was purple and finally she said, What you went through. It makes me so angry.

She went in the bag and pulled out a paper bird and it was half chewed and mouldy and then another, which was unfolded and all the writing was smeared.

Charity Sonia's face was hard and she said, I'm going to get you a lawyer and you're going to send these people to jail, all of them.

Then Charity Sonia was crying and the bag fell open and more mouldy birds fell out. Charity Sonia's body was shaking but it was far away so Nina went over and touched her head. Charity Sonia said, I'm a peaceful person, Nina. But I could kill them.

Nina held her hand and waited for her to stop and Nina said nothing. Charity Sonia kept clenching her fist and her teeth and energy passed through her like radiation. When someone is very angry it is hard to get them to make sense so Nina had to do what Charity Sonia did before and be slow and give a tissue and ask questions.

Then Charity Sonia said, Nina there are pages in here that I can't let you see.

Then another surge went through her, and her teeth were tight and then it passed and she said, Nina, there was food behind the walls, the police tore the plasterboard down. Nina, there was hair and teeth and bandages and shit stuffed in there.

Then another wave of it went through her and she said, Nina. Then Nina again. And her eyes were full of more rage than even Ruth.

Then she stood and said, No, I can't let you see these pages. I'm going to destroy them.

Nina asked why. Charity Sonia said, Because they'll make you sick, Nina. No one should ever see these pages. It will be too much for you. It might be better to forget what they did to you. You should see only good things from now on.

Nina stared at her and remembered Uma saying, Let people live with their lie. And Ruth saying destroy the pages. Nina let go of Charity Sonia's hand and took the bag of paper birds and Nina said, Nina will read them, it is up to Nina.

Charity Sonia said she could not stop Nina, but she begged Nina not to. But Nina said, Everyone has been rubbing out for too long. Nina has to see.

Charity Sonia shook her head and said she would sit in the corner watching over Nina till Nina was done, just in case.

Nina unfolded the birds and Nina was not as afraid of the basement as Charity Sonia. Most of the pages were about being hungry and listening and waiting and peeing and food passed under the door and making blood come. And Nina felt nothing to read it.

Then Nina came across an old scruffy swan, badly folded, and nearly all the words were in tiny writing and nearly rubbed out or faded, and Nina remembered that it was one of the bad ones with the torn edge from jotter sixty-eight.

This is what it said,

The Project has to apologise and must tell the truth because The Project's lies and wanting has caused the many sad problems and The Project made the Pigs come to the Collective. The Project must write it all down so there will be no more lies and the Collective can agree on the one story to tell. Then The Project and all Comrades will erase this story.

On the sad day The Project went to the window to be quiet and The Project got a surprise because Comrade Jeni was there already. Comrade Jeni had broken the rules because she was still unwell of mind and should have been in the getting better basement. Comrade Jeni said, Don't look so scared, it's OK, Ruth and Uma let me out so you and me can have a chat, come here.

Comrade Jeni was not wearing proper clothes but just a shirt and no pants and she had blood scabs on her hands and bruises on her face and The Project felt sick in the belly for her. She looked like the Christ man in the picture of bleeding feet and The Project was not supposed to know this but he was in National Geographic.

Comrade Jeni was sitting next to the window and she smiled at The Project. She said, Let me hold your hand, I won't bite. I see why you come here. It's so lovely up here, you can see so far. There are so many pigeons and their nests, it's amazing. And all the baby ones too, I had no idea. And the kids down there have a swing. Look, and she pointed through the window.

The Project didn't look because it is The Project's window and Comrade Jeni had no right.

Comrade Jeni said, I should have taken you to meet those kids. Why didn't I do that? I'm so sorry. And then she tried to touch The Project's face and called The Project, Darling.

Comrade Jeni squeezed The Project very tight and her red hair was in The Project's face. Comrade Jeni said very close to The Project's ear, We had a secret meeting, Uma and Ruth and me, and they've agreed, they're going to let me go, and I'm going to go up north to the countryside and start again, but I don't want to go anywhere without you, Darling. The Project feared

The page finished and Nina had to look for a time through the other folded birds to find the one that went after this one and it had the opposite shape of torn edge. And it said,

the reactionary words and was confused and looked and Comrade Uma was in the doorway but her face said it wasn't a trick.

Comrade Jeni was on her knees then and stroking The Project's arms and her eyes were big and she said, I know I've not been there for you and I'll never forgive myself for that. And then her eyes went wet.

Comrade Jeni said, That's why I think it's only right that I give you the choice. I won't snatch you again, I promise, but I have to leave here today, so do you want to come with me to a lovely farm with animals, just you and me? We have to go before Chen gets back.

The Project was very shocked that Comrades Ruth and Uma were letting this deception happen. The Project focused very hard to stop the feelings coming and to remember every word for the report.

Comrade Jeni smiled with wet eyes and stroking The Project's hair and she said, It's your choice, Nina. Do you want to stay here or do you want to come and we can start again and I'll be your proper mummy?

The Project stared at Comrade Jeni, and back at Comrade Uma but Comrade Uma hid her eyes.

Comrade Jeni said, We can go now, right away, out the front door. Ruth and Uma have said it's OK. We can put on coats and go and buy some nice new shoes. Will you come with me, Darling?

She squeezed The Project's hand and The Project saw radiation clouds gathering out the window and heard Project Uma sniffing. Then The Project had a feeling of being pulled and Comrade Jeni's eyes were so sad and emotions came and emotions are counter-revolutionary, so The Project pushed Comrade Jeni's stroking hand away and shouted, No, You are a traitor.

The Project felt energy inside and felt proud because lots of words came and they were all correct for once. The Project shouted, You are a slut and a decadent and a class enemy.

The Project shouted, No, I will not go away with you. I hate you.

Comrade Jeni's face was very lost and Comrade Jeni tried to grip The Project but The Project hit her with the bad hand and yelled, Let go! I hope you are hit by radiation. And Comrade Jeni cried, Please, Nina, come with your mummy.

The Project got very hot and yelled, My mummy is dead! And kicked Comrade Jeni very hard and broke free. The Project yelled, Traitor! I am going to tell Comrade Chen. I wish you were dead.

And Comrade Jeni fell back and bashed against the window. And The Project ran to the corridor and crouched in the dark place.

Then The Project had a sleep with a special pill and then there was noise in the downstairs and The Project went to investigate and it was very dark. The Project thought it was

Comrade Jeni attempting to escape again and went to the back door. Comrade Uma was there and Comrade Jeni was lying on the ground on the back steps in the pigeon poo and her eyes were all white with no black parts and her mouth had white foam and there was a blood scrape on her head and Comrade Uma was trying to drag her.

The Project stood and a feather fell down going round and round in circles very slow and then it landed on Comrade Jeni's face.

Then the Comrades put The Project in the kitchen and they said The Project did not see Comrade Jeni, and that Comrade Jeni had most certainly not fallen from the top window, and it was not because The Project pushed her and that The Project was making up stories and that The Project had to repeat the new story that Comrade Jeni had never lived here and that The Project had never heard of Comrade Jeni.

This is the end of this report. The Project is very tired.

Note from Comrade Uma: I am sorry The Project caught me with Jeni at the back steps and now she's getting both incidents completely mixed up. When she was little she saw a baby bird outside the window and it fell from its nest and died, a little incident but she cried for days. She's got this memory all muddled up with Jeni, she thinks everything that dies must have fallen.

Nina sat with the page. The hollow started inside and Nina cried. Nina cried in the arms of Charity Sonia then had to have no one touching. And it was like a filling up and emptying and like a thing had been done and undone and Nina cried until no more wetness would come and the throat was a dry scrape, like still puking when there is nothing left. Nina said the banished words. I. Me. I did.

And Nina cried and the eyes were getting empty.

And another nurse came and she said, Shall we get some help? And Nina said, leave me alone. And so Charity Sonia left too and the nurse gave a box of tissues and someone stood at the door watching and Nina cried until it was very dark and then some more. Nina cried in the toilet and in the bed, and at the window, then another nurse lady touched Nina's head and said, Poor love. What did they do to you?

And Nina said, No, I did it.

Nina cried for Jeni and Chen and the lie Jeni told Chen to make him a father. Nina cried for Uma's lies to save other people from the truth. Nina cried because all these years angry Nina had protected The Project, just like Chen and Uma did. And still they were lying and would die in jail for The Project.

And the nurse said, Miss, I can give you something to help you sleep, and Nina said, It's really OK, Nina has not cried for a long time and it's OK, just let me do it for a bit longer please.

Nina flushed the crying tissues away and felt sorry for Chen and Uma and Comrade Ruth.

Then Nina was in the bathroom and said poor Nina out loud and Nina felt sorry for Nina and saw Nina's ugly red face in the mirror but something was wrong. Nina's face did not seem like Nina any more. Not just the wrinkles and the scars and the word Nina and the word Face and the tears on the face and on the hands.

Nina asked, Who is it that weeps for Nina, whose tears are these that choke in the throat, and then Nina realised they were mine.

Me.

And the words went in circles over and over in the head. Then it was I and I have and I love. And I and Hate.

And then Nina cried for this little guilty thing that was so sacred and knew nothing like a baby bird from an egg, up high that didn't even know if it could fly. This little I. And it was the person I was before I could write or kill with words. But Nina didn't know who this I was. It is a very small thing and so timid and it didn't even have a name and was mostly rubbed out. A thing hiding beneath everything else, that came before words.

And Nina cried for it and held it tight in my arms.

And I called it I.

Jotter #249 2019

Doctor Webber was cross at first but said Charity Sonia's unorthodox methods may have kick-started neurological development as many memories came flooding and there was crying for months, sometimes even when eating and this makes it hard to swallow and then I was just sick of crying and bored of it. Doctor Webber says this is all very good news and the brain is made of plastic and that he has noticed a freeing up of emotional communication since the day and he thinks that a new door might be opening up in the corridor.

The Police took away all paper birds and they were pleased because they make the case against Chen much stronger. All the pages from all the jotters had to be gathered from all their hiding places and the words in the jotters are not Nina's or The Project's any more but are out being independent in the world.

Chen goes to trial in six months' time.

It has been nine months and the itchy stitches are just silver skin now and I have been feeling more and more like a Me and every day I say I more and more. Though Nina had to grow from being eleven to being twenty-eight very fast.

When I look at I and Me on the page, I have to resist the wanting to rub them out, and when I succeed I give myself a treat which is not always chocolate.

The hacks have gone away for a while and I really have to find a new name for myself because they will come back and want to put me on the cover of the government information magazines and ask me what food I eat and what I think of boob jobs and my top dieting tips and who I think is hot and who is not. To be honest I am not so excited about Freedom as before because everyone is always competing and arguing and no one has the answer and it is not for everybody.

I have a new house and it is quite far from London and it has a garden and a guard who comes once a day to make sure I am OK but the rest of the time it is just me and the birds and my new neighbours who are Ali and Sylvia and Omar and they are vulnerable people too but we are free to walk out our own doors.

I have to choose a new name but I can't decide. I'm thinking of Dorothy or Dot but not Dottie because this means profound learning disabilities.

I got to the end of The Wizard of Oz and this is what happens.

Dorothy and her friends go back to the Wizard of Oz to prove they killed the witch but then they discover he is all a fake and just a small normal man pretending he is a wizard with some tricks because he was just a magician in the old Capitalist world. But he gives special medals to the Lion and the Scarecrow and the Tin Man and Dorothy and like Doctor Webber he tells the Lion that he has disorganised attachment disorder and too much flight or fight hormone. And the Tin Man suffered from childhood neglect and that's why they thought he couldn't have emotions but now he does. Then Dorothy is happy with some tears and she has fond farewells to her friends. Then the Wizard gets her to leave with him in his balloon for Kansas and so they must say goodbye to the false ideology of Oz.

But Toto jumps out and Dorothy goes to get him and the balloon takes off and she is stranded in Oz again. And this made me more happy because, compared to Freedom, Oz is a bit more interesting.

But then Glinda the Good Witch came in an outfit of reactionary pink and she made Dorothy click her ruby heels three times and say, There's no place like home, there's no place like home. And I was angry that the Good Witch had kept it secret all along that she could just magic Dorothy back anytime she liked. And saying There's no place like home makes the hollow open up again, even after pink pills. Then Dorothy woke up back in Kansas and it had all just been a dream because she had banged her head. But I knew Dorothy would never be able to survive in normal Kansas again because she had Complex PTSD like me, from killing the Witch.

The ending was very disappointing and I had to cry again. It was like I had only been pretending there were other endings. But that's OK. Charity Sonia says, having to wait twenty years to find out the finale is quite unique and she wishes she had some more mystery in her life.

Charity Sonia was also very angry about the results of the disability benefit test I did two months ago. She said, The bastards, I can't believe it. And she read it out and it was about me and it said,

> You said you had difficulties with moving around. Informal observation noted you to walk 23 metres at a moderate pace with a steady gait. Musculoskeletal observations noted no restrictions and I have decided that you can stand and move more than 200 metres unaided.

Charity Sonia shouted, Bloody bureaucrats. Then she read more and it said,

You said you have difficulties engaging with others and making budgetary decisions. Mental state examination noted good eye contact, rapport, no need for prompting or a cognitive impairment and an ability to make numerical calculations adequately. I have decided that you can engage with other people and manage complex budgeting decisions unaided. We received your GP patient summary sheet letter, your psychological report and case summaries from Women's Aid, and the Department of Social Care. I looked at all the information available. As your needs vary my decision is based on the help you need most days. We are declining your application for PIP assistance.

Charity Sonia said, Unbelievable. What have you got to have to get disability benefit these days, no head?

Nina said, It's OK. The government just want me to get better all by myself so I will have to get a job now.

And Charity Sonia said, Did you just make another joke, Nina?

Charity Sonia has got me a new solicitor to get compensation and he is not No Fee Pendergast who is back in the ring chasing ambulances.

Social Work Phil still says he would do things differently if it wasn't for the system and Cas pops in sometimes and says if I keep eating yoghurt at that bleeding rate I'll need to get a new wardrobe.

Every day I repeat Doctor Webber's coping self statements and slowly the feared words and places are getting fewer though I am still scared of the sky since I found out that lightning is real and to not use an umbrella. Everywhere I go I ask what is the worst thing that can happen and then I wait for it to happen and it never does and then I step forward and in this way I have gone alone to a shopping mall and a hairdresser and Marks and Spencer's and to a pub and stood in the rain for ten minutes just to get wet because it is not radiation.

Crying is like a virus. Charity Sonia cries every time she visits, which does not make her very good at her job because she is supposed to care for me but that will come to an end soon too. She is starting me on Social Skills training and has left lots of bright pages with pictures of people smiling which I am supposed to copy. She said, That bloody internet is a curse, I wish Cas had never given you that stupid phone, and she made me promise never to go on dating sites or post a picture of my face, because when I have a new name I have to be anonymous, like a secret.

The government says I can apply for a car and free driving lessons and a flat with a washing machine, but this is still a long way off.

What I have to write in my diary from now on is the opposite. Instead of writing about the past I have to make plans but I don't really want to make too many. You can never be a perfect person. Charity Sonia says, Remember when you first got out you wrote your list? The DSS can pay for you to do some, but not all of them. I said it was a silly list. Get married, have an affair, see all the birds in the world. She said, Not silly, don't be so harsh on yourself.

I said, Well I don't think the DSS can afford to let me fly a plane.

She laughed and stared and wiped her nose and said, Nina, I think you just made another joke.

She still calls me Nina but Nina has had to die, like The Project did. Nina was just a middle person, a name my mother gave me but she didn't want me. Nina was a dangerous person who had to protect The Project.

Nina isn't I.

I will have to live even though I am scared of many things and it is true that freedom is a lonely place. People are quite confused, it is not just me. I don't know why they are so obsessed with sex and love and photos and they all want different clothes and they all love shopping and they all say look at me and I wish they'd look at each other more and not be on their phones so much but you can't stop them because when you try to make one plan for everyone and turn them into projects it all goes wrong.

Let people live their lies.

I decided to try some new experiences like Doctor Webber said but not too hard and so this week when I visit Doctor Webber by myself on the bus I want to buy some bread for the old man and the birds at the Hospital pond if he is still alive, and thank him.

He was the first normal person I met by myself. I will try some conversation with him and ask if the big white birds are swans or geese. And then I will ask him his name. And when he asks me my name I will just say me, or I don't know just yet. Or maybe I'll ask him if he knows any good names.

And I will not be suspicious of him or think that he wants to lock me in a basement because I must learn to trust people, but not everyone. Then maybe, if he would like it, we will chat and there will be no forbidden words because even though people are still trying to ban words in the news this is Freedom. And we also don't have to talk. Not if he doesn't want to. Because that is OK too. We might just sit and look at the birds. And that will be more than enough for one day.

Charity Sonia was right and maybe writing is part of the problem and it is the last basement to escape from. Normal people don't write reports. So I'm going to see if I can do these things and not write about them. It will be hard but I'm going to go to the pond and not write about it. Just feed the birds and breathe and not try to work out whether Chen will give me a gold star or erase my words. There won't be any record of it, not anywhere at all. And I'll do this day after day like normal people do and life will just have to be like that, incorrect and not recorded. And that will have to be fine.

I know I'm going to miss it but I know writing is holding me back.

Even writing this is not helping.

The leaves are flying and so are the birds. I have learned the names and colours of thrushes, swallows, starlings and magpies. I have a nice window and a view of a street. So I'm going to stop now and watch for a bit then step outside and try to take part and I'll look just like all the thousands in the streets and people will pass me by and not even know it's me. That's my biggest plan, to be just like them and to have nothing to report.

I will say goodbye to Nina now. Goodbye to The Project.

This has been more than enough for one day.

Acknowledgements

The author would like to acknowledge the people and organisations who have made the composition of this book possible:

The Royal Society of Literature, Marian Donaldson and Drumchapel Women's Aid, Jenni Fagan, Peter Cox, Rachael Kerr, Fay Weldon, Nick Fox, Luke Rhinehart, Stuart Kelly, Hanif Kureishi, Ian Rankin, Lettice Franklin, Irvine Welsh, Sue Martin, David Petherick, Roza Nazipova, Dan Franklin, Chris Gray of Lansdowne Psychotherapy, Sally Harrower and the National Library of Scotland, Marie-Odile Pittin-Hedon, Nathan Coley, Tim Lott, Sara Hunt, Ross Murray, Creative Scotland, Emily Ballou, Zoe Hood, Grace Vincent, Rhiannon Smith and Ursula Doyle.

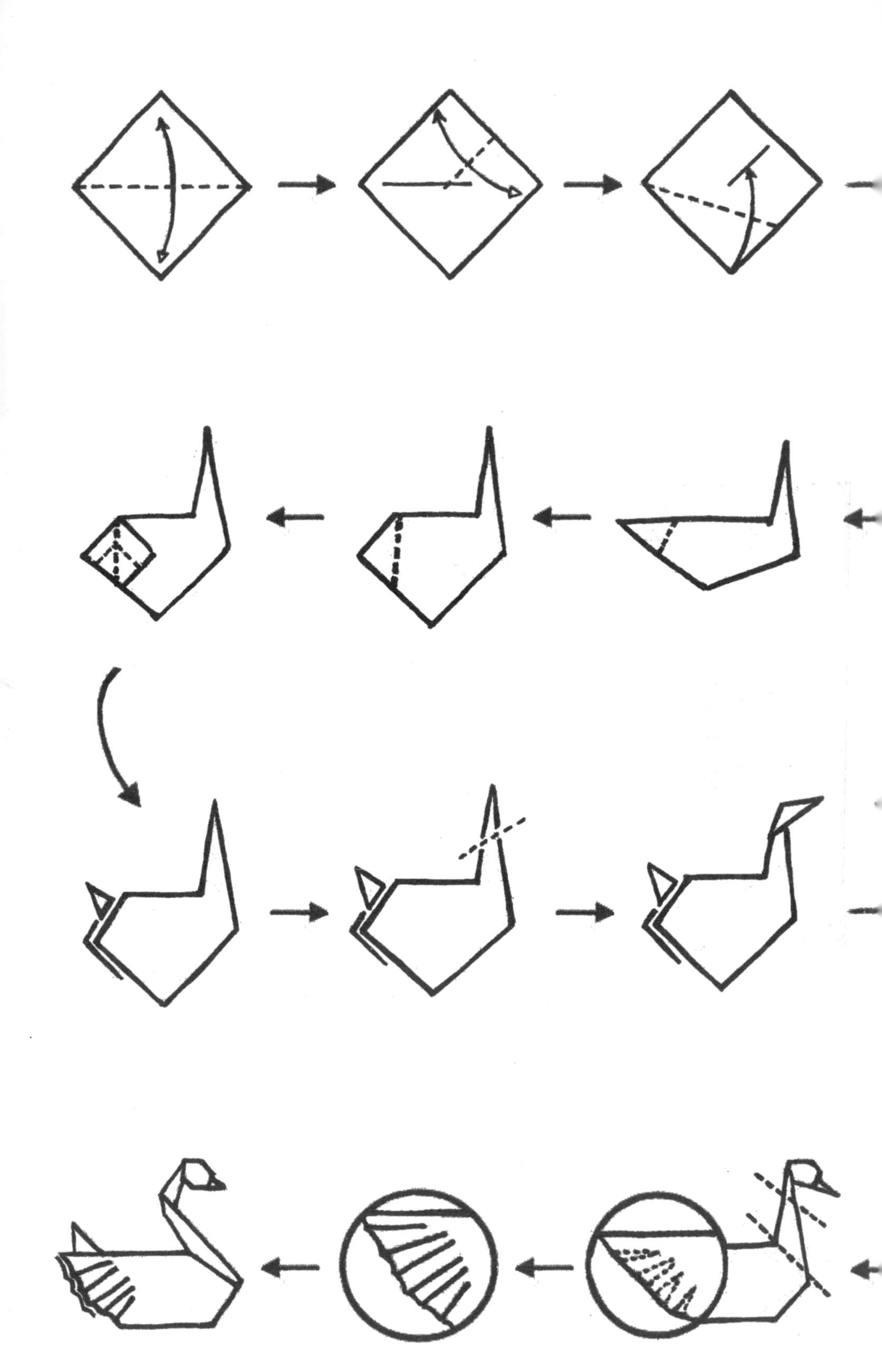